THE HEART NOT ONLY BEATS

Marilyn —
Best wishes!
Lester Rivers

THE HEART NOT ONLY BEATS

LESTER RIVERS

TATE PUBLISHING
AND ENTERPRISES, LLC

The Heart Not Only Beats

Scripture quotations used in this book have come from the New Revised Standard Version.

The opinions expressed by the author are not necessarily those of Tate Publishing, LLC.

Published by Tate Publishing & Enterprises, LLC
127 E. Trade Center Terrace | Mustang, Oklahoma 73064 USA
1.888.361.9473 | www.tatepublishing.com

Tate Publishing is committed to excellence in the publishing industry. The company reflects the philosophy established by the founders, based on Psalm 68:11,
"The Lord gave the word and great was the company of those who published it."

Cover design by Jim Villaflores
Interior design by Jake Muelle

Published in the United States of America

ISBN: 978-1-62994-494-4
1. Fiction / Coming of Age
2. Fiction / General
13.12.26

I dedicate this book to my Swedish Grandmother,
who gave me inspiration for my life.

CHAPTER ONE

The first thought about writing this book came at a difficult time in my young life, after my beloved blueberry-picking, Swedish flatbread baking, stout-hearted grandmother Hildur died of cancer at seventy six. She had been my primary fountain of feminine love and affection while I was growing up and then I was fourteen and felt her loss hugely. She came to me in a dream three nights later, in the early hours of the deepest night, sitting upright in her favorite cotton blue print dress, hem so grandmotherly well below the knee, hands clasped in her lap, her left ring finger still wearing the gold band of matrimony to Black Emil my grandfather, now there she sat firmly in her chair, looking at me and telling me: "You'll be alright, Nash—you were born to write a book about your Father."

When my eyes opened the next morning my mind was obsessed by the notion so unexpectedly dropped onto my yet-undeveloped consciousness that I was to write a book about my father. My Dad was her son, and my father, so thusly I presumed, and with no further obvious supernatural instruction, I went about observing my Dad, Eddie Edwards, for seven years, until the day he finally died in 1972 from that shrapnel hit he took on the right side of his head on D-Day, Omaha Beach, 1944.

It took twenty eight years to kill him, and for that time I was glad, since after all my own existence was due to his seed, and furthermore, I was glad he lived that long because Eddie Edwards was a great dad.

He introduced me into all sorts of sports, took me into the woods and lakes at an early age; at twelve, canoeing in a northern lake about thirty feet away from a mama moose swimming across the lake with us a while, we slowed down while she paddled not more than twenty feet off, then she turned and took up another course. I still have a photo with my first catch of about ten bluefish and crappies at five years old. That was the day when my Dad started baiting my hook for me, and taking my catches off my hook, until I was reeling them in so fast he didn't have time to dip his own rod in the water. "Whoa," he said slightly aggravated, "From now on you bait your own hook and take your own catch off. I want to catch some too," (trailing off into a gentle laugh.) That seemed reasonable enough to me but did slow me down in my five-year-old quest for more fish. But my Dad wasn't just about fishing.

Eddie Edwards was a sturdy Swedish immigrant who came over (at two years of age) from the old country in 1915 with his parents Black Emil and Hildur and he grew up in Hibbing, on the famous Iron Range of northeastern Minnesota, from whence came millions of tons of iron ore for steel for trains and boats and tanks and American victories, and a continent–wide auto industry that touched every one of our lives, not to mention a certain Bobby Zimmerman who a few decades later forged his own fire from the red soul of those yawning iron pits.

My Dad, Eddie Edwards, was born on September 19, 1913. By the time he was thirteen it was already 1926 and things were speeding up even as far north as Hibbing for dark of night Prohibition era whiskey runs. Bootleggers hired twelve-year-olds to drive truck for their legally illicit runs; young Eddie took them up on it as a way to improve his driving skills, and to make a couple of bucks, hard to come by in that remote hardscrabble mining town.

Back then his name was Clarence, which with his Virgo sensitivity seemed a bit effeminate to some of the others, rugged drinking immigrant northerners who trimmed their fingernails with their jackknifes. So he took to calling himself Eddie, short for Edward, a perfectly respectable name even in 1920s red iron tinged Hibbing. But still he had to scrap with some bullies, and along the way he learned he had some pretty fair foot speed, so his preferred method of self -defense was to not back down from the brute challenger, but to engage, quickly, to kick the bully in his nuts and then turn and run like Mary let the dog out…until the brute finally ran out of breath chasing fast Eddie, who upon seeing that, returned to his victim and clocked him with a quick right and then a left uppercut. His Golden Gloves organized boxing experience a few years later would stem from those first apprentice fighter days over a dumb name.

Being a former Golden Gloves boxer, my Dad was eager to show me the ropes. For Christmas 1956—I was five—one of my Christmas presents from my Dad was a pair of boxing gloves, my size, red, so when he stationed us in the basement, in the playroom, where years later he would install a pool table, he began gently to show me how to box. His hands were too big for the junior gloves so he left his thumbs out. Me, I could put all my fighting digits snuggly into the shiny new padded red gloves. Whack! Across my face comes his left hand, batting at my face! I put up my dukes, naively at first but along the way I learned how to use my arms to deflect most of his shots. So he got faster. Thwack! Thwack! Thwack! I ducked and bobbed and weaved and tried my best to return blows, but for about three years he always, always overcame me at the end with a furious flurry of fists that reduced me to a crumpled blob of laughing blather on the floor.

Each time I went upstairs to bed, my face red from his thwacking, feeling on top of the world, after all I had just spent an intense quality hour with my Dad.

And then one day three years later, we were in the playroom, him on his knees and me standing, trading blows, when suddenly he thwacked me with a shot that was sharper than any before, and I felt an immediate rise of red rage and before I knew it I hauled off and punched him right in the nose. We both paused, me for sure uncertain of what came next, which turned out to be blood running from my Dad's nose, and me with a growing sense of dread, he lifted a bare hand to his nose, discovered the blood, looked at shriveling me and threw his head back, partly to stem the flow of blood, and partly to let out such a laugh that droplets of the red stuff spewed all over the place. His eyes beamed at me as he pronounced "The boxing lesson is over." We never boxed again, although that wasn't the last time I saw his rough railroader fists, which you'll hear about a little later.

Hunting? At seven my steps were following my Dad along the rufflecrunch leafy October November trails down by Floodwood, along the oak ridges, where you could scare up some rabbits or partridges to shoot, and take them home to clean in the basement washtub, and with the rabbits my Dad just made a couple of swift expert cuts with a knife, and then just grabbed and pulled the skin and turned the whole animal inside out. The first time I watched him do that, I rubbed my eyes in disbelief but when he did it again and again, each time slit, slit, grab, pull inside out, he turned me into a believer. When we ate it for supper we had to be careful not to bite into the shot that had been left inside; we'd just spit them clank onto our plates and go right back to gnawing on that incredibly tasty gamy fare.

My Dad put a .410 shotgun in my hand at ten years of age and took me to Gun Safety Class, upon which certification permitted me to shoot it legally. It really was a neat gun. You could use it as a shotgun for rabbit, partridge or pheasant, or for heavier game like deer, you just inserted slug bullets. So when deer season came around in 1961 he got me up when it was still dark outside one November Saturday, and packed me and the guns and all his hunting gear into his 1954 powder blue Ford station wagon with round headlights and off we went, out of Duluth and into the countryside, I knew not where, but he did.

I just sat in the passenger seat and watched the stars not moving in the sky although the station wagon flew along the road; that thought remained with me for several minutes. He liked the fact that I stayed awake in the dark, telling me" You're a good traveler." Little did either of us know how prophetic that statement would turn out to be.

We arrived just before dawn at the hunting site, and after a hefty hike up into the woods Dad stationed me at the edge of a clearing, across which was a thick woods, into which he walked, telling me to keep my eyes peeled, he was going to try to scare up some deer. It was a very cold November day and my feet stamped into the frozen ground to keep them warm. Several minutes had elapsed since Dad disappeared into the thicket, and his exact location was unknown to me. Time stood still with cold silence as my watchful youthful eyes scanned the snowy thick woods for signs of life. Something about the winter silence, it's like pure radio waves into deep listening. I don't really know how much cold woods time went by when suddenly, to my right—a crashing in the brush.

From the far right end of the clearing, out of the bush bounded a deer, no, two deer, one after the other, magnificent, bounding, white tails bouncing, right in front of me, less than a hundred feet away. I took my safety off and aimed my .410 with slugs at the neck of the second one and followed it through my gun sight as they bounded all the way across the clearing and out of sight. My finger never pulled the trigger, thinking where the heck is Dad and anyway, they were so beautiful to ten year old me.

My thoughts turned to Abe Lincoln at fourteen not shooting the wild turkey through the chink in his log home, saying his heart wasn't into killing it. By even ten years old I was a very minor expert on the life of Lincoln, for some reason he felt very close to me and my interest already had devoured several books on him.

After about an hour Dad reemerged from the woods and sauntered over to me. "See anything?" I told him about my first deer hunting experience and he understood. Many times I thought he'd be mad at me and then was surprised to be the beneficiary of his tender heart.

You wouldn't know it from his exterior appearance. Standing 6'2" in his socks, he always weighed one hundred eighty six sinewy pounds, no matter if he pigged out or fasted for days. One hundred eighty six was his weight. Zip body fat. He had what he called sloping shoulders, not straight across like some of the Finnish farmers, but slowly rounding down to his arms, giving him unusual power for his size. His hands were railroader rough, knuckles flat from punching, his fingernails he trimmed with a jackknife. His hazel eyes revealed a secret sadness from unspeakable trials in his past, or in his present, for all I knew. Some of the beat-down sense about him had to have been his own teenage years, which we'll get to a bit later. His thin lips turned a little sideways when he smiled, rather, grinned; his teeth showed the neglect of wartime.

His nose, as he liked to put it, was a Roman nose, "roamin' all over my face," broken so many times in boxing and hockey. Thin close cropped sandy butch hair revealed a scar on the right side of his head, of which I would learn much more later on. He loved to dance, and he wore baggy pants, so when he danced his funny jig the coins in his pockets jingled to his grin, which just made his grin grow wider, and then his eyes shone pure happiness when he saw me grinning too.

Dad kept a big top-loading freezer in the basement that was stocked year-round with partridge, pheasant, rabbit, beef, venison, trout, walleye, northern pike, smelt. A word, if you don't mind, about smelting. At seven I had my own hip waders for stream fishing and for the annual smelt run at the mouth of the river on the north end of Duluth. Hundreds of eager smelt dippers would every mid to late April flock to the rocky beach mouth of the river, to intercept in nets as they raced helter skelter upstream to spawn, the famous Lake Superior rainbow smelt, actually an exotic species to the Great Lakes, a silver fish about five to nine inches long. My Dad brought a garbage can from home in the station wagon, and it took him and me about ten minutes to fill the garbage can with smelt. We both used a stiff wire conical net on a pole; dip the net in, pull it lake-ward, and then hold tight to the pole (so full and heavy I needed help to lift it out) as it fills up with smelt. To be cooked, mind you, in an iron skillet, with a little Crisco Oil, the smelt de-headed, cleaned, washed, dipped in flour and fried crispy, to be eaten almost like French fries, maybe dipped in ketchup.

To the right of the six-foot freezer Dad had built a corner of shelves, upon which were lined up, arranged by type of product, various cans of soup, canned peas, canned corn, canned milk, canned beans. Canned fruit cocktail, canned peaches, cans of all types. Canned water—this area of the basement served as our official family bomb shelter in the event of a nuclear blast over the strategically important (yeah, right) remote northern city of Duluth. From the victory garden he planted behind the garage we had beans, carrots, potatoes, tomatoes, lettuce, onions. He didn't mind if his boy pulled a baby carrot out of the ground, cleaned it off with the garden hose over by my sandbox, and crunched into it right there in my backyard, crunch, crunch, oh those baby carrots were sweet. To this day I stand in awe of his self-reliance. He shot, caught, grew, skinned, scaled, and cooked his own food by dint of sheer habit from a hardened youth.

On top of that he showed me how to survive in the northern wilderness. He turned a basic chore of pruning the pair of balsams in our backyard into a real life survival lesson. "See, you take these boughs we just cut off and spread them on the ground between the trees for a bed that will insulate you from the frozen ground;

and then you take the other boughs and lean them up against each other between the trees and interlock them this way and you end up with a pine bough lean-to" to protect against the wind, in front of which the lesson continued, "not too close to the lean-to, but close enough to feel the heat, you start a fire and keep it going all night if ever you find yourself lost in the northern winter woods."

Some of that knowledge was used in Boy Scouts and winter camping but to this day this son hasn't yet faced the hardships his father endured.

Sports? Dad started teaching me sports before I even knew it. In my fifth summer he led me to the end of the concrete alley behind our Lakeside house in the east end of Duluth. At the end of the alley was a break, a crack in the concrete, and he had figured from that crack to the gate in our white picket fence was about fifty yards. So he showed me how to line up at the line, to get ready, set, and run! I took off, my little legs churning, but his long loping gait easily overtook me and he made it to the gate first by a long shot.

We raced like that for five years. He'd say "Wanna race?" and I readily took him up on it; it was fun. One year, my tenth, he issued his challenge and off we went to line up at the crack. Ready set GO! As usual, I was off first, and approaching the gate my wonder arose, where are those long legs to overtake me? I kept digging, and suddenly he let out a big laugh behind me as he realized that for the first time his son had beaten him. We walked silently back to the house, my heart choking with pride and also his with my having beaten my forty-seven-year old Dad in the race he had taught me to run. Crack in the concrete to the gate in the fence. Hurray!

Later that summer he sat at the kitchen table reading the sports page and said "Hey Nash, I see they're having a citywide playground track meet over at Ordean Junior High, you want to go?" My heart stopped as I stood in the doorway, feeling a morbid dread come over me at the fearful prospect of competing against other boys, but at the same time I knew I couldn't say no to him, so yes came out. I was just a short little bookworm who sat on his porch or, more often, in the maple tree in the backyard, reading books. In my eleventh summer, I read 127 books, five a week, which was all the library would permit me to take out; carried in a blue and green striped cloth book bag hanging from the handlebars of my one-speed fat tire bike. The thought of actual physical competition with my peers scared me half out of my wits. But the fateful day arrived and I rode my bike the eight blocks to Ordean where the track meet would be held, and ignorantly signed up for five events: standing broad jump, fifty yard dash, high jump, base run and shot put. There were hundreds of kids from all the playgrounds all over Duluth, which is a city twenty nine miles long. What was little me doing there?

So I did what I could in the various competitions and came away with four blue ribbons and one green one, fifth place in the shot put, my puny frame was undersized for that one. I said nothing to my mother at home and went up to my room to look at my ribbons and replayed my events in my head. That's what we used to do before being constantly plugged-in to outside entertainment; we used our brains all day, which may be connected to the apparent dumbing-down of America during my lifetime, as hardly any child ever lives as we did anymore.

My Dad called from work to see how his kid had done, my Mom answered the phone and called me down to ask me. To my mother: "four blue ribbons and a green one." She repeated that into the phone, and I went back to my room. A couple hours later Dad got home from work, I was then in the living room, he rounded the corner out of the kitchen and wide eyed looked at me and almost shouted "CHAMP!" grinning and running up to me and lifting me up in the air. For the first time it dawned on me that I was a champion, a city champion in four events. That first track meet would become the first of many over the next ten years, with some wins, some losses, as in all sports, and my Dad took the time to be at almost every one. Even leaning on his cane, toward the end, he witnessed my best long jump ever, twenty-two feet six inches, in the MIAC conference meet at Macalester College in 1971. Unfortunately I scratched by a hair and it didn't count, but in looking back at his hazel eyes beaming with pride as he leaned on the cane at his side I knew it was a good jump anyway and I was glad he saw it and heard the crowd go ooh.

Shortly after my initial success at my first track meet at age ten, playing down at Portman Square, the city park just a half-block from my house, came my first exposure to Jack Lourdes. Jack was a grade ahead of me, dark haired, with an intense look about him even at age eleven. He had heard about my time in the fifty-yard dash at the track meet and challenged me. "Edwards, you wanna race?" Even with four citywide blue ribbons my shrinking violet nature remained, and I shook him off.

Ice skating? My first skates were second-hand speed skating skates with the long blades like the Olympians race in. Laces tied together, slung skates over my shoulder, and wearing my half-buckled galoshes over my two pairs of regular socks and a thick woolen pair of skating socks, my brother Jesse and I walked the half-block to Portman where the softball fields were frozen over in winter to make a great big skating rink. We went skating for hours on end every winter growing up. When Christmas two-week break came around, it was all day every day at the rink, until the early dark of Duluth winter (about 4:00 p.m.) sent us home for supper, then back out to skate under the lights until they threw us off the rink and turned off the music and lights for the night. Back in those days they even had music piped over the loudspeakers, Doris Day, how much is that doggy in the window?

We had strong ankles, Jesse and me, and Ralphie, Jesse's friend and sometimes Ron Skyler, my friend, whose dad ran the YMCA in Duluth. They were good people, I remember Mr. Skyler checking me out at first to see if I were good enough to be hanging around with his most excellent boy, and then Mr. Skyler and I enjoyed a cordial adult relationship long after Ron had left town for his Honeywell career. Ron was always the first one of my friends in high school to talk about deciding on a career.

Heck, we were all good people. Some lasting impressions, some lasting friendships, sharing frozen toes and nippy cheeks, and then there was the boys' trick of stealing a pretty girl's hat and skating away with it. She chased them in her figure skates, pushing off from her toes, but their hockey skates were too fast, they were too fast, and they tossed her hat back and forth between them laughing until she gave up and just watched them. And a funny thing happened. Whenever the offended girl just dropped it, lost interest in the game, one of the guys would skate to her to return her hat. She possesses more power than she knows, I thought at the time. Any way you slice it, skating is fun.

I look at kids in winter now, sitting in front of their electronic gadgets and can't help thinking they're missing out on the fabulous snowbound outdoors with frosty breath, strong ankles, good cheer, high physical speeds, great friends and glad hearts in glorious icy beauty. Come to think of it, it would be tragic to miss that for anyone wishing to experience life fully, at least in the north.

But back to Eddie Edwards. When he was sixteen his dad, Black Emil, laid off at the mine, took off for Chicago to find work and never returned. Black Emil—they called him that because he was a fearsome bull-strong mean-spirited black mustached drunk—left his sweet wife Hildur with their four kids and no money. Eddie's older brother Pat, older sister Alma, and younger brother Floyd all lived under that humble roof supported now by the meager earnings of Hildur's immigrant floor scrubbing jobs. To make matters worse, also in 1929 the Barnes family's clapboard house down the street burned to the ground, killing both parents and stranding four orphans. Hildur took them in too.

The pressures on the family were so great that Eddie decided he needed to quit high school and go looking for work himself. His big brother Pat couldn't do it because he was lame, having had his right leg crushed when he was run over by a truck when he was twelve. So Eddie Edwards left high school in his sophomore year and found himself riding the rails with myriad Great Depression hoboes, learning how to cook hobo stew with chunks of whatever vegetable or hunk of meat was available in a coffee can over a small fire behind bushes along the tracks or inside the boxcar as it progressed down the line, and how to sleep on top of the railroad cars by loosening his belt and looping it through the grates on the runways that ran along the top of the cars, and then rebuckling it to hold him there while he slept. Sometimes he'd wake up three states away. He picked cotton in Alabama, potatoes in Idaho, oranges in California, and he carried only an extra pair of socks, in which he kept the small money he earned, and every few months he would ride the rails back to Hibbing, where his grateful mother cooked him a big supper, washed his clothes, darned his socks and let him sleep in his own bed for a night.

Then, before the crack of dawn he was off again, leaving his hard-earned money on the kitchen table for his mom to find. By the time he was eighteen he'd been in every one of the forty eight states, and spent ninety five percent of his time on the road for three years. He finally went back home to finish his high school education, graduated at twenty-two, and went to work as a gandy dancer for the Great Northern railroad. That was actually a pretty good job for a young buck, bunk and meals provided in a traveling caboose, and plenty of hard outdoors work, swinging sledges and knocking rails into place as the railroad was built tie by tie, bolt by bolt. My Dad ended up working thirty eight years for that railroad and its successor, the Burlington Northern.

CHAPTER TWO

I suppose it's time to introduce my mother. The time: February-March 1943. The place: Springfield, Ohio, where the U.S. Army had a boot camp for new soldiers drafted to fight Hitler. On the weekends the soldiers got passes to go into town for the dances that were held at the Marigold Ballroom near Wittenberg University. Many of the young ladies of Springfield found work in the secretarial pool on the base, and that's where twenty-two-year-old Susan Marie Grover tried to lose herself on the rebound from Captain Richard Swenson, the tall blond medical school graduate from a good professional Springfield family, who pledged to marry her as soon as he returned from the war.

Young Susan, a shapely dark-haired spitting image of the movie star Merle Oberon except for the small gap between her front teeth, was impatient and wanted to get married before he shipped out. Can't let a swell catch like that get away, she thought. But Richard said no, his duty came first, and he wouldn't take the chance of leaving her a war widow if he didn't make it back. The thought was honorable but the split was utterly painful to sensitive Susan, who then heard about the secretarial job on the base from her girlfriends Dorothy and Wanda, and she signed up the very next week. After all, she was an up and coming twenty-two-year-old dark-haired shapely fox on the loose in Springfield and she needed to make some money.

Saturday night rolled around and Dorothy and Wanda dragged the brooding Susan to the dance at the Marigold. There they melted into the age-old protocol of shy men standing in small groups on one side of the ballroom, and the women all bunched up tittering in little groups of their own on the other. But when the band struck up a swinging set all bets were off, as the soldiers knew their time, maybe on earth, was limited. They broke up their little groups and crossed the floor to pick out a daisy from the flower bed and dance their troubles away, careful not to crush the petals. Some guys were shyer, and the bolder women, including Wanda, being a redhead, walked over to them, took them by the hand and dragged them onto the dance floor. It wasn't always pretty. Some of the soldiers were farmers who knew nothing of the difference between a waltz and a schmaltz. But there was one tall soldier, with a commanding presence like a sergeant, which he was already, quieter than the rest, not bad looking but for a roaming nose, who not only knew how to dance, but he danced with such glee that he wore the young ladies out.

"Susan, you need to dance with that tall one over there, he's a wonderful dancer," Wanda breathlessly advised. Slightly snooty Susan deigned a glance in Eddie Edwards' direction and sniffed "well, he's not Richard." "Richard's gone, get him out of your head," the still breathless redhead sniped. "Anyway, isn't it our duty to see to it these soldiers have some fun before they ship out?" Susan put her cigarette down and diffidently noticed the tall one approaching her. "Dance, miss?" Eddie Edwards gave her a short bow. Something about his eyes, she thought, this one's seen a lot. He carried a cool strong confidence, unlike the other momma's boys in uniform there. Well ok, it was her duty, so she accepted.

That was all it took. Eddie and Susan had such a good time dancing they made a date for next Saturday, and then the Saturday after that, and then the Saturday after that; and then on March 22 fast Eddie proposed and in that crazy mad upside down wartime world, after knowing each other for a total of six weeks, she forgot Richard for a moment, blushed and accepted so on April Fool's day 1943 they got married in the Wittenberg chapel. He was thirty, she was twenty-two.

That was an insane time in America; the national martial obsession with war, rationing, Rosie the Riveter, the whole world was off balance and people got caught up in it and did things like get married after just six weeks of dancing. Two weeks later Eddie, a solid 204 pounds of dancing Iron Range steel, shipped overseas to help defeat the worst evil known to humankind, at that time anyway. The dark-haired pretty young Mrs. Edwards accepted his checks mailed from the government and had a ball driving all over the country with Wanda and other girlfriends on endless vacations, Grand Canyon, San Francisco, to the Lincoln Memorial in Washington, D.C., while he lay in an English hospital one click from checking out. He was in the hospital due to the shrapnel hit he took to his head during the D-Day assault on Omaha Beach June 6, 1944. The slug he took in his thigh was no big deal; it went straight through and missed the bone. But when that grenade blew up just meters away from him, one fatal hunk of metal flew in his direction and sealed his ultimate fate. They patched him up—it took eight months—and sent him back out to the front, where he marched all the way to Czechoslovakia and, I think, back.

When Eddie Edwards received his honorable discharge and Purple Hearts and was sent home after Hitler succumbed to his fate, he arrived back in Hibbing weighing one hundred forty pounds. From June of 1943 to August of 1945, the war sapped him of sixty four pounds. His pretty young wife, in her gross disappointment over what seemed to her the crummy dirty red northern remote boring town of Hibbing, wasn't interested in nursing him back to health, so his mother did. Six months of care under the watchful wonderful Hildur brought Eddie back to the one hundred eighty six pounds he carried from that day forward.

By 1948 petulant ambitious Susan had cajoled her husband into transferring his railroad job to Duluth, where at least they had a symphony orchestra and lots of doctors who worked at the hospitals there. She picked up a secretary-receptionist job at the Duluth Clinic where she could get her daily cultural fix with the doctors and he began his Duluth career hand-loading boxcars full of sacks of grain at the rail yard, including the day he was struck by lightning while walking for shelter in a torrential downpour. He fell flat on the ground, out like a light (had hit him) and lay there for a couple of minutes, while his co-workers, in their own fright, remained huddled in the boxcars, thinking he may be dead. And then Eddie Edwards got up, and rubbing his arm walked toward the astonished faces. He sat down a while and then went back to work.

In November 1949 their fates were locked together for good with the birth of their daughter, who they named Lila Jane Edwards, my big sister. Baby Lila showed signs of a brilliant mind even at two months of age. Then at fourteen months after Lila was born, her brother Nash arrived on January 17, 1951, as my elders relayed, apparently I was in quite a hurry, almost popping out in the elevator, and when they brought me home from the hospital Lila later claimed she remembered the traumatic event, right down to the dress our grandmother was wearing as she held Lila on her lap at the window; my sister somehow interpreted my arrival as supplanting her roost as the most popular baby in the house, like a jealous feline. Lila lived and died thinking she was in competition with me.

What Lila didn't know and couldn't know is that before they left the hospital with me, my own mother tried to give me up, saying to her husband Eddie "Now I have my girl and you have your boy; let's get a divorce, you take the boy and I'll take the girl." She said that to him on the day I was born, according to what my Aunt Alma told me years later. Why would she tell me that? The Edwards women took little truck from puffed up ladies like her. Eddie Edwards looked wanly at his pretty wife and felt his heart in his throat. He had already forgiven her for spending all the money he'd sent home during the war. And even for not helping him to get well. But this, he couldn't accept this. "N-Nooo" he stammered. "We have to stay together for the kids if nothing else." She didn't answer him, turning a cold Ohio eye to the blank Duluth hospital room wall, trying as hard as she could to remember Richard's face, the face she feared slowly slipping into dark rumors of fading memory.

Eddie drove slowly as he left the hospital, finding his car almost involuntary finding a parking spot next to the Kozy bar on First Street. He walked blankly into the bar and took a seat at the end. "What'll it be, friend?" The bartender could see the sad look of someone who is coming to terms with a bummer. "A bump and a brew," Eddie replied stoically. The radio was on and the Minneapolis Lakers were winning their game that day by scoring twenty two points, led by George Mikan. That Mikan, Eddie thought, he'll probably go down in history as one of the best. "Another one?" The bartender lifted an eyebrow at Eddie. "No, thanks, gotta be going." He knew in his heart the answers weren't to be found there. Funny how bars give themselves appealing names, like the Kozy or Moby's or Beachcomber or the Kom On Inn.

Eddie's mother Hildur looked at him upon his return home and instantly felt his pain as only a true mother could. "You sit down now," she softly said, "and I'll fix you a plate." She knew he probably hadn't eaten for hours, and those Swedish women like their men to eat. When she put it before him, she took a seat facing him at the kitchen table. She said nothing as he scarfed his food, avoiding her glances. When he was finished, pushing back from the table to give his stuffed belly more room to sit expanded, she got to the point.

"What did she say to you?" She knew already, or sensed it.

"Ma, she wants a divorce, she wants to take Lila and leave Nash with me."

Hildur's Swedish started to rise, faster than flatbread; she got up and started moving around, then sternly announced she was going out for a walk.

As the tale was told years later, the tide was turned in the family's favor when my grandmother Hildur walked in her sturdy shoes to St. Luke's hospital on a cold January afternoon and found Susan in her room, where she read her a particularly Swedish riot act. "You little hussy, you stay with your husband and be a mother to your children!" Whatever she said to her, it worked, and together my Dad and Mom brought me home from the hospital that cold grey January day. I think from the get-go she pretty much left me on my own, which may help explain certain melancholies that affect me, but we're getting ahead of ourselves here. Plenty of psychoanalysis ahead.

In March of my fourth year my brother Jesse was born in 1955. Now he rightly claimed his spotlight and my mother took to making him into a cuddly curly-haired cute little Jesse. As the years passed, as big brother to Jesse, I encouraged him and did whatever I could to help him; not to mention the times I tortured him; he readily cried at the slightest mean thing that came out of me. He was a blue eyed blond, brightly sensitive to the feelings of those around him, while my sister and I were dark eyed, dark haired like our mother, both tending to be self-motivated over-achievers. The joke around the house was that Jesse was the milkman's kid (or some doctor's?). Years later, by the way, Jesse's resemblance to his Dad became so strong it wiped out any possibility of foul play.

He was just a sensitive kid, easily hurt, and so he eventually became the family clown to mask his sorrows by acting so goofy he reduced me to clutching my stomach and Lila to cutting the air with her hideous shrieking laughter as he cavorted past our bedroom doors acting the fool.

In the spring of 1963 I rode my bike over to Ordean, to watch the seventh-grade boys trying the high jump. Still in sixth grade, all of four feet ten inches tall, and wearing clodhopper hunting boots, I stood there silently observing as one by one the older boys went at the bamboo pole and knocked it down. Jack Lourdes was one of them, and suddenly in a loud voice he turned to his teammates: "Hey, that little Edwards kid can make it."—He knew that I had won the high jump last summer—turning to me, "wanna try?" The other boys nodded their acquiescence so I sat on the grass and took off my boots and socks, then stood up, rubbed my bare soles on the cool grass, eyed the bar, set at four feet, ran up on the grass and cleared it, Valery Brumel style, landing crunch on my right forearm in the sand pile. They let me do it a couple more times, and then I happily rode my bike back home. That was the first of many times Jack went out of his way to help promote my interests.

My work every day world started that summer, when I became a full-time caddy at the country club. During the coming school year my concentrations included my class work, track, basketball, volleyball and football teams at Ordean, playing the cello in the seventh grade orchestra, Senior Patrol Leader of my Boy Scout Troop, but summertime was work time. Every day my morning walk took me seven blocks to the course, usually early enough to get my shoes wet in the morning dew, across the par 3 17th up the long first fairway to the clubhouse, behind the clubhouse to the caddy shack, where I put my name into play with the cool cats at the old wooden counter who barely looked up from their blackjack game to register me. I took a seat on the bench with my back to the wall, and soon enough old Nick Starling would sit beside me and gently rub my little back while he murmured "yes that's right, yes that's right." At thirteen my height was still stuck at five feet two, the shortest kid in my class.

Nick was eighty years old, stooped, swarthy, wrinkled and both hard and gentle; he had been a caddy all his life. The first time I learned that it surprised me, but then Nick was just one of us. Sometimes his name would be called for the same foursome as I drew, and then when our players were teeing off he always implored me to "watch my ball and let me know where it ends up," since his eyesight wasn't what it used to be. Yes, that's right. I usually carried one bag, although after a couple of years a couple of us liked to carry two whenever we could—we called it doubling—for more money.

My Northland Country Club career is worth noting, partly because of my own hole-in-one at age thirteen on the Par 3 fifth hole at Northland in the summer of 1964, witnessed by another caddie, Dick Durgan, who ran over to the hole from the next tee, looked down into the hole and started jumping up and down on the green, signaling me that my drive took one hop and went in the cup; and partly to tell how my caddie skills improved so that I got my own golfer a hole-in-one. Dwayne Jenson was an insurance man in downtown Duluth, and a regular member at NCC; one day I drew his bag and carried it around for him through sixteen pretty miserable holes. On the tee at the par-3 Seventeenth, 176 yards over a deep gulley to the green, you can't be short and you can't go long. I knew his game by then and had pulled the six-iron halfway out of the bag when he turned to me and walked to the bag asking for the five. The six started to drop back into the bag and he said no, wait. "I've been shooting so poorly today I guess I'll go with your call." So what did Dwayne Jenson do with the six-iron but knock a one-hop hole-in-one and turn to me with the biggest smile you ever saw on an insurance salesman. By the time we got up to the clubhouse the word had already spread—and the custom was for the hole-in-one shooter to buy a drink for all the non-hole-in-one shooters—a game I never did quite comprehend. He tipped me *ten dollars* and we were all celebrating.

One day Dick Durgan, the caddie who witnessed my ace, talked me into hiking up the service trail where we found the service truck parked with open windows and a small box of Crookette rum-soaked cigars on the dash. Dick reached in and swiped them and we took off running down the road, back to the caddy shack, where outside, in back, we laid on our backs in the grass and lit rum-soaked cigar after another, until we were turning green in the gills. Now I sat up and woo, I was dizzy, and then to my dismay I realized my wool jacket (hey, it was summer in Duluth) stank of cigars, my breath stank of cigars, my short crew cut hair stank of cigars…I went into the caddy shack and bought a box of Junior Mints to eat and cover up the smell, of course what it did was make me even sicker.

Neither of us were called out that day so I walked home early burping rum soaked cigars and mints, and the moment I walked into the kitchen my mother said "You've been smoking!" and made me sit at the kitchen table, not to move until my Dad got home. Next to the table was a counter with some fresh bananas, so when she left the kitchen I plowed thorough a couple of those, ignorantly increasing my distress. A couple of miserable hours passed before my Dad came home from work; my mother told him why she made me sit there, he looked at me, visibly softened, and said "Don't do that again, I expect better of you" and I was off the hook, much to the chagrin of the Ice Maiden.

It needs to be noted that my caddying also was initiated by my Dad, who took me with him golfing when I was seven; sometimes he let me pull the handcart. It was my Dad who, reading his sports page, notified me of the big country club tournament where they needed one hundred caddies for four days. That was my official start date of employment, in my eleventh summer. For the tournament my rookie caddy status drew a golfer from Minneapolis whose medal round had placed him in the 113th flight. What did I know if they were hacks?

We just carried the bags. We were at the ninth hole, they were putting, I was standing by the green, and my Dad was in the gallery watching when a man next to him said "That's a sharp looking boy there, look at those piano legs." My Dad smiled and let him know that was his boy. From all our races in the alley, from my own genes from my Uncle Pat and even Black Emil, I had big strong legs, and for the next three summers I wore clodhopper hunting boots to caddy, specifically to build up my "piano" legs to defend my city championship in the high jump, which I held or shared for five straight years.

Funny things happen to me a lot, and one was when I was sitting around the caddy shack, I overheard another caddy, a kid from West Duluth, I knew him from city track meets. This was in the summer of 1964, right after school let out, and after I had won the seventh grade city high jump to win my first athletic letter; Ricky Glenn, the kid from West Duluth, was telling his friends down the row that he had won the seventh grade city championship in the high jump. I sat there stunned, knowing the blue ribbon was on my wall in my room. A little bit indignant, too, that someone else would be falsely claiming my glory, so I stood up and walked over to Ricky and asked "how could you be the seventh grade city champ in the high jump, when I am?" He looked aghast at me, speechless, his friends leaning in to hear his not very soon forthcoming response; I turned and walked outside, finished with my confrontation, feeling a little shook up myself. What's the difference between courage and fear?

Let it be recorded here that my home in Lakeside, on McCulloch Street, eastern Duluth in the 1950s and 1960s, was not a warm place. Oh sure, we were in Duluth, where they have nine months of winter and three months of tough sledding, and sure, for fun in April we went down to the lake to climb the seventy foot high ice chunk mountains blown in by overnight massive northeasterners, but inside our home it was also cold. As in no affection. My Dad and Mom slept in separate beds, and shared nothing in common except us kids. At least I got some of my Mom's good genes, (by which I'm told relates me to old-time movie stars and even a president!) But for all the meals our family shared every night at the kitchen table (she was an excellent and consistent cook) there was precious little love spoken, so we all grew up sort of deprived. I've since heard of families who at the dinner table all talked throughout the meal; we ate in silence.

How does a kid learn about love if he's never shown it or never told it? My most notable memory of my mother at the dinner table was her using the heavy end of her butter knife to rap my elbows off the table; that hurt. How does a family operate if they always eat in either silence or strict correction? Yes, my Dad showed me in so many ways. One night I was in bed, maybe eight years old, and heard my Dad creaking up the stairs; you could tell who was coming up the stairs by the heaviness of the creaks. He silently padded into my room in his stocking feet, over to my bed, where I pretended to be asleep; he leaned over and kissed me on my forehead, then turned and left the room and creaked back down the stairs without saying a word. Who's gonna tell me my Dad didn't love me?

My Mom was another story. Her parenting consisted of writing and posting lists of chores for us kids to do. Grandma Hildur hated that. My first chore, directed to me when I was seven, was to scrub the kitchen floor and down the linoleum lined stairs to the basement once a week; and if she disapproved of any portion of it, I had to do it all over again before I could go outside. After two years she was moved with compassion and brought me a rubber mat from the clinic to kneel on as I scrubbed, just like my grandmother. Also at seven I became the regular dish-washer or dish-dryer, switching off with Lila; but when I washed, I was not quite tall enough to reach the faucet without rubbing my belt buckle against the wooden front of the sink. My mother was very angry about the crease my buckle had worn into the wood; all I could think was, hey, is it my fault I'm short? After all, I was seven!

My mother was a great cook, I got some smarts from her and very useful discipline, which has indeed come in handy in this ever more lackadaisical world of ours. But a hug, a kiss, an "I love you," a caress, even just a warm touch, a pat of affection, a touch of kindness, a glance of warmth, a wink, a nod, were not in her power to give me.

She surprised me one day when Nicky France threw a rock that hit me in the head and drew blood while I was playing with other kids at Portman, the park where we skated in winter. When I returned home my mother took one look at my bloodied head and packed me into her Pink Bomb—a Studebaker brush-painted pink, which she loved—and drove me to France's house where she walked me up to the front door and challenged Nicky in front of his mother, her hands trembling on my shoulders. It made me feel like she cared about me, for the first and maybe only time.

Looking back across the decades, I do see a golden thread that has run throughout my life. For as my mother was unable to show me love, I have found solace in the most unlikely places. I was five years old when I found myself in the basement, by the big old octopus furnace, and for some reason I took a raincoat from the hooks by the stairs, put it over my head and sat with my back to the warm rumbling furnace, leaving just a tiny crack of light to penetrate the interior sanctum, and sat there, silently, feeling the warmth on my back, rumbling, just a bare crack of light coming in, so warm and safe and nice, when one day all of a sudden a cascade of goose bumps ran up my left arm, around my shoulders and down my right arm. For all the world in me, it felt like someone or something was putting its arm around me.

The next time I would eagerly await its return under that raincoat. It came back every time. I came to call it my Furnace Room Friend, and could summon it at will whenever I sat there in the almost totally dark under the raincoat. I later discovered my FRF was portable, when I found various other spots, always with a dark rumbling, where the cascade surrounded me. All I knew for certain at five was that it felt warm and safe. My Furnace Room Friend was my refuge then, and is still by me, when my mind is right.

The Ice Maiden went back to work at the Clinic when Jesse was in second grade; she drove me to Ordean Junior High in the mornings on her way to work. Until one day when I was in eighth grade, and for some irrational reason she was angry at me and refused to take me to school, even though she drove right past it, and this came at a moment when we were just about to get in the car and I would be late for class if she didn't take me. Ice refused and moved toward her car door.

Out of my mouth involuntarily spurted a blue streak consisting of every cuss word I had heard at the caddy shack; she looked at me in horrified indignant surprise, barely able in her rage to say in lowered evil tones, "Wait 'til your father hears what you said to me," getting into her car and gunning it down the driveway so heatedly the back bumper scraped the concrete at the bottom as she turned and gunned it into the street, leaving me standing there in the driveway. My thumb got me to school that day. Come to think of it, that was my first time hitch-hiking. That night, when my Dad came home from work, she filled him in on my filthy mouth, and he rushed up the stairs to my room, not in a friendly mood, chased me into a corner of my room with his hard Iron Ranger fists raised, ready to strike. I cowered in the corner as his fists loomed over me and he said "If anyone ever called my mother those names I woulda knocked his block off." I meekly looked up at him from my submissive crouch, my arms raised in defense and said "Your mother's not my mother." His fists slowly dropped to his side as he acknowledged my point, "I know" and turned and silently left my room and slowly descended the stairs. I quietly rose from my crouch, profoundly impressed that he loved his mother so much and how much I wished I could love mine just a little.

The shrapnel piece that had lodged in my Dad's head in 1944 really began to trouble him by 1966, having evolved from a bloody attack to scar tissue to a cyst that impeded the blood flow to his brain. He had promised to buy me a steak dinner if we won half our games in sophomore football; we did, and then some, so one autumn day in 1966 he drove me up the scenic colors in full blast North Shore of Lake Superior to the Shoreline Restaurant and we enjoyed thick slabs of broiled sirloin with baked potatoes, green beans, oh man it was a great meal, delicious.

On the drive home he began to speak in terms I had never heard him talk about before—about how he thought he was going to die in that English hospital—it left my heart troubled when I went to bed that night. In the middle of that night, I awoke to the sound of my mother frantically calling Lila to come downstairs.

"It's your father."

Upon hearing those words I leaped out of bed and flew down the stairs and ran to their bedroom, where my Dad lay with his back on the floor, gurgling in his own spit. He was having an epileptic seizure. Lila grabbed a spoon and made sure he didn't swallow his tongue. She was like cold steel in crisis.

I stood there dumbstruck looking down at my hunting fishing sprinting boxing big strong hard-fisted lightning-surviving Dad lying twitching helplessly in front of me on the floor. I went with him in the ambulance, and he woke up while we were enroute to the hospital. "Sorry about the scare," he rasped, looking cheerfully into my worried eyes. We clasped hands and held tightly all the way to the hospital, where they diagnosed it as an epileptic seizure caused by a blockage of blood to that part of the brain.

My aunt Alma came to stay with us to help nurse him back to health. We sat at the kitchen table and talked for hours, for days. That's when I learned, from her, about my Dad's teenage travels during the Depression. He had never ever talked about it to me. I said "Wow, I wish I could have been there." He looked at me sadly across the table, the afternoon fast dropping sun behind him, and said "No you don't." The sheer weight of his words on the air between us told me far more than what was actually said. Alma later told me that our neighbor on the corner Mrs. Magnum, whose father once had been a candidate for governor, told Alma that Ice had said to her she "wasn't about to stick around and take care of a sick old man." He eventually came around, saying "I don't know how to spell the word quit," and went back to work. But the die was cast, and over the next five years his health diminished, and through three different painful debilitating "exploratory" brain surgeries at the VA hospital in St. Paul they prepared him finally to quit after all.

It was early in pre-football season 1968, my senior year at East, when I heard the Ice Maiden talking on the phone, and she started crying, which was a first for me to witness. Almost telepathically I knew Dad was telling her he wasn't coming home; he'd met another woman who wanted to take care of him. My friend Cathy and Jesse and I took him pots and pans, rugs and towels for his little forlorn West Duluth apartment, for which he was surprisingly grateful.

Meanwhile, at home, Ice saw her newly divorced state as requiring some new discipline around the house. Proof positive that she didn't know me in the slightest, she took to getting my attention by hitting me in the face and neck and shoulders with a thick yardstick that had been used to measure my growth in the kitchen since my childhood. Wack! Wack! Wack! That quarter-inch yardstick hailed down on me over and over, time after time that senior year at Duluth East High. I stood six feet tall by then and faced her, standing elbows out, fists at my waist like Superman, laughing down in her face to show her she couldn't hurt me. Wack! Wack! Right on my face, my head, my neck, Wack! Wack! Why was she beating me? Wack! Wack! I honestly didn't know, unless she made the biggest mistake ever, thinking she could instill her brand of new discipline into a hormone-raging seventeen year old bent for Europe.

Jesse, then thirteen, sometimes sat on the couch watching the beatings, and confided to me many years later that I was his hero, for just standing there and taking it. After each beating I would run up to my room, sob into my pillow and then run out the door all the way to Cathy's house, a little over a mile away, where her parents understood my plight and allowed me to sit on the floor, just inside their front door, back to the wall, with the hall light off, by myself hugging my knees for as long as I needed to. Then I would thank them and run home in dark streets to bed.

Those were the days I was getting up at 5:20 a.m. by my clock radio to run outside, over to Forty Seventh avenue and then sprint up, jog down, sprint up, jog down, ten times and then run home and get ready for school. It may sound like a cliché but it is so true that the main difference between a champion and an also-ran is very often sheer hard work and self-discipline.

One day Ice attacked me again and just as I had felt rage erupting in me when my Dad taught me to box, I felt it rise now, and I grabbed the hated stick out of her hand, held it over her head (she instinctively ducked)—I was hurt to see that she actually thought I would hit her. Instead I just held it over her head and snapped the stick in two, and then put the two pieces together over her head and snapped them into four, surprised at my own strength, threw them clattering onto the couch and informed astounded speechless Ice "you will never hit me with that again." Stunned Susan never hit me again.

Within a year she had ditched the house, bailed out of Duluth, left fifty two pairs of shoes all neatly lined up along the basement playroom wall, married a doctor and moved to Scottsdale, Arizona with him. He had the marriage annulled after a month and kicked her out; her brother Charlie drove over from San Diego and took her home with him, where she eventually got her own apartment and a job and lived out her tragic brief life on Balboa Avenue.

Dad moved back into the house on McCulloch Street with Nan, the woman who had been caring for him; he drove her to Hibbing where they had some kind of self-devised ceremony, but they had just eight months together before the shrapnel finally took him down. Sometimes he would be sitting quietly drugged at the kitchen table, when abruptly he would turn, head jerked up, eyes opened wide, convinced the Germans were attacking, involuntarily recreating scarred memories.

About seven a.m. on July 8, 1972 somehow we all—Lila, Jesse, me, Nan and Alma—found ourselves silently standing at the foot of Eddie Edwards' bed. He faintly looked in Jesse's direction and sighed, barely audible, "Jesse," and then his breath gurgled, his eyes went vacant, his chest heaved, rattled, heaved, rattled and then in the longest moment of a life which had survived the Longest Day, he was gone, an American war hero at fifty-nine. We stood there silently looking at his corpse. Lila went to the phone to call our mother to tell her the news; Lila was cold. I walked around to the side of the bed, and as in the movies, gently pulled his eyelids closed. They popped right back open, and I walked away cursing the movies. I walked out to the front door and looked out the window at the street where I had grown up. Now a strange tug in my gut told me this had been my home for seventeen years but might not be for much longer.

I was twenty-one, Jesse was seventeen, Lila had already moved out, she just came home for the death. The mortgage wasn't yet paid off. Most of his $10,000 life insurance went to my mother, and I had asked him why. He told me he still loved her. I looked out at the street wondering what I would do now. On my own at twenty one, thankfully prepared for survival by my Dad, painfully unaware of how unprepared for love by my Mom, a whole life ahead of me I couldn't see, and didn't have anyone to turn to for advice.

Given the nature of the journey you are about to read, perhaps a word about spiritual training is in order. In my house there was none. I never saw a Bible or any other religious book in my house. On Sunday mornings when I was little, my Dad would pack us into the car and drive to Hibbing to go to church with his mother. From Duluth the trip was about one hour fifteen minutes. When we arrived at her modest subsidized apartment, we could instantly smell fresh bread baking. Fresh, piping hot Swedish flatbread, prepared with love from the early morning so that when we walked in the door, all three of us kids got our own small circular loaf, with our initials carved in the bottom. I would quickly find the one with an N on the bottom and grab it, butter a steaming slice and devour it. Mmmm.

Then we would take Grandma to her Lutheran church, and sit through one of those dry dead ritual services that drive so many young people away. "Turn to Hymn 234 and stand and sing" the pastor blandly intoned. My mother would go through the motions so everyone could see she her, holding the hymnal up high ostensibly so I could read the words…ah naaah da tooda, mmm who all belgraaa… making up the words as I hummed along. They meant nothing to me. My mother would attend church in Duluth on Easter and Christmas, and was sure to be there as well for the church directory photos. Firsthand I saw hypocrisy leaking out of sheer stockings.

Otherwise they sent me and Lila to the Presbyterian church just a half block away on Forty Fifth avenue east. They sat at home and drank coffee and read the newspapers while Lila and I endured Sunday school. My mother let Jesse off, he stayed home. Lila actually found refuge there in the young teens' group, and spent many hours avoiding our home at the church. Me, I was more interested in my Boy Scout troop which met weekly in the fellowship hall.

For ninth grade confirmation my classmates and I were trained to memorize and recite the Apostle's Creed, which frankly did not resonate in me, so that when confirmation time came around that spring, I was sitting in the church pew with my classmates, thinking what on earth will I do? I can't get up and say I believe this and I believe that when I don't, I thought. I had it memorized but not internalized. Sweating bullets, I waited for the Pastor to come down from his pulpit, invite us all to stand in a line facing the church (Oh God, should I run out now?)

and turn to us to simply ask us if we wanted to be members of that congregation. Yes! I could say yes to that! And the crisis passed, but soon thereafter I walked away from church, from Boy Scouts, to play basketball and listen to my Beatles 65 album "...I'm a looooser..." The lyrics of which, by the way, Ice thoroughly disapproved.

Earlier I alluded to myself as one "bent on Europe."That wasn't actually my first trip on my own; the first one was a Christmas break free train trip (as a family member of my Dad the railroader I rode the train for free). I was sixteen, and on that trip, for some reason, I felt compelled to visit my beloved two years deceased grandmother's older sister, Helga, at her small rural home in Chewelah, Washington. I took the train to Spokane, and when I disembarked from the train I was met by a very nice man, clearly a friend of my Dad's, who he had called to see if he could meet me and make sure I find the bus to Chewelah. So he showed me around the corner to the bus station, shook my hand and wished me well. My Dad has some nice friends, I thought, but I could have found it myself.

When I got to Chewelah I walked up a quiet almost farmland cattle path, there were horses in back yards, and found her address and knocked on the door. When she came to the door and looked down at me from her stoop (she was tall and wearing her own stout grandma shoes) my mouth dropped in amazement. For the first time in two years I was looking at my grandmother's face, the sisters resembled each other that much. "And who might you be?" she sweetly inquired. "I'm Nash Edwards, Eddie's boy," I replied. "Oh my land," she gasped, holding her large Swedish hands to her face. "Well, come in, come in." She had met me before I was old enough to know her, so this was my chance to meet her. We sat around and chatted about all sorts of things for a couple of days; she fixed me chicken and dumplings. When we parted I offered a handshake and was given a hug. And so I returned for the second half of my sophomore year of high school, never to see her again, happy that I had.

One final note about my early spiritual life was that at seventeen, my intuition somehow told me that this entity referred to as "I" possesses both a spirit and a physical body, and that it would be wise to assign a higher value to the spiritual side than to the physical side. I trusted that intuition then and do still. To maintain it in perfect balance was easier said than done, as my physical body grew stronger and faster and more confident, my mind ever more audacious each passing year. As the years pass, most of our contemporaries lose their balance and don't even try to regain it, sinking instead to a sense-obsessed materialism. To maintain one's balance, as the Buddhist saying goes, one must do more than not fall over. It is truly a "razor's edge" we walk between conscious discernment and sense-overload. I refuse to believe that humans were made merely to consume. I concurrently do believe that humans usually live far beneath their potential. Therefore my pursuit must be to encourage all who will pay heed to utilize more of their minds, more of their hearts, more of their souls.

CHAPTER THREE

The idea of hitch-hiking around Europe came to me while I was still in ninth grade, reading maps of the world for fun. Several of the books I had read included the lives and times of Europeans like Columbus, Pizzaro, Napoleon, DaVinci and Michelangelo along with tales of American mountain men like Kit Carson and Jim Bridger. Twenty feet up in my backyard maple tree where I sat for hours reading my books in a natural cradle of branches, if you turned slightly to look out at the lake, Lake Superior, you could see the long iron ore boats chugging out of port and within an hour they were out of sight, just as young Christopher Columbus watched the ocean vessels sailing from Genoa, which got him reportedly interested in seeing perhaps if the world were not flat.

I saved every dime I made caddying and then working two summers at the country club pool as a "snack bar operator," a friendly euphemism for a student dollar an hour assistant to the pool manager. An interesting feature of that job was that I had the key to the pool area, the snack bar and even to the lights in that lit the pool from under water. Most of my classmates from school, the brightest ones, were members' kids and had privileges there where I worked.

My click with them was at least partially due to my ability and willingness to turn the pool lights on for them at night. In those days, I had at least $500 in one dollar bills saved in my sock drawer. Sometimes I would take my dollar bills out, spread them out on the living room floor, and just stand there and look at them. My Dad was so impressed he even borrowed a hundred from me at one point, much to my surprise, and then he paid it back from his next paycheck.

My big break for making money for Europe came in my seventeenth summer, when my Dad (who else) got me a job as a fireman on the Great Northern railway. First I was sent to the railroad doctor for a "physical." I was sitting in his office when the oldest doctor on the planet shuffled in and wanted to check my hearing by holding his ancient railroader's watch up to my ear tick-tock-tick-tock and asking me in his scraggly voice, "Hear that?" Yup, I nod. "Okay, your hearing's fine," he informed me in his weak monotone, pocketing his watch.

The only other revelation received from that "physical" was his laconic report about my back x-ray, telling me that "you'll have trouble with your lower back later in life, your lowest two vertebra are fused together." Huh, I said. Never bothered me in football, long jumping, sprinting, high jumping, and that was when we landed on sand piles. Oh well, maybe later. (Only I discovered much to my amazement decades after that railroad doctor's advice, that even though my lower back is not what it used to be, my lower two vertebra are NOT fused together.) So I passed with flying colors and reported to duty at the railyard the next day.

My advantage as a high school kid out there was that I was happy to work two shifts a day, which I did many days, finishing up my first eight hours on the locomotive when a voice would come over the radio, "yeah, Edwards, you wanna double out?" They'd give me forty-five minutes for "beans," which usually consisted of me walking over to the Shack for a fried chicken dinner and then back to climb aboard my new locomotive still wiping my fried chicken greasy fingers on my overalls and meet my new hoghead (engineer) for the next eight hours.

I'll just say that my fireman job was pretty cushy and a little bit absurd. I mean, I appreciate union wages, the idea of collective bargaining makes a lot of sense, I feel an affinity with working men and women everywhere. But when firemen on the locomotives were grandfathered under the union contract with the switchover from coal-fired to diesel locomotives, that ushered in a new level of uselessness. Firemen used to stoke the fire with coal for the whole run, that's how they were named. But with a diesel engine the fireman mostly just sits there and keeps the hoghead company. I actually did cross-word puzzles at my window, especially when my hoghead pushed a train of cars a snail's pace over the scales on the way up to the docks. It took a good two hours to first gather up all the cars from various tracks, there occasionally I was needed to watch for the switchman's signals ahead, then push the thirty-eight car train of iron ore cars to the scales, then slow down; and then the hoghead drove the locomotive with his head leaning out the window to watch as his first contact with the scales incurred with every car, inching all thirty eight cars over the scales at a snail's pace.

My only certain duty on the whole shift was to watch for the switchman's signals up ahead when we took a corner left. The hoghead could see him if it bent right. The nonsense of it did not escape even this kid grateful for union wages, namely that I could be replaced by one or two strategically placed mirrors, as my hoghead was not bashful to tell me. After a few days on the extra board, which meant I could be called to work for any shift, at the last minute, I took a whole month of replacing two firemen on vacation, and got a regular shift out of it—4:00 p.m. to midnight, then to 8:00 a.m. if I doubled out. That regular shift allowed me to make my travel plans; I didn't have a car yet, so I left our house in Lakeside at 1:30 in the afternoon, hitch-hiked to the railyard outside of Superior, Wisconsin, we're talking about maybe fifteen miles through two towns and over an interstate bridge, often getting there just at 4:00, then when I got off, either at midnight or at 8:00 a.m., I hitch-hiked back home to sleep for a few hours, then repeated the process. For a high-schooler in 1968 in Duluth to be pulling down one hundred dollars a day was unheard of. By the end of the summer my bank account was filled enough to take my ten-week Europe trip and to pay for my first year of college at the University of Minnesota in Duluth. That summer I read for the first time Jack Kerouac's On the Road, which really fired me up to take my pack to Europe, although at that time I knew nothing of Sal Paradise's vices and definitely didn't understand what Dean Cassidy was really up to, me being just a pure jock rock hard innocent squeaky clean student athlete from Duluth Minnesota.

When my high school graduation came in June 1969, Ice stayed home and Cathy drove me to the ceremony in her white Volkswagen beetle; she got Ice's ticket and watched from the peanut gallery. Two days later I visited my Dad in the VA hospital in St. Paul, recovering from his first brain surgery. My first time there, I walked down the sterile–smelling shiny floors through semi-lit hallways of the VA hospital to enter a long room of probably forty beds, in the first one to my left, behind a drab white half-drawn curtain, lay my once invincible Dad. He was not conscious, just lying there propped up on the pillow, head mashed in from the top of his skull to the middle of his cheek, every inch black and blue from a fall he had taken after ringing to no avail for a nurse. As I stood there somberly looking at him he opened his eyes, reached for my hand, and slurred from the drugs "itz good ju came." I just stood there, held his hand and looked into his eyes, so grateful to him, as his eyes closed peacefully, leaving me unsure whether he would be alive when I returned from my summer in Europe. I figured he would want me to go. All summer I thought of him and tried not to until I returned from Europe.

Three nights later I checked into a hotel in Luxembourg to begin my ten-week hitch-hiking trip I had planned since ninth grade. My cost was $387 round-trip fare on Icelandic Airways, which was a turbo-prop which caught on fire as we circled out of JFK airport, returned to fix the problem while we remained on the plane, then took off again three hours later; I fell asleep even in my excitement but was awakened by a nice stewardess who offered me cognac at 4 a.m.. Sure, I said, never having been drunk in my life. By the time we got to Reykjavik in Iceland, I was feeling the cognac, and did enjoy looking at the thick-haired Icelandic girls with their hair braided up in lovely rolls of yellow, and slept almost the rest of the flight to Luxembourg.

My thinking was that my two years of high school German language study, particularly under my German teacher (and track coach) Gerhard Schlector, a strict, understanding coach and excellent teacher, no nonsense, but not without fun, like when he taught us the beer-drinking songs of the Hofbrauhaus in Munich, "ein, zwei, gezuffa," I figured I could get around Europe on my own.

So the next morning, I repacked my pack—a daily ritual I had learned from something I had read, it's good to stay on top of your stuff on the road. My backpack was purchased for nineteen dollars from my friend Deke Sturro who worked at the surplus store in downtown Duluth, with a magic marker and a piece of cardboard to write on. Each city and country would be inscribed on the pack as my travels unfolded.

On the road out of Luxembourg the next morning, bound for Belgium, I took my cardboard and marker out and wrote in large letters "Brussels." Almost no sooner than I stuck my right thumb out while holding my sign in my left hand did a big truck roll to a stop and I picked up my pack yelling yippee and ran to sit up with the driver, a big round red-cheeked German who turned out to speak no English so the test was upon me to have a conversation auf Deutsch. He drove me almost one hundred kilometers toward my goal of Brussels, and along the way we had a heart to heart talk as we drove through the Ardennes Forest, itself a huge battleground during the War, about how he had to fight for his Furher and my Dad had to fight for his, but thankfully we all can live in peace now. He nodded repeatedly. "Ja, Ja."

My German friend dropped me at a crossroads, he was continuing east but Brussels was north from there, so we bid auf Deutsch farewell and I lifted my pack onto my back and began to hike down the road, several miles until coming upon a tiny pastoral town which boasted a tiny pastoral storefront into which I walked and bought a slab of salami, a loaf of French bread, and a bottle of red wine, all for about two dollars. Then I hiked up a row of stones that led to a split rail fence leading to a breezy shady knoll under a big oak tree, where I sat and enjoyed my first European lunch, overlooking a delightful flower-strewn Belgian meadow on a beautiful sunny June day. First time my lips ever touched wine. Didn't take much to make my cheeks warm. I packed the leftovers into my pack and roamed down the meadow on my wine legs, getting out my BRUSSELS sign for the road.

A well dressed businessman in a sweet gray Mercedes picked me up still a little tipsy from my afternoon wine tasting, which I found to my amazement contributed to a generally cordial visit all the way to downtown Brussels. This gentleman spoke English, so I spoke German to him and he replied in English, that way we both could practice. Before he dropped me off he gave me his card and encouraged me to call him if I were ever in Brussels again. I said thank you in English, he said Bitte, and we parted ways.

Perhaps the most amazing thing about Brussels is the incredibly well-thought-out system of concentric streets and avenues, full of great old buildings, almost every one of which predates the United States. It's really no wonder an international system of justice runs through those concentric streets, completely rational professional articulate barristers arguing their intricately constructed cases before the international tribunals. I stayed in my first youth hostel there, and found it totally adequate for this former hunter boy scout camper fisherman. We all had to do some work around the hostel to pay for our keep, about thirty cents for the night for a good clean-sheeted bunk and a shower in the morning. Guys and gals stayed in separate rooms, at least in this hostel. I picked up a broom and started sweeping for my part. Everyone else found something to do.

These were travelers like me, many from the States like me, a few Germans or Dutch or English on holiday. Most, I found out quickly, were older than I was, and they all commented on it, until I thought well, am I too young to be here at eighteen? I didn't think so, not with three years of planning and saving. Anyway they were all there on Daddy's dime, I was there on mine. After Brussels it was to the coast, to England, home of King Arthur, Herman's Hermits and the Beatles, by way of Oostende, a bustling port city.

Oostende is the kind of city you pass through on one trip and make a note to one day return for a closer look. The activity of the waterfront generates a buzz of culture in wonderful buildings with beautiful women everywhere. At any rate I passed through it to the ferry across the English Channel, before anyone ever dreamed of a tunnel under it, this was still the ancient way of travelers to England. The high winds from the Channel reminded me of Lake Superior, but much warmer, so I stood outside and faced into the wind, searching the seas for signs of land; in the spray I felt the need to find a restroom, in England called WCs for water closets, anyway to my chagrin I had to pay to use the WC. That was a first. I dutifully entered it into my pocket spiral notebook which served as the record of every nickel I spent on that trip. Finally, the grays of the Channel faded and the white cliffs of Dover appeared and soon we were all disembarking the ferry, first among them myself, eager not to be hemmed in by a traffic jam. I was on a mission.

This night would be spent in London or else. Right away I hitched a ride out of Dover onto the road to London. Then I stood for a couple of hours learning the patience of the road, and finally a lorry stopped and I ran up to it, jumped into it, pulled my pack onto my lap, and said "Thanks a lot…I'm headed for London." "Waell then, myte, yur in a big wye of luck, ewe are" He spoke the first Cockney I had ever heard, and although it was English he was speaking, in England at that, I had great difficulty understanding what he was saying. So the next couple of hours were a diversion of major import. I may have even learned a little Cockn'y meself.

But London it was, I stood there as an eighteen-year-old at Piccadilly Circus and said "wow." I found a youth hostel not far from there and one night I was out walking and just came upon the famous place, where I stood around observing the environs until I moved on to the next neighborhood. Stay with me dear reader as I take you through many diverse neighborhoods. After whipping around to see Parliament, Big Ben, Windsor Castle, the Tower of London, on a more imprudent twist, my discoveries included the self-proclaimed oldest little pub in Great Britain, where I was politely informed that a pint of brew could remove your cap, two would make you sit, three would see that you have to pee, four and you're out the door. I didn't drink any that day; still had never tasted beer in my life. After a couple of days roaming London I headed north to the home of Shakespeare, Stratford on Avon. Fantastic. I couldn't believe I was standing on the very ground he trod. Such creativity. Such genius. Such a treat to be here. I lingered there with the Bard a while and then moseyed out of town, heading north to find my night.

The roads north in England are Roman roads; when the Romans were controlling England a thousand years ago, they built these absolutely straight one-lane roads that didn't turn or hitch or bend anywhere, for miles and miles they ran straight, true as a Roman spear. The real thrill came when the car you were in approached another one coming the other direction, and as the two got closer, they each inched toward the side and barely missed each other when passing. The Romans didn't think to build two-lane highways, but their roads certainly have stood the test of durability.

A small truck picked me up and took me all the way north to Derby; along the way observing a sign pass by "Sherwood Forest this way." I mean, the real Sherwood Forest, with Nottingham (I wondered if they still had a sheriff) just an hour from Derby, not a movie, not a TV show, not a condo development south of Ridgedale in Minnetonka Minnesota, it was the real Sherwood Forest. Robin Hood was one of my favorite heroes; I remember reading "The Silver Arrow" twice as a kid and still couldn't believe Robin would die. Finally I was hiking up a country road in a hilly area in northern England, well not that far north, as my trusty map showed that I wasn't even halfway to Scotland, anyway there were plenty of dairy cows in the pasture, sharing moos with me, and then I stopped at a small store and asked if they had cold milk. It had previously been my lesson that in Jolly Olde England they don't like to drink cold beverages, except the occasional pint at a pub. The round-faced aproned woman nodded yes, and turned and reached up and took the pitcher of milk from where it had been resting on top of the icebox, not in it. She brought it over to me and poured me a glass as I bemusedly watched and ordered a donut too. When in Derby, I thought to myself, and stood around there eating my donut, drinking my "cool" milk and beginning to wonder where I would sleep tonight.

That's a feeling peculiar to the road, I think, and if one has not been there one cannot possibly experience it except through the expressions of others who have. This much I offer: after a week, two weeks, four weeks, six weeks...every night needing to find someplace to sleep, you get hardened in a way but also deepened. Still yearning. Your truest night is elusive. Solitary nights are fertile. There will never be enough nights to do all that you want to do, but I am grateful and glad to know the special solitude of the road, counting stars overhead.

A short hike out of town as the afternoon sun began to set and I got a ride to a little town called Uttoxeter, and there the driver of the lift, a skinny long-eared chap who ran a little farm up the road, allowed me to stay the night in his barn, up in the hayloft. Not very far north, as I mentioned, but the nights up there were cool, and I rolled up in my (East) Indian blanket in the hayloft, and slept soundly until the rising sun woke me through the shutters. I got up, repacked my pack, walked over to my long lobed benefactor's house to thank him and he gave me directions south to Birmingham, then it took me all day to get there.

Birmingham's youth hostel was a bit grungy, but the bed was clean and it only cost me twenty five cents to stay the night. It's a big industrial city that occupied my fancy for a couple of hours in the morning; then I hit the road heading south again, this time heading for Bristol.

My plan was to cover a lot of ground in ten weeks and I was on schedule. I was lucky again, getting a ride all the way, but the driver, a quiet chap who preferred to drive in silence, was going to Chepstow, a little town across the Bristol Channel from Bristol, where I found a hostel near the water, and walked around that town for the night, observing small town English folk as they strolled casually along the waterfront enjoying their ice cream in the warm summer night (far enough south to feel warmer). Stopping into a tiny restaurant for supper, the proprietor warmly greeted me, a very friendly fellow from India whose name was Ducknow, and he explained to me that that was the same name of the town in India from which he came. He was one of those Indians with dark skin, black eyes, and teeth so white they dazzled. I told him I didn't like any hot spicy stuff so he chuckled "no curry then?" "If it's hot, I don't want it," I replied. Something about spicy food makes me sweat on top of my head, pooling into a sort of Lake Edwards, that's just me. So he indulged me and fixed me a good English chicken pot pie. When I finished and paid the bill, we shook hands as he warmly invited me to visit him in the future.

The next morning was a short hop to Bristol, another fairly large city, which was incorporated as a town in 1155. The medieval city was full of history; including a dark era of slave trading in the 17th and 18th centuries, then importing sugar and molasses from Jamaica, making Bristol a sugar and chocolate center, and a cathedral church which was once an abbey of St. Augustine. There were all sorts of pretty girls walking around too, making it a fun place to see history and modern marvels. I stayed one night at the hostel there and the next morning took me to Bath.

Now, Bath is a special city. Those arcing large limestone many-columned buildings known officially as the Royal Crescent are awesome. This is the city named for the hot natural springs which the Romans found, and where the Saxons built the abbey on the site where Edgar, the first King of England, was crowned in 973. By the Seventeenth Century it was a popular spa and resort for the well heeled of that day. But another neat thing about Bath is that it's less than a day's hitching to Stonehenge, and that's where I headed next.

I had read about Stonehenge, and knew it had a mysterious tale behind it, with Neolithic people scratching out an immense circular ditch using deer antlers for picks, to later erection of the large sarcen stones for purposes exactly of which remain to this day unknown. As I stood there in mid-June 1969, you could still walk right up to and around the huge stones, and various pieces of rock and rubble lay around just part of the landscape. Since then I have heard it's been picked clean by human vultures with insatiable appetites. But then it was free and open, and I stayed around for a few hours to check out the shadows the moving sun was making on the ground. It has been said that Stonehenge was built as a temple and predictor of the sunrise of the summer solstice. To be there, sitting cross-legged on the grass in the middle of the sarcen circle, one is taken to worlds away, times past, memories long since wiped from our minds. You are surrounded by twelve foot high stones which somehow were put there by humans like you, only with certain knowledge long forgotten. You feel very small in this immense universe with more questions than answers. And to feel that at eighteen held a particular wonder.

It was late afternoon before I could pull myself away from the Druid riddle, and I once again got lucky and caught a lift with a nice elderly couple on holiday from Liverpool. I sat in the back seat with my pack and just listened to their wonderful accents, and they got me as far as Southampton, where I found a hostel in a funky neighborhood and got a bunk for fifty cents. The daily protocol was like that: find a bunk, stow my pack (keep my money and passport on me at all times), and go for a grand walkabout through the town my feet temporarily trod. Southampton's fortunes lie with her position near the head of a viable waterway, where the Romans had a settlement in AD 43. In the European Middle Ages she was already a major port, and by 1980 had become the second biggest port by tonnage in the whole of England. I spent some time down by the waterfront, watching the fishermen tossing out their nets in the early morning fog.

Then I set out again hiking south until I scored another big truck ride that took me all the way through Portsmouth and over to Brighton, where I was dropped off two blocks from the hostel and found it quickly. Brighton is another one of those charming English resort areas, right on the English Channel, with seven miles of beaches, mostly rocky. King George IV had a colossal Royal Pavilion built for his use there, with an Indian exterior and intricate Chinese interior decorations. I tried to skip a few rocks but it wasn't the same as tossing thin eroded stones onto a placid Lake Superior cove; back home we could consistently throw "motorboats," which took a big hop, another hop, then another, then settling into a thuda thuda thuda thuda series of small hops that carried far. By now, however, I was looking ahead to re-crossing the Channel but first I would stay a night in Hastings.

My reason for wanting to spend a night in Hastings had to do with the silly fact that in twelfth grade I took myself out of advanced classes in history, tired of the same old kids in my classes year after year, wanting to taste a bit more of the mainstream, and then soon discovering my mistake by way not only of the gigantic difference in the quality of instruction but also the comparative lights of the students. So that I only learned two things my senior year in history, and one of them was that the Battle of Hastings was won by the Normans in 1066. So I caught a lift outside of Brighton that took me straight to Hastings, where a most delightful hostel awaited my arrival, it was very nice and quaint, right down by the seaside. Bunk and a shower for forty cents. The ruins of Castle Hill, on the sandstone cliffs overlooking the old port, are a great place to sit and watch the sunset's magic red hour glint off the glass windows of the antique stores below.

The next morning I picked up a short lift to Dover, where I climbed aboard the ferry back to Oostende. You could easily spend all ten weeks in England but there were eleven other countries on my radar and my schedule would not keep. From Oostende I hitched east to Antwerp and spent a night on a walkabout through my first neighborhood where I couldn't understand what people were saying. These Belgians speak Flemish, or Dutch, and it's vaguely related to German but beyond my comprehension. Fortunately I was able to find speakers of German or even English. Antwerp is a pretty big city, over a million, only one night spent there. But I will tell one funny story from that day.

After my first lift, I was hiking on the road with my pack on my back, a bounce in my step, happy in my heart, then a bus of schoolkids drove by and it appeared to me they were laughing at me and pointing to my legs, I thought. Hey, short cut-off jeans revealed my thunder thighs and big calves, so what's the big deal, I thought. A short way down the road I was stopped by a couple of Belgian troopers; I immediately pleaded ignorance, pretended only to speak English, but what they had stopped me for blew my mind. They said, smiling at me, in Belgium in 1969, "wearing white socks is a signal that you are a homo on the hunt." So that's what the kids on the bus were pointing at? Baloney, in America white socks are worn by strong jocks, rugged hunters and even some leftover beatniks from the Fifties. That was just a chance to confirm to myself that other people's assumptions do not define me.

That afternoon I entered the Netherlands, still wearing my white socks; heck, dark socks looked goofy to me. I found a hostel in Rotterdam. Wooden shoes, dikes, tulips, canals, windmills, and lo and behold, English speakers. The Dutch I met spoke English perfectly and I asked one of them how long he studied it. "For six years, from primary all the way to graduation," he perfectly replied.

Rotterdam is a big port city, with an inner city which was almost totally rebuilt from the ashes of WWII, including one of the first pedestrian only walkways. But its harbor is most impressive, one of the largest in the world, and Rotterdam has access to the North Sea, Rhine and Maas Rivers, adding up to one of the great ports of Europe.

In the morning I caught a series of short lifts for the fairly short distance to Amsterdam. The youth hostel there was right in the center of old town, which is a cobbled close-knit bundle of neighborhoods, and on my walkabout that night my observations included women sitting on chairs in windows, each with a bare red light bulb casting a mood over their heads, giving them a subtle aura. Almost too innocent to know what they were, bashfully I walked on by after one of them unsettled me with a sweet red-lipped smile. The next day I decided to hang around Amsterdam for another day, it's really pretty, and discovered a brewery near a canal, in a park where I just took in the sun, this time drinking a bottle of Heineken beer, brewed in the brewery right over there, for just thirteen cents a bottle. Life was good.

As I lay there in the sun on the grass, my elbows propping me up to view the canal, my big Rushabout temporally on hold, someone called out to me from his bench behind me. "You drinking Heineken?" I turned and looked at my questioner, a blond Dutchman about twenty five, slender, in jeans, smiling at me. "Yeah." "You know, they make Amstel beer in the same vat, put different labels on them, and you can drink Amstels for eleven cents a bottle." I considered myself educated on that local note and switched to Amstel. Erik and I drank three each as he marveled at me hitching around Europe at my age. When standing up to go, I wobbled, under the influence of forty five cents of really good beer. Eric laughed at me and pointed me to the street that went back to the hostel. I slept like a log that night and woke up with Germany on my mind.

Out of Amsterdam the traffic was heavy but I got a lift from two students who were going to Arnhem, where they dropped me on the road to the German border. From there it was a short hop to the first town on the German side, Kleve, where I spent the afternoon and night. There's not that much to tell about Kleve, other than that it is in Germany, they speak German there, and I found a little sports field with a long jump pit, so I took off my shoes and socks and stretched out before attempting a long jump, speed plus height equals distance, but the best I could pop was about 16 feet. Off my high school best by about five feet.

The morning found me on the road again, this time bound for Munster. With my usual good fortune I pulled into Munster at 3:00 in the afternoon, so after I paid forty five cents for my bunk and shower, stowed my pack in a locker, I was free for the rest of the day and night to roam around this great German town. It was originally founded in AD 804 when Charlemagne sent a missionary there to found a bishopric and then chartered as Munster in 1127. Its location at a confluence of important waterways made it influential during the period of the Hanseatic League in the thirteenth and fourteenth centuries. In modern times it is a city more than two and a half times as large as my hometown, so the additional diversions I ate up like a lollapalooza.

After about two hours of my walkabout, a lovely spot by a small park beckoned me to sit for a while, then a guitar playing began behind me. I turned and there was a solo male guitarist, picking out melodies with all ten digits flying, and it was mesmerizing. After a time he noticed me watching him and he looked at me with blue eyes and blond Aryan hair and said, in English,

"You're an American aren't you?"

"Yes."

"How long have you been on the road?"

"Um, just two or three weeks so far."

"Did you know that this is your Independence Day?"

"My independence day?" I was perplexed.

"Today is your Fourth of July," he explained.

"The Fourth of July?" I smiled, "That's cool, I'm here in Germany for the Fourth." "My name is Dieter," he offered his hand. "My name is Nash" I gave him mine and we shook on it. Dieter was in graduate school at the university and just played guitar for fun.

"You hungry?"

"I'm always hungry," I replied with a grin.

"Want to go with me to this little wienerschnitzel restaurant?" Now I hesitated.

"Don't worry, I'm buying, I just want to help you celebrate your Fourth of July!"

I shook my head at his kindness and accepted, and I followed him around the corner and down a block, where he opened the door for me and we went inside. The waiter showed us to a table on the side of a very typical German restaurant, right down to the lederhosen. Oompa music was playing somewhere in the back room. We had barely started to talk when the waiter was back with two steaming plates of the house special, wienerschnitzel. Dieter ordered a bottle of Rhine wine. Needless to say I was up for a good meal, and wow was that wienerschnitzel good with that wine! Upon my third glass of wine I started to get warm. Dieter noticed that and abruptly, as Germans do, said "Let's get out of here where it's cooler." We were pretty much done with the meal and the wine so sure, I said, let's go.

When we got outside we walked back up the street, and suddenly Dieter put his arm around my waist, a little too friendly, which instantly and forcefully received my repulsion. I looked at him and said "I really thank you for the food and the wine but don't ever touch me like that again." I was a little taller than he was and maybe twenty pounds of muscle heavier, so I steadied myself. Dieter looked at his feet sheepishly, jammed his hands in his pockets and apologized, mumbling something about white socks. We parted as friends.

In the morning I was on the road south and again fortunately caught a ride with a truck driver all the way through the industrial pocket of Dortmund, Essen, Düsseldorf and he finally let me out at Cologne, which they call Koln. I found a hostel right around the corner from the Cologne Cathedral, which was built between the Thirteenth and Sixteenth Centuries, and is the largest Gothic church in northern Europe. Ninety percent of Cologne's central city was destroyed during WWII; you wouldn't know it to see it now. But maybe the coolest thing about Cologne is that one could hop aboard a boat and ride it down the Rhine River all day to end up in Mainz.

So there I was, lying on my back in the sun on the deck of this touring boat, bright blue German skies, the Rhine all around me, surrounded by hills full of the grapes that make the wine I drank with Dieter. And not too far down the river, here come the castles. I didn't count them but they were quite a few, one on this corner overlooking the turn of the river, then another on the opposite side just out of view of the first, leading me to thoughts of little fiefdoms ruled by local lords supported by dozens of peasant laborers. Were all the rulers related, as was the case with

England, France and Spain? Or did they eye each other warily across the water? Or what if they both were related *and* eyed each other warily? I pondered on the shifting intrigue that seeps out of medieval history books.

Next up along the Rhine: Bonn, then the capital of West Germany, and the birthplace of Beethoven. One of the older travelers on our barge was explaining some of Bonn's history to his grandson, and as I sat right next to them this is what I heard. The city developers in the nineteenth century took pains to keep heavy industry out, in order to preserve the city for rich residents, so that Bonn today is a vibrant administrative and business center with some light industry, indeed a lovely city to watch from the barge as we chugged slowly by on the Rhine.

It was several hours more of the slowed-down time of being on water before we reached Mainz. It seems that being on water for a short time makes time speed up, as when we are surprised to already be at the end of a pretty canoe run; and other times, longer time spent on a boat, time slows down, so that when you are there for a week it feels like a month, and a month on the water feels much longer. Even just an eight-hour run down the Rhine River felt like I'd been on it long enough, and I was happy to get my land legs under me again as I trooped up the hill to find the youth hostel. Hostelling was definitely the way to go, every city had at least one, and they were all listed in the AYH handbook I bought back home and brought with me. So far the most I had paid for a bunk was sixty cents.

My walkabout led me to understand that Mainz is the birthplace of Johannes Gutenberg, whose invention of the moveable type printing press launched the Reformation as the populace could now read the Bible for themselves. Think about that; before moveable type, books could only be printed from individual presses, one painstaking page at a time. In fact, in 1440, when Gutenberg's Bible was printed, many scribes were still making books with calligraphy. Heck, in 1969 we have electric typewriters, how far we have come, my thoughts exploded with the possibilities.

The next morning found me following the regulars to the autobahn entrance. It had gradually become apparent that there was a large pack of hitchhikers that moved from city to city pretty much on the same timetable, so that familiar faces showed up down the road. We separated at this road because we all knew nobody would pick up a bunch of us; I hiked down to find my own spot to hitch, took out my cardboard and marker and wrote: HEIDELBERG. I was standing just at the end of the exit where the traffic was picking up steam to motor down the no-speed-limit autobahn, and about forty minutes and one hundred cars had accelerated past me, a bright red convertible saw me, swerved to the right, screeched to a halt and a gorgeous woman tossed her blond hair as she turned to wave me up. I picked up my pack and ran to the car, plopped into the passenger seat, my pack in my lap, and looked into the dreamiest blue eyes I had ever seen. "Where are you headed, baby?" she asked me in German. "Uh," I stammered, "I'm going to Heidelberg to see old town and the castle." "Mmmmm" she purred, "I'm going to Heidelberg myself," now in English. "Why don't you put your pack in the back seat so you can be more comfortable," she asked, batting those baby blues at me. So I did, and settled in for a ninety-mile-an-hour rush down the autobahn, trying not to look at her but unable to help myself, I gawked.

Her hair was thick and looked naturally wavy, pure blond. Her shades wrapped around to disappear into the blond waves. She had a very cute nose and round luscious lips, and she wore a tight pink t-shirt that was too short so it hung down from her ponderous breasts and you could see her navel. She noticed me staring at her and smiled "I'll bet you get picked up by a lot of girls." "Well, no, not exactly," doing my best at that precise moment to keep my mind on the truck right behind us, threatening our existence. Nobody drives ninety miles an hour in Duluth. Suddenly *Whoose*!

A car passed us on our left like we were standing still. Good grief, how fast was he going? My blonde driver reached down to turn on the radio, and who do you think came on but the Rolling Stones: "Hoooonky tonk woman"... She cranked it up, stepped on the gas and took her convertible to one hundred mph. About four miles down the autobahn we cruised by two men in long white coats looking under the engine of the Mercedes that had wooshed past us. The factory was just up the road.

"So what's your name, cutie?" she shouted over Mick Jagger's screams.

"Nash."

"Hi Nash, I'm Gretchen."

"Nice to meet you" I said to my now favorite name in the world.

"Say, how old are you?" the jig was almost up.

"Eighteen."

"Eighteen! I thought you were about 22...well, you're a hunk anyway," she smiled. I smiled too. I was totally unsure of myself, thinking if she had put her hand on my leg I would have jumped out of the car. So basically I forced myself to ignore her for the rest of the ride to Heidelberg, a really cool old city inside a big modern city with a great castle overlooking the whole city, the Heidelberger Schloss. When Gretchen pulled off the autobahn she automatically turned for the old town area. "Have you seen the castle?" Gretchen locked eyes with me for a second. "N-no." "Want me to be your personal tour guide?" "S-sure." She parked the car and we got out and walked around old town about two miles together, she was about five foot seven inches, hourglass figure, maybe twenty three, tan, and a smile so warm it could melt an iceberg, or maybe even the son of Ice.

"Did you know that the university here is the oldest in Europe?" her voice was soft and fluffy.

"No, I didn't. When was it founded?"

"1386." I said nothing, just shook my head in amazement. In Duluth they talk about hundred-year-old structures being old.

Her stride was keeping perfect time with mine and we cruised along, arms swinging, her long yellow hair bouncing. As we approached the castle, we turned to look back. The castle sits over three hundred feet up from the river Neckar, and from that height you can look over the entire city, old and new. Not to mention the sunset, which I was about to discover. Gretchen took my hand and pulled me out of my daydream and we walked hand in hand to the castle entrance. We paid Dutch, and the first thing she did once inside was to whirl around and plant a warm kiss on my lips, pressing her breasts against me. Then she stood back with a little smirk, a flip of her hair and she was off, this puppy following. I didn't count the steps to the top.

Once out on the top parapet, we walked out to the edge and side by side leaned our elbows on the red sandstone railing, and for about ten minutes we just looked out at the city, each of us silent in our thoughts. And as we stood there silently next to each other, the hairs on our forearms touching on the railing, the sun dropped quickly, leaving us in magical red hour, as the sun's rays bend over the horizon on longer waves to frame the most perfect time of day.

By July 17 my trek had taken me to Basel and Bern and back to Munich, a city I stayed in for four days, partly because I was tired of constantly being on the move, and partly because it is a beautiful area to hang out for a few days. I took one day trip and returned to the hostel at Rotkruet Platz, which was a little different from other hostels as it was situated directly across the street from a half-block city park, with tree hedges all around and a big fountain. After spending the maximum two nights at the hostel, I just checked out and walked across the street, picked a spot to lie down along the back hedge, and rolled up in my Indian blanket and my poncho and slept free on the ground. My Indian blanket, lighter like a sheet but warmer, tightly knit, red print.

In the mornings we were all awakened precisely at 7 a.m. by Munich policemen who sauntered down the row of sleepers, rapping each on the bottom of their feet with their walking sticks, repeating to all in precise Germanic tradition: "Sieben uhr, absteigen!" (7:00, get up!) Then, when the police weren't looking, we would wash up and brush our teeth in the fountain. Pack up your stuff, take your pack across the street and secure it in a locker (you could still rent lockers even after you checked out) and take off for a whole day walkabout.

On my last evening in Munich I visited the famous Hofbrauhaus, a big working class beer hall. It was noisy. I took a seat in the rear corner so as to survey the whole room; it was my custom to sit with my back to a wall, just a habit formed from reading about the death of Wild Bill Hickok. My table, the chairs as well, were solid oak, substantial. The railings holding the oompa band in the middle of the big room also were solid oak, as were all of the scores of other tables and chairs and booths, which gave the big room a warm and natural feel. These were solid people, these Germans. A big-haired buxom waitress in a peasant blouse slid up to me on a slippery floor to take my order. "Bier?"

"Ja, bitte," I affirmed, and she slid off on her rounds. The oompa band was playing traditional German folk songs and beer drinking songs like we had listened to in Herr Schlector's class. Hey, I recognize that one: "ein, zwei, gezuffa," How about that? The date was July 20, 1969—the day Neal Armstrong took one small step for man, one giant leap for mankind. German kids had been let out of school throughout the country that day so they could watch the landing on TV; the German people rightfully felt a pride in the mission, Werner Von Braun being one of their own.

Well into my second twenty-ounce twelve percent smooth German brew in a clay mug emblazoned with the HB logo, the band was playing, the voices were getting louder, and then suddenly one man came running down the aisle, holding his beer over his head, sloshing as he strode, yelling in German "*They landed on the moon*! *They landed on the moon!*" He screeched to a halt in front of me and stuck his finger out at me and addressed me "Bist du Amerikaner?" "Ja, ich bin Amerikaner," I replied, uncertain of what would happen next. "Hurrraahhh fur Amerikaner! They landed on the moon!" And he bid me to get up on my table so I did, clutching my mug, and the whole room went silent as I stood on my corner table. For just a second. Then the oompa band started playing Yankee Doodle Dandy and the entire Hofbrauhaus establishment lifted a mug and cheered me! "Hip Hip Hurray!" I'm not making this up.

It was several hours later when my fortunes found me sitting on the grass slumped against a tool shed under a starry night, still clutching my HB mug, somewhere in Munich. Sitting there in my cloud I was approached by two ladies. One of them spoke to me in English. "Are you all right? Do you know it's three a.m.?" I looked up at her, she was pretty, both were pretty, shapely, scantily dressed, and both were taking pity on me, you could see it in their painted eyes. I just said "Jugendherberge?" (youth hostel) They immediately understood and saw me to the tram that took me back to the hostel, their wistful eyes watching me go, where I got my pack out of hock, took out my blanket and poncho, and crashed in the park.

What effect do sixty ounces of twelve percent beer have on an eighteen-year-old's brain? On previously brew ignorance? The closest I can come to expressing in words what I felt like upon awakening is simply to say it felt like the old cliché, death warmed-over. Such a colossal headache, I had never known before. Some graduation, I sarcastically grimaced. Dying of thirst, I got up and walked with my four-hundred-pound head perched on my aching neck to the fountain, where I leaned forward and from the weight of my head fell face first into the water, where I drank and drank and drank. Dragging my wet carcass out of the water, away from the fountain, lent just enough momentum to shift the direction of the tilt of my monster head back to my crash spot, where my light went out again for several hours. Finally my eyes opened in the heat of the sun; by its place in the sky I could tell it was almost noon. I was alone in the park, except for a couple of pairs of other stragglers next to the hedges. I sat up slowly, packed my pack slowly, picked it up slowly, put it on slowly, and slowly walked out of the park, past the hostel, across a busy street, and stuck out my thumb for Garmisch-Partenkirchen.

Where exactly I had read about Garmisch-Partenkirchen I wasn't sure, but as I rode with my new driver, a salesman on his way to Innsbruck for a conference, he told me he was passing right by GP, the scenery becoming more and more beautiful with mountains behind valleys and forests, and gradually my low mood slowly began to think about considering the potentially possible action of somehow lifting from my brow. The youth hostel in GP shared the spaces with other visitors, it was a family resort in a beautiful corner of Bavaria. That sunny afternoon caught me sitting around the outdoor common area, just lolling in the sun, still pretty low, wearing shades for extended reasons.

Two young men in their mid-twenties came out and sat across from me, both carrying guitars. My shades lowered just a bit to watch as they proceeded to make music on those guitars, so sweet, so lyrical, a duet, picking those notes with their fingers, not with a pick like a rock n roller. This was classical music on classical guitars and it drew a crowd of onlookers. The two virtuosos played for us for about thirty minutes, we applauded, and I resolved to buy a guitar.

One of the temporary inhabitants of those semi-rustic surroundings was a five-year-old boy on holiday with his parents. I met Peter when the two guitarists broke up and being just five, he spoke only German, and so I spoke German to him for our conversation. "And what is your name?" I opened.

"Peter, and what is yours?" He brightly responded.

"My name is Nash," I tossed back to him. "And" I added, "where do you live?"

"We live in Munich," looking over his shoulder as if to confirm with his parents.

"Oh really, I've just come from Munich myself."

"Ja?"

"Ja." And how old are you, I asked him.

"Five." And he asked me how old I was.

"Eighteen." And he asked me, where do I live?

"America." His eyes widened as he eagerly asked me "Kennen Sie (Do you know) Ben Cartwright?" I was sorry to disappoint him, but got a good lesson in the effect of television on children even six thousand miles away.

The next morning I was off to Innsbruck. It didn't take very long to get there but the terrain was rapidly becoming much higher and more rugged. The trucker who picked me up about five miles south of GP had to shift down to take the upturn of some of those Austrian mountains, truly some of the most beautiful in the world. This is the land of Hayden, Mozart, Schubert, Strauss, and they say if it's alpine, it's probably Austrian.

The shower at the hostel in Innsbruck was ice cold, no heated water upstairs in that old wooden building, and at that elevation the warm water was not coming upstairs. So a one-limb method of showering presented itself to me, which consisted of holding one arm in as long a as painfully possible in the freezing water, then quickly pull it out and soap up, then quickly back in to rinse, and so forth through the four limbs. Then for the head and torso, just man-up and step in breathless and finish that shower in record time.

Innsbruck is another really cool city. I was digging Europe because there were so many awesome, ancient, important places so close together. Now this Alpine resort, with an old town with narrow streets, colors bright in the light dancing off the nearby snowy peaks, some of them over 10,000 feet, lit its street lights for me to wander about. The following day would take me to Italy. Much on my mind that night was about the major difference between my country and Europe was simply about 1,000 years of social and agricultural development, and many of the original buildings in Europe give firsthand evidence. The civilizational vibration is higher in Europe. When then was the last political assassination in Europe? In America I had witnessed, on TV, three from 1963 to 1968, four counting Malcolm X's murder, which received much less coverage.

The mountain roads south of Innsbruck run through the Tyrol Pass, at thousands of feet elevation. But gradually rock gives way to forest gives way to meadows and rolling hills. The elevation is still pretty high in Brunico, the first Italian village where I enjoyed an actual Italian meal. I don't know about you, but where I come from, spaghetti is a main course. Not in Brunico. The spaghetti comes out in steaming bowls as the appetizer, then the chicken and the sausage and the salads and the breads. Whoo! I was stuffed, and needed to sit there for some time before attempting to rise. Fortunately time slows down here in this Italian mountain town the way it does on water so they aren't looking to move my table out from under me, the way some places do in America.

But I wasn't staying in Brunico that night. I went for a big push to Venice, and got as far as the cornfields outside of Venice just after dark, so I rolled up in my poncho and slept in the cornfield, a couple rows in from the road to stay out of sight. Pretty soon the mosquitoes started attacking me; I used my bug spray and covered all the exposed skin and drifted off to sleep until early morning. When my eyes opened, my pack was repacked, slung over my shoulders and I set out to hike to Venice. A small ferry putted me a short distance over to the sidewalks of Venezia, literally a city of lights on the water. I asked around a bit and found the hostel, a cavernous place in a very old gray stone building. Looking across the water, the visitor could see Fifteenth

Century architecture gleaming, visibly closer to the water than it most likely used to be.

After checking into the hostel and stowing my pack, my steps led me right back outside and caught a gondola to the other side of the opulently designed street, to San Marco Piaza, visions of Sophia Loren, a grand plaza almost overbearing in its five hundred year old architectural power, and here, a little restaurant in the shade looking out on the plaza. I ordered spaghetti, just to see what Venice had to offer.

As I sat there gazing across the shadows, my ankles started to itch. One ankle scratched the other, then vice versa, then I reached under the table to scratch, then I pulled my socks down and discovered almost solid mosquito bites over a two-inch band around each of my ankles, where they had bitten through my unsprayed socks. Both ankles were on fire. I tried to ignore them. I barely succeeded through my meal, which for some reason didn't really set too well with me, and I had to push it away as a strange warmth came over me, or was it a shiver? I got up and stepped into the sun to warm up, I felt dizzy, whoa, better get back to the hostel. So I managed to retrace my steps to the gondola, and retreated to my bunk where I stretched out on my back.

Things went downhill from there. By four hours later, 5pm, I lay there in a cold sweat and wanted someone to amputate me above those accursed ankles, not really but it felt good to formulate it in my mind. Finally I couldn't stand it anymore and got up and went downstairs to the office, which consisted of one desk and two chairs, and a fat laconic gentleman who looked perplexed as I tried to ask him if he had anything for mosquito bites. We batted stupidities back and forth a minute and then a dim light appeared in his swarthy eyes. "I do know of something that will help the itch," he said, "but your girlfriend won't like it."

"I don't have a girlfriend, so what is it?"

I wiped my brow.

"Pickle juice," he pokerfaced.

"Pickle juice?" I double checked.

"Pickle juice," he confirmed. Then he held up a fleshy finger telling me to wait, and ducked out of sight through a door beyond which I heard banging and clattering and then he reemerged triumphantly with a small plastic jug of pickle juice. When my eyes still searched he showed me to pour some onto a cloth, then apply the cloth to the inflamed area, and oohh, that cools it right down…put some over there. I soaked my ankles with it and I stank like a state fair pickle on a stick but didn't care. Once back to my bunk and stretched out again, waiting for the fever to break, it didn't. It got worse. Finally Gary, a fellow hitchhiker from Colorado, who had shown up with some of the regulars, saw me there and came over and asked me if I were alright.

"I can't seem to shake this fever, and I have a splitting headache." My report was grim.

"Have you taken any medicine?"

"No, I don't have any." I admitted.

Here, I'll give you a penicillin pill, trust me, my Dad's a doctor, I have plenty for myself." It was a magnanimous gesture.

"You would do that for me?"

"Of course, that's what medicine's for." He ran over to his bunk and pulled out a small bag, out of which he unwrapped various pills, found the one he was giving to me, and came right over to me with it. "This is penicillin. It will reduce your fever," he explained. I gratefully swallowed it with a half glass of water and laid my head down as my pickle ankles smelled up the whole room.

By the time I woke up I must have slept ten hours. True to Gary's prediction, the fever was reduced, but not gone, and my headache continued to concentrate right behind my eyes. I'll bet this is the kind of mosquito bite that struck down many a conquistador. I went outside to sit in the sun on a bench overlooking the Piaza San Marco across the way. It was another beautiful sunny day but I couldn't enjoy it. Over the loudspeaker

I heard the flip side of the Stones' record I heard in Germany: "Brown Sugar" was topping the charts this week. After a while even the Stones couldn't help me and I went inside to get an address of a local doctor. Take a right out the door and down the sidewalk. Lightheaded I walked down the sidewalk, water at my left, holding a scrap of paper with the doctor's address scribbled on it, watching the numbers on the doors until whoop, here it is. Double check the paper. Double-check the doorway. I took a deep breath, raised my right hand to knock on his door when suddenly, like curtains coming down, the fever dropped out of me. I stopped, lowered my hand, listened, looked around, drew a deep breath of wonder, checked myself again and walked back to the hostel happy not to have amputated.

In the morning I did my chores around the hostel, packed up and thanked Gary again for helping me out. "Where are you off to?" he asked.

"Florence,"

"I don't know," he said, "we talked about going to Florence or going straight to Rome and spending more time there."

"I'm going to Florence to see a couple of things my reading told me about."

"Oh, well, probably see you in Rome," he bid me farewell, my hand clasping his in remarkably better health than last night. The lone remaining diablo in me was a lingering headache right behind my eyes. My vision was limited due to having to give up lateral looks because that hurt. So I was hiking along the highway, sort of airing out my head, not really trying to catch a ride but then a big truck careened to a stop right ahead of me, and I ran to it with pack in hand and jumped into the cab, to find the driver at the wheel and wife and twelve year old son in the extra cab behind.

The whole family was on the road. We had a blast talking about our travels. The driver, Gregor, tanned like an Austrian skier, was from near Innsbruck, and Rosa, his amiable wife, was from the Netherlands. Their son, Johan, was traveling with his parents during his one month hiatus from the school year. In Europe they are smart for a reason—they place a high social and governmental value on education as being of intrinsic merit.

The trucking family dropped me off walking distance to the hostel in Florence, and now I was really getting excited to see Brunelleschi's Duomo and Lorenzo Ghiberti's bronze doors, which he began to work on at age twenty in 1420 and it took him twenty years to finish. Up a street I walked on my way to the Duomo, which when built was the largest dome in the world. As I approached the corner, I began to see the Duomo looming over the tops of other buildings to my right, and then whoop! I almost ran into three girls who were rounding the corner going the other way. They stopped, I stopped, we looked at each other and then one of them blurted "What on earth are you doing here?" They were Lakeside girls from Bridgeman's, the milk store on the corner just on the other side of the Portman skating rink, from whom I had bought many a gallon of milk and a few lollapaloozas over my adolescent years. Here they were on their college-girl European venture, riding the Eurorail and visiting cities, while I was traipsing with my pack through cornfields and meadows.

"I'm traveling." I replied.

"You're too young to be here!" they protested.

I shrugged my shoulders and grinned back at them. "Well, I'm here."

They still couldn't believe their college adventure had to be punctuated by this youth from Duluth, and they walked on by. "Well have fun, and be safe," they tossed back at me. "Thanks." Just like that a connection from 6,000 miles back home was past. I walked chuckling up to the corner, looked right at the massive Duomo, left to the Baptistery of St. John, whose north wall was illuminated by the amazingly intricate details of Ghiberti's bronze paneled doors, and was pulled to them to look intently at how in the world did he make those figures so realistic and so small, and make them in bronze? For twenty years?

Later that day I found Michelangelo's David, inside the Accademia, standing up on a pedestal, and I stood there in awe of the fineness of the work, the polish, the hair, the eyes, the hands, the legs, all so realistic, cut from stone. Cut, chiseled, sanded, buffed, rubbed to such a polish it took my breath away. When the authorities weren't looking I reached up and touched David's big toe, right where Michelangelo's hand had once been, and silently noticed so many others had done the same thing over the past five hundred-plus years that the end of the toe was worn down a bit. My subsequent walkabout included visitation of the tombs of the Medici's, the eminent patrons of art.

Chicken parmesan Italian style was my supper that night; usually on the road I tried to eat a solid meal at a restaurant once a day. Some were better than others, this one was superb. My headache was just about gone by now, and life started to get a bit brighter with a good meal in me. So my evening walk took me to the Mercado Centrale, where various vendors of leather goods plied their trade.

Now I was set for a big road day to Rome. It took three different lifts that day, the first two being short hops and the third a keeper all the way to the Appian Way. And once there, I felt the danger level increase strictly on the basis of how Romans drive—like madmen. Traffic whipping around the Coliseum is crazier than Los Angeles, and I kept to the far edge of the walkway around it to get to the hostel.

Rome is different in many ways. It feels imperial, but also unabashedly fun-loving. Beautiful women and impetuous men. Dark-robed, pious old parishioners, bent from the waist, fervently rubbing their rosaries, entering the side door of the Vatican, immediately step into the most egregious display of ostentatious splendor and concentrated wealth I've ever seen. Now I stepped into the Vatican, and was, like the parishioners, overwhelmed by the gold and silver opulence. But just to my right, my breath again was taken away by the sheer polished beauty of Michelangelo's creations, this one being the Pieta, and in the summer of 1969 I was fortunate to see it before some clueless idiot later smashed an arm with a sledge hammer. Intact, the Pieta must be one of the grandest sculptures of all time, with the eternally graceful body of Jesus lying with limbs hanging from the blessed lap of his mother. You can hear it cry if you listen closely.

Right next door to the Vatican is the Sistine Chapel, which had come alive during my senior year when I read "The Agony and the Ecstasy" while listening to Carlos Montoya's guitar. Now standing under the ceiling where Michelangelo labored on his back for four years to complete the wondrous work, I just stared and stared until my neck hurt. I wondered, are there any patrons who sponsor major artists anymore? Or was that a luxury of past days? Could a Michelangelo be successful now?

From Rome a beeline began around the Mediterranean, with a quick stop in Pisa to see how leany the tower is. The funny part was that there was another tower not too far away, which was leaning more than the Leaning Tower of Pisa. The stars were my room that night. The next hostel stay was in Genoa, where Columbus as a young boy watched the ships disappear over the horizon, which gave him a revolutionary thought: the world is not flat. I sat up on one of the hills overlooking the sea and watched the ships just as Columbus had.

Then six rides in a row came at me and blew me through Monaco (couldn't afford it anyway), Nice, Cannes, Marseilles, Montpellier, and Perpignan, where I stopped for a sunny afternoon stroll around that pretty pastel colored city by the sea. Finally in the next hour my feet fell in Spain, and covered the rugged Costa Brava in a Cadillac driven by a blue-haired matron on the way to see her grandchildren; to spend that night in one of the most unusual cities in the world, Barcelona. Here they speak a dialect of Spanish called Catalan. The bottom line was that my

German was temporarily useless, and if they didn't speak English, we innovated.

What an amazing city! I walked down Las Ramblas, maybe half a mile down a hill, with myriad types of vendors, a different type every block. This block, on both sides of the pedestrian-only street, are potters; next block: plants and flowers; next block: aviaries, birds; next block: fruits and fruit juices, fortune tellers, furniture, leather goods, guitars and so on all the way to the bottom, where you run into the tall columned statue of Columbus, for this is where his ship returned from his 1492 voyage, when Ferdinand and Isabella of Spain stayed at their summer palace in Barcelona.

I stayed a night in Lerida on my way to Madrid. Now inland, into Spain, they spoke Spanish, and by my walkabout I discovered that they really do take a siesta at mid-day for a couple of hours, then go back to work, and get off work late, go out to eat late, sit and talk late. It was ten p.m. and every restaurant I passed was packed and noisy. For some reason, I thought, Spaniards talk louder than other nationalities I had heard. Could the difference be the grape?

By the time I checked into the hostel the next day in Madrid it was already late afternoon; it had been a long, hot day of hitching across some pretty formidable countryside. Long means rides were few and far between, so I was able to fully appreciate the reasoning behind the national siesta, having stood helpless under the blazing mid-day sun learning the patience of the road. There was a discussion going on in the lobby of the hostel; I listened in:

"And whatever you do, don't drink, wash up or brush your teeth in the fountains, if you do you will be thrown into a Spanish jail, and you don't want that."

"But will they really arrest us for that?"

"Look, this is Franco's Spain; you ever heard how he gained power in the first place?" (seeing no, he continued) "Just mark my word, you need to keep your noses clean in Madrid."

Franco's Spain, I thought. The old man had been ruler of Spain since he won the Spanish Civil War that Hemingway wrote about. "The last surviving Fascist dictator," he had been called. In 1947 he set up Spain to be a monarchy with himself having lifetime powers. Now this was the year, 1969, that Franco officially designated Prince Juan Carlos, then 32, to be his successor. But until he stepped down, Franco ruled with an iron fist. And that meant no washing up in the fountains. But at the same time that didn't slow down the true Madrid residents, who were a generally happy lot, loud at night, laughing and conversing often until 3:00 a.m. The saying on the street was: "There's a hole in Heaven right over Madrid, so that those who have lived and loved in Madrid may continue to look down upon the endless party with eternal happiness." Quite a lyrical language, this Spanish, I thought to myself. In Madrid I bought my first pair of genuine leather cowboy boots; I've owned a pair ever since.

But now I was facing a bit of a time crunch. I needed to get to Paris ASAP so I could spend a couple days there before heading back to Luxembourg for my Aug. 22 flight back home. I overheard one of the other travelers at the hostel talking about getting university rides. "You can walk up to the transportation board and find postings for someone to share gas to Paris, for example." When I heard that I headed straight outside and asked the quickest way to the University of Madrid. Now, there are usually a lot of young people around youth hostels, and sure enough, someone knew the directions, and it turned out to be just a few blocks away.

So I sprinted to the university and looked around the campus for a few minutes until I came to what appeared to be a student union area with a bulletin board with a huge map of Europe on it, and little scraps of paper stuck next to it, each one posting for a rider to this city or that, split the gas. My eyes scanned the posts and there, there it was! One rider wanted to share gas from Madrid to Paris, with one overnight in Bordeaux. I wrote down the number and got to the nearest pay phone. While it was ringing I remembered I didn't speak Spanish, I'd open with English, then fall back to German if necessary.

"Si? Hola?"

"Si" I parroted, "do you speak English?

"Yes," he answered, "I speak a little English, may I help you?"

"Well, you advertised for someone to share gas to ride with you to Paris, and that's where I'm heading."

"Well, well, you're the first one to respond to my advertisement in two weeks so you are the one to ride with me, as I am leaving tomorrow." Just like that. We made arrangements to meet at a small but noisy restaurant near the campus. He was a professor of history at the university, and his trip to Paris was to do research there. Dr. Philip Saragoza looked the part of a university professor, button-down collar and a forest green summer jacket with brown leather elbow patches. He was about forty, dark haired but starting already to lose his hairline, thin face with a trim moustache, round-rimmed glasses in front of dark thoughtful eyes, slender body, skinny legs, frequently lost in his thoughts.

"So what time in the morning would you like to head north?" I asked him as my words jolted him from his ponderings.

"Eight sharp. I will pick you up at your hostel at eight sharp."

"Excellente, senor Doctor, muchas gracias," I used up my entirely inept Spanish vocabulary on him and he laughed and gave me a thumbs up as we parted ways for the night.

On my way back to the hostel I stopped at a park bench and lay on it, lengthwise on my back, and gazed up at the stars. So many stars. Such a fabulous summer. Such amazing moments, for example when I hitched through Switzerland on my way to Munich. How many Eurorail passengers got to ride on top of a pile of hay in a hay wagon pulled by one horse, driven by an old Swiss farmer, as it rounded the corner of the scenic mountain road slowly, clip clop, clip clop, and there right in front of me was the Matterhorn. "Die Matterhorn?" I asked the driver, pointing.

He smiled and nodded, "Ja, das ist die Matterhorn." I pulled my Kodak instamatic out of its assigned pocket in my pack and snapped a really cool photo. Then I lay back in the hay and watched the Matterhorn walk by, clip clop, clip, clop.

But now it was Madrid and by 7:00 a.m. the next morning I had already cleaned up, packed, grabbed a bite to eat, and sat outside waiting, hoping the good Dr. Saragoza would show up. It was just another beautiful summer day in Spain. I sat and grew quiet. At 7:55 the doctor pulled up, in a Jaguar, no less, I looked twice at the silver beauty. He was in no mood to hang around, so we were off and before long cruising in the smoothest ride I had ever experienced, headed for Segovia. In Segovia, a very pretty place to visit, I thought, but I also now recognized that the good Doctor meant what he had said—drive straight through, allowing only for an overnight in Bordeaux. And so it was that we blasted through San Sebastian, Biarritz, Bayonne and after a tough day on the road riding in air-conditioned luxury, we pulled into Bordeaux. He had pre-arranged a hotel room for himself so he dropped me at the hostel and we agreed to meet at eight sharp in the a.m.

Now, as for France and things French, I wasn't all that well informed on that trip. But I knew that Bordeaux meant good red wine, so I bought a small bottle of cabernet, a short loaf of French bread, a hunk of salami and a couple of hard boiled eggs, then I walked over to a pretty little park overlooking the river, and sat there on a park bench enjoying one of the most satisfactory meals in all of Europe. I had been blessed with fantastic weather, this night being the same, blue skies, white clouds, hardly any rain at all. There was that one time in Munich when it rained while I was sleeping in the park; I spent half the night on a concrete church stairway out of the rain. But hardly a cloud was in the sky that night in Bordeaux, and I thoroughly enjoyed just sitting there and watching the stars come out while listening to gentle laughter and a lone concertina lilting somewhere below in the balmy August night.

The fair doctor was prompt as ever in the morning, and as he pulled his silver Jag up to the sidewalk in front of the youth hostel, I got in with my pack while various other hitchhikers scanned the wheels and wondered whose celebrity son I might be. If only they knew.

"Did you enjoy your night in Bordeaux?" Dr. Saragoza looked well-rested.

"Yes indeed I did," my enthusiasm showed.

"Good, good, I like to see that," he noted.

"Pardon me?" I was slow on the update.

"I like to see visitors enjoying our countries, and I especially I like to see you soaking it all in."

"That's good, that's exactly what I'm doing, soaking it all in."

"Make sure you write it all down," he turned to me, urgently.

"I will." I assured him it would all be written down (and you, dear reader, are witness to that promise kept.)

The Jag sped north past Angouleme, Poitiers, Tours then Orleans as Dr. Saragoza played an audio tape of Italian language lessons for two of the hours; I didn't mind a bit. Molto Bene.

"How many languages do you speak?" I asked him after the lesson.

"Five…Spanish, my own, and also English, as you know, plus German, French and Italian, as you have just seen, I am in the process of learning."

"Is that because you have so many different nations and languages bunched all together as Europe?" I asked. He looked over at me with an eyebrow lifted over his round rimmed glasses and looked as if he would bite his lip.

"That's a very good question. I guess I never thought about living anywhere where there's only one language."

"Well I just speak English and a little German," I said.

"The good news for you is that you're only eighteen," he noted.

"Why is that good news?"

"You have your whole life ahead of you! You're getting a huge jump on life with this trip you're taking."

"I know it'll probably affect me some way but right now I'm on enjoyment mode."

"You go ahead and enjoy, my young friend, and know that you will never again be the same." The professor nodded to himself as the silver Jaguar streaked through the blue night toward Paris.

Professor Saragoza and I said our goodbyes at a little café in Montmartre, where I instantly felt at home, it's full of coffee houses and cafes and bistros, bookstores and bohemian types like me. After he left I looked around there for a room, I didn't always need to stay at a hostel, besides, the hostel map shows the hostel to be way out and I liked it right there. I talked to some students and they directed me to a rooming house up the street a couple of blocks. I walked up there and picked up a private room for $14 a night. I paid two nights up front. It's on a little hill, down which the street takes you to the Champs-Elysees.

Left Bank, Right Bank, it was a bit confusing; fortunately I could walk to the Louvre, whichever bank it was on. Inside the Louvre, which had been a royal residence before Louis IV moved the court to Versailles, you could easily spend three days or more looking at everything, but I hurried to the Mona Lisa first. She just hung on the wall in front of me, behind a cloth rope, no protective glass or any such thing. I could have reached my hand out, leaned forward and touched her, but didn't. So I just stood there and reveled in DaVinci's genius. What, oh what was she thinking? I tried to see the brush strokes, how he did it.

Down the hall I saw Egyptian, Greek and Roman antiquities, and over there, that huge painting by Rembrandt. It was, simply put, the greatest collection of art, sculpture and ancient artifacts that I had ever seen, even imagined. I gave myself four hours to wander through the magnificent museum.

A bright afternoon sun greeted me when I left the Louvre and went to find the Eiffel Tower. I knew it had been built in 1889 for the Centennial Exposition, but not until I overheard some tour guides leading their groups of intently listening tourists did I hear the rest. At the time of its completion, the Eiffel Tower, named for its designer, met with amazement. It was built with advanced knowledge of metal arch and metal truss forms, and until the Chrysler Building in New York City was built in 1930, the Eiffel Tower was the world's tallest building. I chose not to eat at the restaurant a hundred feet up the tower, presuming costliness. I made it this far by living frugally.

There was one more thing I must do while in Paris, walk under the Arc d' Triomph for my Dad. I had seen the old film clips of Allies marching victoriously under the Arc, and I wasn't sure if my Dad had been in a position to make that march, so my intention was to make it for him. As I stood there looking up at the top of the Arc, a gravity came over me, and my heart quieted, with the knowledge that my Dad might actually be gone by now. Sucking my breath in, I slowly began walking, tears rolling down my cheeks, unable to stop them. "Alive or not, Dad, this is for you." It was a short walk but a long thought.

The morning calendar said August 20; time to go. The previous night had been a sublime reflective stroll listening to music along the Seine sidewalk cafes, and now I packed for my last night in Europe. I took a local bus to the outskirts of Paris, wrote out one more sign on my cardboard "Luxembourg," and stuck out my right thumb. In about twenty minutes a black sedan pulled over, and I jumped in with my pack. At the wheel sat a truly fat man, his rotund belly riding on the steering wheel. His small eyes were almost squinting from the fat around them. He talked to me with cheeks that looked like they were full of nuts.

"Where are you going?

"Luxembourg. My flight leaves Wednesday afternoon."

"Well, I'm just going to Verdun."

"That will be fine," I said. I knew from ten weeks of hitching that the rides come as they come and you never sweat the small stuff.

"How long have you been on the road? Oh, by the way, I'm Bert."

"Ten weeks. I'm Nash." I sat up.

"Ten weeks! Good heavens, kid, aren't you homesick?"

"Not really, what I feel now is that I'm kind of ready to go back and go to college." Bert's neck jiggled his approval. Then he wanted to know everything there was to know about American TV and Hollywood. He asked question after question, which must have been, I thought, born of hours on the couch eating chips and cookies. Anyway when we got to Verdun he was enjoying the conversation so much he offered to take me all the way.

"You know, I'm actually going to a place called Etain, just north of Verdun, and then it's only about thirty miles to Luxembourg, why don't I just run you over there?"

"That's very kind, but you don't have to do that for me, I'll be alright," I protested.

"No, no," his neck jiggled, "I insist. I want you to have a good experience as you leave our Europe."

"A really friendly Europe, thank you very much," I settled in for the last run.

My hitchhiking trip was coming to a close the same way it started, with a good-hearted soul giving me a lift, even going out of their way for little old me.

Bert and I shook hands in front of the Luxembourg Hotel where I had stayed way back in June. I actually got my same room, and had time to wander the streets that night and get a big breakfast at a café nearby in the morning before packing up, checking out and making my way to the airport. The years of planning, the working and saving, the reading of books and maps, all catching up to me now as ten weeks on the road were jamming up at the end like a ten-car pileup in my mind. Totaling up my pocket spiral notebook, I determined that I had spent $489 in ten weeks, not including airfare, and I still had plenty of railroad money in the bank to pay for my first year of college.

As the Icelandic turbo prop took off, I leaned my head back and let the instant memories flow through my head. That first conversation in German in the Ardennes Forest, Dover, London, Stratford on Avon, Derby, Birmingham, Bath, Stonehenge, Hastings, Oostende, Amsterdam, Munster, Cologne, Rhine River castles, Mainz, Basel, Bern, Zurich, Innsbruck, Heidelberg, Munich, Garmisch, Venice, Florence, Rome, Pisa, Perpignan, Barcelona, Lerida, Madrid, Paris, Michelangelo, DaVinci, Ghilberti, and all the times, people and spaces in between. All the characters I had met, all the history I had seen and touched. But what kept popping into my head on that plane ride home, August 22, 1969, were Dr. Philip Saragoza's words "you will never again be the same."

It was three a.m. when my final ride dropped me off at the corner of Forty-Fifth Avenue East and Superior Street in Duluth, just a few blocks from my home. As I crossed the street, I saw a familiar figure just closing up shop at Jimmy's Pizza, the neighborhood favorite. It was Don Sturn, a fellow Duluth East graduate who I had known since elementary school.

"Hey, is that you, Nash?" He saw me approaching him with my pack on my back.

"Yeah, Don, how're you doing?"

"Where the heck have you been all summer?"

"I've just hitchhiked through twelve countries in Europe."

"No lie?" Don looked shocked on top of being dog tired from a long day at Jimmy's.

"Yeah, really, it was fantastic."

"Wow, you have to tell me all about it sometime."

"Sure," I laughed, because up to and including that answer ever since Don started talking to me I found the answer in German in my head and translated it to English to answer him. That curious linguistic hangover lasted almost three days. Don was tired and I was tired, my day had started in Luxembourg, so we went our separate ways. After I walked the last three blocks to my house all the doors were locked and there was no key left anywhere and nobody was home. Ice knew I would be home on the twenty-second. Where the heck is she? I went out into my back yard over by the balsams, pulled out my Indian blanket and rolled up in it inside my poncho, wadded up a shirt for my head and curled up survival style.

I woke up about three hours later and got up to stretch, when I noticed a light on in the kitchen at the Olson's across the alley. I had been their babysitter when I was thirteen. I took a chance and walked over there and knocked on the door. Mrs. Olson came right to the door and made a big fuss about well, I had to come in and have a nice breakfast and tell them all about Europe. So yes, my first morning back home was a good one because of the giving nature of good people. I enjoyed Mrs. Olson's cooking (she insisted on being called Serene but I couldn't). Frank Olson didn't call her that either. They were good folks, I had known them for years. After breakfast Frank pulled out his extension ladder and gave it to me to use to get into my house, "just be sure to bring it back when you're done," agreed.

I used the ladder to get to my upper bedroom window; jimmied it open and climbed into my room. The first thing to do was go downstairs, struck at every step by the sheer comfort of our modest home, through the kitchen and out the door to take Frank's ladder back to him with many thanks. Then I took to exploring my drawers and closet, amazed at the amount of clothing I possessed.

After living out of my pack all summer it was an eye-opener. American consumers, what have we become? Thoreau sits there shaking his head, "Simplify, simplify."

It turned out that my Dad was being cared for in Hibbing by his sister Alma, so that's where I hitched next, eager to see him, hoping he was in better shape. When I arrived at the little apartment door which had been my grandmother's when I was little, my aunt Alma opened it and loudly announced my name "*Nash is here!*" For some reason she always got excited when she saw me and spoke in a loud voice to show it. I walked in, gave Alma a hug and looked at my Dad sitting on the edge of the couch looking at me; he was the first to speak.

"You look like hell." He was referring to the fact that I had not shaved or cut my hair since high school. The funny part was, he didn't look so great himself.

"What about my moustache? I bargained for his approval.

"What moustache? Put some cream on that and let a cat lick it off."

"Well how are you anyway, Dad?" He sat back into the couch and softened, and then proceeded to tell me as little as possible about his brain surgery because it raised his blood pressure when he got worked up over certain injustices. I fully accommodated his wishes, except for the personal grooming suggestions.

Over the next couple of years I finished two years of college at UMD, where I also ran for the track team and wrote a weekly column for the student newspaper, observations on life. I had quickly learned that as Dr. Saragoza had said, my life was never the same. Almost everyone I met—they seemed so immature, petty, materialistic, fearful, anxious, full of doubt, no confidence, at least not based in authentic power, I really had nothing to say to them, so I wrote about them in my weekly columns. I rarely spoke to anyone. One day in March of 1971 I surprised myself with the sound of my voice at three in the afternoon when I said hello to a teammate in the locker room after school; I had not spoken yet that day. And so my solitary nature born from much time alone began to solidify in me.

CHAPTER FOUR

"Edwards?"

"Yup," I said.

"Climb up the rope ladder with your duffel." The second mate called out to me from above on the deck. So I slung my duffel over my shoulders and climbed the rope ladder up to the deck, where the mate greeted me.

"Welcome," he said, "your first time out?"

"Yes, I just got my Merchant Marine card."

He walked me to the forward end of the 600-foot iron ore boat and showed me the deckhand's quarters under the pilot house. I picked out a bunk and began to unpack my duffel; it was going to be three months out here, so I figured I'd get settled. This was the first union job my Dad didn't get me; my girlfriend's dad was an attorney for U.S. Steel, and he got me the job. These were the boats I used to watch from up in my book-reading back yard maple, and now I was a deckhand on one, the S.S. August Sherping of U.S. Steel's Great Lakes Fleet. You needed an actual Merchant Marine card to work on one, so this is just another flashback to Kerouac, who wrote that he had worked in the Merchant Marine during WWII. I was twenty years old now.

In my ore boat bunk, as I was finishing parking myself out of my duffel, which carried at least twice as much as my pack carried, another deckhand walked into our tight quarters.

"Jim Parker's my name," he smiled and extended his right hand.

"Nash Edwards. Nice to meet you. Sailed before?"

Jim shook his head, "Nope, first time. You?"

"First time too. We're gonna work on this hatch farm."

"Suits me," said Jim. Jim stood about 5'10", sinewy build, sandy hair, glasses on his narrow nose. It turned out that Jim had a Master's degree in English, and had just returned from a fifteen-month sojourn in northern Ontario, where he had canoed north from Minnesota, leased an acre of woods from Her Majesty's government, cut trees and built his Thoreau-style cabin. He brought with him 100 pounds of flour, 50 pounds of sugar, and 50 pounds of bean seed. He planted the seeds and grew his beans, and ate heartily for over a year while living and pondering in his 8x10 cabin. "I bought a roll of linoleum at an Indian trading post and had a real nice floor," he smiled.

"I mean," he grinned shrugging, "how much do you *need*?" I took it all in, hearing this fellow's tale of doing what Thoreau had done. "Simplify, simplify," I noted. Jim sat up.

"You know Thoreau too?" Within two weeks we had shared a ton of notes and stories about our favorite writer in common. Wake-up was at 7:00, when the deckwatch on duty came in and told the deckhands to get up. We dressed quickly and walked the 600 feet down to the galley at the after end, where John the Porter greeted us with his standard "What'll it be for ya today?" John the Porter was a sickly looking fellow, pale in the face, with thin dark hair sticking out from under his Porter's cap. His pale blue eyes and pale thin blue lips made him appear to be sea-sick twenty four hours a day. He stood a little crooked, tilting to his left side, as if the seas were tossing him, but he probably had one leg shorter than the other. At any rate, he meant what he said. "What'll it be for ya today?" meant whatever your heart desired for breakfast, they'd fix it for you. I went with scrambled eggs, bacon, milk.

"No toast? Hash browns?" John tilted. I accepted his suggestion and ordered both. One couldn't eat too much out here on the hatch farm where the work was long and hard. I had asked for a hatch farm, rather than one of the newer boats with hatch cranes that did most of the work for you. Angus, the Bosn's mate, put the young deckhands to work chipping the paint off the pipes by the pilot house. It didn't occur to me yet that once completely chipped off, fresh paint would be applied, just as something to do when we weren't in port, loading or unloading. The old Nova Scotian regaled his young crew with tales of taking his wife for his carnal needs right in the Volkswagen after she picked him up at the docks after fall tie-up. "Ya gotta take it when ya need it," was his motto. And it was all agreed that his wife probably had her own horns after Angus had been gone four months.

Sailing, as they called it, although the boat was entirely run on coal steam, was really not much of a life for a married man. Heck, one of the wheelsmen, Bill, was on his fifth wife. Bill was off his watch, sleeping in his bunk one afternoon when I looked down the deck and saw it bending back and forth in some pretty rough waves on Lake Superior. Mind you, this was the same kind of boat as the ill-fated Fitz, in the last couple of years that the Edmund Fitzgerald still sailed.

"Hey, hey!" I shouted into the wheelsmen's quarters, and Bill, groggy-eyed and stumbling to the door, asked "what's all the racket?" I pointed and told him breathlessly that "the boat is bending!" Bill looked down the deck, then looked askance at me and wryly advised me, "next time, when you see the boat *not* bending in a storm like this, *then* come and get me." In other words, rookie, it's supposed to bend in a storm, that way it doesn't snap in two.

I stepped sheepishly back into my quarters, where Jim and the other deckhand, Craig, were debating who was the best seaman on the boat. Craig was a dark-haired square-jawed tall handsome drifter from southern California, and it was soon not lost on Jim and me that Craig was a bit simple-minded. First of all, he was from southern California, so he was basically superficial to begin with. He liked to stand in front of the mirror for upwards of an hour, making sure every hair on his head was in place, and he would lather up and shave his face three times to make sure it was smooth as a baby's butt.

With lather still on his face, Craig liked to inform me that Duluth was the best city in the country to be "on the bum." "Get a free meal at the Union Gospel Mission, then go down behind the old Fitger's brewery, where runoff pipes could be tapped into our copper mugs until we lurched drunk as skunks up to a free bed at the Bethel."

To Craig, that was the top of the heap. Jim was having his way intellectually with Craig on the aforesaid debate, and he brought it to a sudden halt with an English major's play on words that "the best seaman on this boat is dried on my sheet." We all broke down at that, but Craig looked away not wanting us to see him laughing.

The first time you ship out of Duluth on your way down the vast waters of Lake Superior, you are mesmerized by the beauty of the hillside town and then amazed at how quickly it recedes from sight. It looks flat but is not, here as in Genoa. Then hour by hour, coal-fired engines built in 1913 drive the boat with 27,000 tons of iron ore to the great steel plants of Chicago, and a simple deckhand can watch up to forty hours of landless horizons before the end of the water is again spotted in northern Michigan. We were heading for Sault Saint Marie, a border town of upper Michigan and lower Ontario, where the Corps of Engineers for the Saint Lawrence Seaway maintains locks that lower the boats from Superior elevation to St. Mary's River elevation, which is the same as Lake Michigan.

While the boat was in the lock and waiting for water levels to change, the mate on watch and usually a deckwatch were swung over on a "Bosn's chair" from a boom on deck, and then were lowered to the concrete deck of the lock. Then they would walk up to the mail station and pick up whatever mail for the men or the officers of the boat was on hand and bring it back. As deckhands we just stood and looked around since our day ended at 5 p.m. unless we were in port.

When we worked we worked hard. They fed us well too. A typical union negotiation gave us a full breakfast, you've met Porter John; then, at 10 a.m., time for coffee break, this time with fresh pastries baked that morning by the second cook, a baker by trade. Cream puffs. Hot strawberry Danish. Noon we broke for a big midday meal with meat, potatoes, beans, chicken, hamburgers, you name your lunch. At two p.m. it was time for afternoon coffee break, which now included cold cut sandwiches, ham, beef, salami. At six p.m. you packed into the galley for the feature of the night. Tuesday night was steak night, with all the trimmings, as many steaks as you could eat. Some of us tossed the bones up in the air off the deck where the seagulls which had followed us from Duluth would swallow them whole in mid-flight. Nobody mentioned that it would kill them.

Looking back now it cannot be missed how stupendously ignorant we were then. We were not paid for our brains anyway. We were paid for our brawn, and after supper was finished, we three deckhands and a deckwatch would gather in the blind tank, which can be thought of as the basement of the front part of the boat, the forward end. This was where the chains for the anchors were kept, and an occasional shackle from one of those chains could be found lying around. At eighty five pounds, it was perfect for one-arm shoulder presses. We tossed them around like Frisbees; we were very strong, adding muscles daily.

Arriving into the port of Chicago with a load of iron ore, while commonplace, is still a big venture. Several miles out, the firemen in the Hades-like engine room were instructed to shovel salt into the coal fires, which made the smokestacks belch white smoke; that way the folks on the shore thought it was clean. I saw the hypocrisy in that immediately, but said nothing. Our boat was pulled by a tugboat around a bend to get the boat to the north slip of the huge U.S. Steel plants; one of my jobs as a deckhand would soon be coming up.

When the bow of the boat came fairly close to the side, they would send me over the side on the Bosn's chair and lower me down onto the deck. Then they would throw me a rope, which I would catch and pull in, since connected to it was the big corded steel cable that I needed to drag and secure over the pile-on and throw up my hands to signal it was time to pull her taut. This whole time the tug boat was straining an eight-inch thick cord of nylon to pull the forward end around the tight corner. Our eyes needed to be trained on that cord as we worked, because once in a while the cord would be strained to breaking "POW" and whipping one end at us with no respect for human life.

Once the boat was tied up on both ends, the deckhand's job was done, and given a good time of day, this might be a good time to take eight hours off and go up the street. In Cleveland one time I went for a run and wound up guest of a man and his son, to sit with them at a Cleveland Indians baseball game, in which Boog Powell hit a home run for the visiting Orioles, all while my boat was being unloaded, so who knows what the City of Big Shoulders could offer?

The mates told a story to us newbies about how two of them once walked three blocks up the street from the plant to the local tavern, but one mate lagged behind and followed after them a few minutes later. He was mugged in the first block by a thug who took his money. He figured, well, it's just two blocks to the tavern, my buddies can cover for me, and continued until in the second block, a different thug suddenly appeared in his face and demanded his money.

"The last guy took my money," the mate jerked his head toward the last block.

"Well, then gimme your shoes!" And that's how the poor mate approached the third block, heck, he could see the tavern lights from there, so he continued in his stocking feet. Half a block to go, he was shuddering with relief, when out of a tree right in front of him dropped menacingly a third thug.

"Gimme your munny!"

"The first guy took it."

"Wha first guy? Man, where's you shoes?"

"The second guy took them."

"*First guy second guy, shit*!" Thug number three clocked the mate right on the chin and knocked him off his stocking feet. Then he kicked him in the ribs a couple of times for good measure. He turned and slunk away muttering to himself *first guy second guy shi*. The wheezing mate picked himself up, limped across the street to the tavern, where he was greeted by the astonished faces of his mates.

The moral of the story being, don't go up the street by yourself. So when it came time to head up the street in South Chicago I was joined by Craig, Jim and Warren, one of the wipers who worked in the engine room in the after end. Warren was sort of a mamma's boy in his overall demeanor who jumped at the chance for some real adventure with the guys. We walked briskly, feeling free, away from the plant and our boat, just exploring our way. They found a cathouse and I followed them inside. There was a huge room almost like a bus station, with a black and white checkered tile floor, and a long low breakfast counter running down the right side of the room and a creaky staircase at the end of the room led to unknown parts upstairs.

One particularly doleful pallid-skinned seedy character in a ragged blue bowling shirt stood askance looking at us from his vantage point behind the counter. While the others followed Seedy's dirty-nailed finger pointing up the stairs, up they went, one behind the other, to take care of their business, I stayed behind at the counter and figured I'd better order something so I asked Seedy for a cup of coffee. "You're not going up?" He was confused at first; then he looked at me as if he were serving a Martian.

Seedy eyed me suspiciously from behind the counter as I sat there maybe forty minutes; the smell was unlike anything I'd ever had the pleasure of encountering, maybe the closest was that flophouse in downtown Bern, Switzerland that reeked of dried condoms. Warren was first downstairs, ruefully admitting he didn't get to penetrate her because of a sore she found on his organ, but then kept mooning about her for the rest of the day. Craig the California stud was next in thirty minutes, all grins, thumbs stuck in his waistband. Jim took the longest; I figured the smiling English major probably talked to her half the time. But who knows these mysteries? All I knew was that as a twenty-year-old virgin I really didn't want my first time to be a cash deal.

The air outside was refreshing after forty minutes sitting in that smelly dank cruddy hole. We walked down to the bar, I think the legal drinking age was eighteen in Illinois at the time; anyway I easily passed for older in those days, anywhere. So we all trooped in to an all-black bar and took a seat at a table. As I walked across the room to the table, I felt like every eye was on me. We sat down at the table and the bartender called out to us from behind the bar.

"You fellas want somethin?" I for one was not sure we were welcome there.

"Four beers please," Jim answered him.

"Ya gotta come up here to the bar to get em."

"OK," Jim said and smiling his way across the floor, followed by the room's eyes, paid for the beers and adroitly carried the mugs all by their handles across to our table. We sat there and made a toast to Warren's new love, to which he blushed and turned away. After a few minutes the normal buzz of the room kicked back in and we melted into the crowd.

Walking back to the boat that night, I was thinking about that. Where I had grown up and gone to school, there was one black kid in our whole class. Yes, it was pretty far north so the black percentage of the city's population was only about three percent, and except for the one family who thought it would be an advantage for their son William to go to eastern Duluth schools, every other black kid went to Central. It was truly a social, economic, geographical, and racial divide that defined Duluth; sadly, it still does today.

So it was that I felt on unfamiliar ground when the majority/minority was switched around and I was seeing them as they see us. What if they had all been white and I had been black? That was my first lesson in my own built-in racism, even though I didn't feel a shred of hostility toward non-whites. But I was learning to be aware of how I should be seeing others, through their words, actions and eyes, not just by the color of their skin. But purely on the idea of race, which in the full measure of anyone doesn't amount to a hill of beans, we too often base our perceptions of each other. God help us.

We all walked together back to the boat, not because of the mates' story, well, not entirely because of it. It just sort of made sense, walking together, and little did I suspect at that moment that I would one day see that as normal, and my instinctive solitary tendencies were not normal.

By the time we all got up the ladder to the deck of our boat, it was time for the deckwatch to sound the ballast. A deckwatch worked with the deckhands when opening or closing hatches, but otherwise he had his own set of duties on his watch, which was either eight-noon, noon-four, or four-eight, each time their watch came around, twice a day, they would be on, and between their watches they enjoyed eight hours off. This particular deckwatch had clearly ingested some drugs, as he discovered in our presence that he was unable to fit a quarter-inch rod into a four-inch opening. The low end of the rod kept missing the hole, as we all stood still and stared. Finally, in a pure fit of frustration, the first and only time I ever heard it, he threw down the rod and rope and blurted, in a single sentence, the same word used as a noun, adverb and verb.

"Well, fuck the fucking fucker."

Jim and I looked at each other, suppressing our laughter, in wonder at such an astonishing gift of verbal communication. It was not unheard of, in fact as a former railroad fireman and switchman, and now a deckhand with thirty-six working men on a 600-foot boat, some of the habits of the others had a way of rubbing off on me. So that when I was invited to a friend's family Thanksgiving one year, there were about fourteen people seated around the table, and I found myself asking very politely if someone could "please pass the fucking potatoes." You could have heard a pin drop. The inevitable pregnant pause, then Ted, the patriarch, the man who got me the job on the boats in the first place, said:

"Nash has been on the boats." Which was followed by hearty laughter and clinking of wine glasses.

But back to Lake Michigan. Now we were leaving Chicago and the wind was picking up. As soon as we cast off we—three deckhands, a deckwatch and Angus the Bosn's mate—went to work closing the hatches over the now empty cargo hold and rolling huge canvas tarps over the closed hatches and securing them with wooden spikes pounded by a mallet each of us wielded. All five of us worked on one hatch at a time, and with weather picking up as we got further out into Lake Michigan, the job became more urgent. We couldn't let the boat get into really deep water in a storm with any hatches open.

So it was with breakneck speed we pulled, we dragged, we pounded and leaped over the hatch to the next one, which had just been closed, and pull, drag, pound, leap, and pull, drag, pound, leap and we were only finished with three hatches—34 remained, and now cold rain was driving into our cheeks. We lost all sense of everyday existence and kicked it into hyper drive to take care of the work at hand; my eyelids were glazing over with the sideways rain and I swung the mallet harder, swifter, driving the stake firmly into place, securing the tarp against the seas. Then crouching up to the next stake, pull the tarp, pound that one in. It took about three hours to tarp down thirty seven hatches in the same manner as they did it when the boat was new in 1913. This was what I had signed up for—to work a hatch farm. After one especially brutal three plus hours in a driving snow storm the captain himself came down to our quarters to tell us what a good job we had done.

We worked hard, they played hard; I saved hard, and spent not a dime in Chicago or any other port. I went on with a twenty dollar bill and left three months later with the same twenty in my pocket. This was paying for my next year of college, and what was to end up being my last year on the track team. Actually, that was the year the school paid me to run for them, with a tuition scholarship that covered two of three quarters that year, so that with my boats money I had enough to pay what I needed at school and buy my first car so I could get a driver's license. My first car was a ten-year-old 1961 Karmann Ghia, for which I paid $500 and drove to school my final year as a full time student at UMD.

It wasn't all work and no fun. I drove that Ghia all the way around Lake Superior, taking the northern, more pristine route first. One cool thing about the Ghia was that the passenger seat folded way forward so that if I placed a wooden drawing board to span the distance between the back seat and the front seat, I could sack out in the car with my feet in the wayback, very comfortably. So there I was, asleep in my car in a small park in the Ontario town of North Bay, it must have been two a.m., and a RAP RAP on my window right next to my head jolted me out of my sleep. Flashlights in my eyes. Her Majesty's servants. I rolled down my window and looked up at two Mounties.

"Is this your car?"

"Yes."

"Did you know that it's against the law to sleep in this park?"

"No."

"Had enough rest?"

"Yes."

"Well then, best be moving along," and that's how I left North Bay, and drove through the night and by the next afternoon pulled into one of the nicest cities I have ever visited, Toronto. Before long I discovered a youth hostel, where for $2 Canadian—a looney—I got a bunk and a shower and a place to store my stuff, while most of my gear remained in the Ghia. A short walkabout, very clean, very nice, I liked, and still do like Canadians, for their friendliness and openness. Ultimately I went back to my stoop, as I was now accustomed to do, take a perch and watch the world pass by. Sometimes I would just look at feet, how many different sizes and shoes, and how the feet landed on the ground—plodding, striding, limping, cruising, gingerly, absent-mindedly—you can tell a lot about a person's history by their shoes and how their steps fall if you know how to pay attention.

After a while, a well dressed silver-haired gentleman took up a spot near me. He watched the passersby with me for a few minutes and then he spoke.

"Would you mind a little conversation, sir?" He bowed to me.

"No, I wouldn't mind," I thought, much to gain, what's to lose?

He sidled over to my concrete perch and began to ask me arcane intelligent questions; I found myself momentarily being drawn into his web. Then I thought of Dr. Philip Saragoza's line, I will never again be the same, which in this instance meant don't be gullible.

"You have such a beautiful mind," he beamed up at me on my perch.

"Why do you say that? I haven't said anything so remarkable."

"Ohh, there you go again." Dramatically he drew an arm across his forehead.

"Ok, what's up with you? What do you want?" I was losing patience.

"I'm inviting you to a party in Hamilton." He smiled, his silver moustache turning up at the edges.

"Hamilton? Where's that?"

"Ooohh, just down the road a ways," he affirmed, nodding to his right.

"What kind of party will it be?"

"Oh, music and dancing and drinking and whatever." He was getting excited.

"And who will be there besides you and me?" I waited as he paused.

"No one," he admitted. "But you have such a beautiful mind." I thanked him and bid him goodnight and turned up the stairs into the hostel. Poor guy. But not so poor, after a while I went back outside to double check my car. Strange what ownership of property does to a person's attitude. In this small case, an unreasonable fear, a lack of trust. But therein lies the rub—are we not innately trustful? Does a newborn hold a distrust of others? My effort is to trust until that trust is broken, so I walk up to any individual anywhere with trust in my heart. It's up to them to un-earn it. When I'm properly balanced, that is.

After Toronto I drove to London, where the University of Western Ontario is located. One of the girls I had met in Munich was a tall Canadian, pretty and fun to dance with. Chloe and I had corresponded a couple of times, and now I just dropped in on her life at the university. She was gracious and allowed me to sleep on the porch for a couple of nights, after which she asked me, "Just what do you want?" I took that as my signal to split, and so the Ghia was soon speeding toward the Windsor Tunnel, Detroit, Chicago, all the way north to Duluth.

CHAPTER FIVE

The end of the necessity to use a student deferment to stay out of Vietnam came in June of 1973. I had needed to get the deferment based on my attendance as a full-time student at UMD, but I put it off deliberately, to see if I might squeak through, even with lottery number 54. I read first the history of Indochina and learned right away that America was just the latest in a steady line of imperial colonizers like Great Britain and more recently, France. It seemed to me that Ho Chi Minh was like his country's George Washington. I just knew the war was wrong when I was eighteen, and then thirty years later my judgment was vindicated when none other than Robert McNamara, the Secretary of Defense during Vietnam, published his own admission that it had been wrong. (How could we have known that at eighteen and the "best and the brightest" didn't?)

Next I read the draft law, learning that if I didn't take a deferment and avoided being called, I was off the hook at twenty-six. But take a deferment and extend your liability to age thirty-five.

So it was that one day in 1972 I was with my third mate from the second boat I worked on, I had worked my way up to deckwatch so I walked with him to get the mail at the Soo. We stood against the counter waiting, his big belly pressing against it. This third mate was fat, very fat. He also chewed tobacco, and was forever hawking a mouthful of beetlejuice over the side; he'd been chewing so many years there was a neat little pocket under his lower lip for the chaw to sit, and that made him talk a little funny. He took up a little mail sack and threw it over his ample shoulder and left me to manage several different large sized boxes. On the way back to the boat I had to ask him.

"Say, Mate, how come I'm carrying all these big boxes and you've just got that little sack?"

"Becuz ah git paid fur whet ah know an you git paid fur whet you do, and ah know that those boxes er heavier then this here satchel." Such was the wisdom of my boat mates. Anyway, we got back up to the deck and the Mate started handing out the mail.

"Edwards, here's one for you."

I took the official looking letter wondering and opened it.

"Greetings from Uncle Sam. Report to your Draft Board." I told the Mate who told the Captain who allowed me to jump off there with my stuff and hitchhike back to Duluth. I left my duffel packed at home that August day 1972 and wore my UMD letter jacket buttoned up in the Federal Building of Duluth, which by then still had not installed air conditioning. Such folly in the air-conditioned city, the city fathers intoned. Sweat rolling down my arms under my jacket, I sat there and fielded a few hostile questions from fellow citizens who looked at me suspiciously, apparently having never read the history of Indochina. I went home and sat by the phone for two days with my duffel packed and my route to Canada planned. I simply would not fight in an immoral war of imperialism.

Then the deferment came through and I unpacked my duffel and took up my final year at UMD. I had been elected co-captain of the track team but didn't go out due to the changing conditions of my life and partly because of the coaching methods of one of the few female track coaches of a collegiate men's team.

Just to give one brief example, to motivate her pole vaulter at his final collegiate event, she came right out and said "Well, Don, this is the conference meet; for heaven's sakes, beat somebody!" As a result of methods like that I spent most of my time that year being editor-in-chief of the student weekly newspaper, which allowed me virtually unlimited freedom of expression, something I very much appreciated. It was fun to be the exclusive interviewer of such names as Christine Jorgensen, the world's first transsexual, whose birth name was George, who was changed into a woman in a series of operations beginning in 1951, and now was a theatrical feminine lady whose silver earrings jingled as she spoke.

In those days I also studied people closely while sitting on a ledge at UMD and found a number of axioms in the bargain. Physical attractiveness, for example, can be a curse rather than a blessing, not because it brings one to the attention of others, but rather because it tends to bring one's attention to oneself. People are funny when they stand under their showers and then sprint for the bus to avoid the rain. People are strange when they call dogs dumb animals and then forget their friend's name. People are pitiful when they cough all the way to the cigarette machine. To live according to how other people think is to lose my self-esteem; but to live without compassion for other people's feelings is to live without respect for myself. To follow the judgment of someone else is to allow them to lead my way; but to live a life without the aid of advice is likely to be difficult. Finally, the people who say the most are likely to do the least. If I listen while I work, I will hear, they will not. I will work, they will talk. And when the job is done, they will continue to talk about how quickly I managed to finish.

That was the year Eddie Edwards died, and now I was in charge of paying off the mortgage and supplying the food for me and Jesse. I got paid a little by the Statesman, I had some boats money in the bank, back then I always kept at least $1,000 in a bank somewhere. But what year was it? 1972. What became my crutch after losing my Dad?

MaryJane. Weed. Grass. Pot. It was everywhere, and I got so into it I bought a couple of pounds one time and Jesse and I, sitting at our kitchen table where we both had grown up, were sorting out sticks, weighing three-finger lids and then selling them for $13 a lid, with plenty left for us to smoke for free.

I smoked it every day for a year and a half. I would roll a doob before I went to bed; and wake up, walk over to the window, sit on the stool I left there, light the pre-rolled doob and watch my thoughts unfold as I retraced my life on that street. From the first time I looked out that window at four years of age to the present, seventeen years of growing up on that street. When my mind had processed the entire linear string of my life to the present day, I got up from the stool and went to the bathroom and got on with my day.

Sooner or later it has to be brought up, so this is just as good a time as any. How does a Boy Scout good clean morally straight boy like I was turn into a long-haired, heavy drinking pothead? The answer, to this day remains the same as it always was: I don't know, other than the weed worked somehow to dull the pain of loss I felt, and the drinking—well, I was Black Emil's grandson. From a curiosity, weed became a weekly party thing, and then an every day thing, and then a just be high all the time routine. In the beginning it was a great challenge to see how well I could perform my everyday life while stoned. I also discovered that with constant practice my guitar playing was improving, and for some reason that's where weed drove me—to my guitar. I remember once seriously thinking, I wonder what it would be like to be straight again?

I smoked so much I hallucinated right in front of the mirror in my bathroom. This is only weed, mind you, I had never tried anything stronger than that. But this one time, looking at myself in the mirror, my face turned into a werewolf's face, fur and all. I blinked. It blinked. I turned my head. The werewolf turned its head. The hair began to stand up on the back of my neck. I felt a cool breeze sneaking in the window. I closed my eyes and held them tight for a minute, then opened them to see myself back in the mirror. Whew. That was a close one, I thought. That was about the time the movie "The Exorcist" came out and was all the rage. The book came out first and was scarier than the movie. So I was aware of those ideas. But in addition, there seemed to be an almost invisible loosely aligned occult network roaming the streets of Duluth at that time, and I came into contact with a number of them. We all smoked reefer together and swapped occult stories, of which I had none to offer. One bejeweled sorceress predicted to me that I might soon see a white goat and when that happened, my life would be destroyed. Don't worry, old beaded one in moccasins, I made it this far; how are those crystals working out for ya?

In June of '73 I ran a little miniature golf course on London Road. In those days my reading had turned to Buddhism. I also was reaching the end of my rope in terms of just keeping it all together. The past twelve months had been, well, challenging: the house, the mortgage, the food, and keeping Jesse off the street as much as possible, which was not at all; he had tried all kind of drugs out in the gravel pit, where I never ventured. I had been sort of a big man on a small campus, and as one brief dark-eyed flame told me, I "threw it all away." She didn't know the half of it. But now the universe seemed to be closing in on me; it was like my mind was the hub of a bike wheel, and until that summer I had been able just through native ability to work with all the spokes, but now they were too numerous, I was overloaded.

Sitting on my stool at the mini-golf shack, looking out at Lake Superior, that huge calming body of big blue water that had shaped me over the years, I decided right then and there to come up with a way to handle the phenomena, a way to keep my mind in control no matter what the world threw at me. The concept of four was borrowed from the Buddha. Strip away the layer upon layer upon layer of Buddhist tradition and you are left with the four noble truths: Suffering exists. Suffering is caused by craving. There is an end to suffering. The end of suffering is the cessation of craving. Seekers would travel long distances to meet the Buddha and ask him questions, and for every question he felt did not apply to his four noble truths, he would simply reply "That does not apply." That's what I needed, a gatekeeper.

Then, what four tenets resonate in me? To what ideals do I want to dedicate my life? First came Truth. Without the truth we are in the dark. Next I chose Understanding, since that quality was much needed in my own development, and as I conceived it to be a universal need. Next came Kindness, also needed in my quiver, borrowed from Jesus, who represented to me then a master of life, and ultimately of kindness. Finally I chose Peace, for that must be what all humans want, which was what I chose to believe at twenty-two.

Then I adapted a yogic system of breathing, in which you breathe out Truth, you breathe in Understanding, you breathe out Kindness, you breathe in Peace. Or vice-versa. Either way it works in the way Emerson wrote about boys in church repeating a word in their heads until the word dissolved and only the idea remained[1].

"Truth, Understanding, Kindness, Peace."

"Truth, Understanding, Kindness, Peace."

"Truth, Understanding, Kindness, Peace." I read somewhere that it is possible for an individual to come upon his own mantra, and this is mine. When I meditate on these concepts, the words fall away very quickly, and after decades it does feel that these qualities are mine indeed. I certainly find peace within them.

But we get ahead of the story. During the 1972-73 school years, nobody knew that I was not completing any courses; I would register for a full load, then two weeks later drop all my classes, take the refund, and live off it. That way I figured I could spend the year running the paper. Nobody checked. Except for two people. One was my first journalism instructor and faculty advisor, who discovered the ruse late that spring, walking into the newspaper office and urgently informing me that I had not completed a single credit that year.

The other one, by some hidden hand of luck, was my former high school girlfriend Cathy, who now worked in the Registrar's office and actually was the one person across whose desk came the list of student deferments for each quarter, and part of her job was to verify that all had completed the credits required. She checked my name off as completed for three straight quarters in which I didn't, during a time when the draft was very much still in force. I didn't know about this until years later, when we ran into each other and she told me I owed her big time. I really did.

When the U.S. finally got the picture and evacuated Saigon, and the draft law was set to officially expire in 1973, I made plans immediately to finish up my Statesman year, then catch a boat to run a full season. There was still time for parties. It seemed like during that year every week at one friend's house up on east Fifth Street, shared by four guys, there was a huge party, kegs of beer on the first floor, everybody passing joints on the second floor, and me sitting on a bed in a third floor room, playing my guitar, after working my way through the first two levels. I bought my guitar in 1971. Hour upon hour upon hour of practicing got me into a space where I actually was pretty good at a modest type of finger-picking after a couple of years. I would bring the guitar to parties and go off into some room and start playing and singing, and before long the room would be full of stoned groupies who watched and listened in varying degrees of self-medication.

One night in February 1973, after I was finished playing, everyone left the room except one pretty girl from Albert Lea, Annette was her name; she was a brunette with a hot streak. She liked the guitar player and we started making out on the bed. Clothes came off, flesh on flesh, oh, oh, oh, good grief it's over already! My virginity lay used up on the sheet as I lay back listening to Annette from Albert Lea quietly leave the room and go downstairs to another guy, a more experienced guy. I figured it wasn't time for me yet, even though I had turned twenty two the month prior. Since then I have read that heavy marijuana usage will reduce one's libido, but that's no excuse.

In July 1973 the boat dispatcher called me and told me if I could get up to Two Harbors in an hour I could sign onto the S.S. Nicholas Darias. I called my boss at the mini golf and apologized for a quick exit, he was cool about it; he eventually sold that parcel of land to McDonald's and made a bundle, which I'm fairly certain was his aim from the start. I quickly packed my duffel, keeping in mind I would be out there through November this year, and that meant, for one thing, an extra parka to wear over my first one; the Lake Superior winds were very cold, and went right through just one measly parka over a wool shirt over a sweatshirt over a cotton shirt. I caught a ride from the first car I saw and got to the Darias in plenty of time. There I went on as an experienced seaman, so they put me to work as a deckwatch, and I took over the four to eight watch.

That was the best watch to work, I thought, since I was done work before breakfast, then had all day off before going back on duty at 4:00 to 8:00. One of my duties was to make the coffee for the pilot house crew on that watch. I asked the watchman how they liked their coffee made.

"You know where the coffee urn is?" He asked me.

"Yup."

"You know in the drawer those bags that say use one?"

"Yup." "Use two. We want it strong enough to take the paint off the bulkheads."

"Okay." Another of my duties was to hose down the fantail early in the watch. Soot from the coal-fired smokestacks covered the deck; it was sort of a Zen experience to hose it down, leaving a perfectly clean deck. Once I made the coffee and delivered it, and hosed down the fantail, I would give myself a break in the still-starry morning and lean over the fantail, watching the dark churning of the waters behind the boat and feeling the big rumbling from the engine room under me as my Furnace Room Friend returned to comfort me just as it reliably did over the past seventeen years. Goosebumps all up and down my arms and back somehow gave me a peaceful mind. I had a few other chores, such as sounding the ballast, and I never had any problem with getting the rod into the hole, and raising the flag at sunrise and taking it down at sunset. I actually got to watch the sun rise and set over a mostly landless horizon for ninety days in a row.

It would be a shame to write about life on the boats without sharing a little more about the stars. When your horizon is water in all directions, that means fully half the night sky is visible to you. A great arc of millions of stars, constellations, planets was my perspective when I lay on my back on top of a hatch about a third of the way down the six-hundred-foot boat. At night, in southern Lake Michigan in summer, or Lake Erie, my ears strained for sounds other than the breaking of water against our bulkheads. All of the answers to all of the riddles of all of the eras of humankind shone above me, as far as I could see. My eyes feasted for hours at the inscrutable sky, surmising that Plato and Socrates saw very much the same sky, as southern Lake Michigan is almost at the same latitude as Greece, as odd as that may seem. Every time I submerged myself in that exercise my return to smallness was sudden.

In the galley of that boat I was exposed to tuberculosis. One of the wipers from the engine room was a small, wiry, almost spindly fellow named Charlie, but we all called him Coughing Charlie, because he had a wicked, no stopping, deep, wheezing cough. He had black stringy hair that stuck out under his filthy Phillies baseball cap, and when he smiled or laughed, he opened his mouth to show about half of his teeth missing, but there was no mistaking his laugh. His eyes lit up with glee and he laughed and laughed until the coughing kicked in. I felt concern for him; he was a sad sight. Whenever I walked into the galley and he was sitting there alone, sipping his coffee, our eyes would meet, my eyebrows would rise, and with a silly grin on my face I started to dance a jig right there in front of poor Charlie, who eyes lit up and he laughed and laughed, then coughed and coughed. I felt badly making him cough, but he had so much joy in his beady little eyes when he saw me, I had to indulge him. Years later, during a routine physical, the test came back that I had been exposed to tuberculosis, and I knew precisely where.

That wasn't the only new thing I exposed myself to. One trip down to south Chicago found me walking up the street on my own, despite the stories the mates on my first boat told, more due to my ever-increasing solitary nature. I found a little neighborhood tavern with a pool table on the side. It was mostly populated by locals, who mostly happened to be black, and I was cool if they were, keeping mindful of what I learned my lesson the previous year. I picked up a pool partner in a beautiful black girl who was sitting and watching me play on my own for a while before she asked me if I wanted to play her. She was very dark skinned, fine features, poured into her jeans and strikingly voluptuous in a royal blue blouse, and was also rather serious. I wondered what made her tick so I asked her my then standard astrology-related opener.

"What's your birthday?"

"January 17," she replied.

"January 17? What year?" I was stunned.

"1951." This ultra foxy woman from the 'hood arrived on the planet the very same day as I did, and by accident of birth she lived here and I was a lucky traveler. I told her we were born on the exact same day, we probably have a lot of similarities, but she wasn't ready to buy it. We played on, and talked, and then she invited me to go with her to her apartment, but wait, she paused, and told me well, her man might stop in and that wouldn't be good. So I didn't leave with her, even though she was about the hottest woman I'd ever seen. I played another game of pool and had another beer, then hiked back to the boat, where I was a bit later informed by a wiper who had been in the same tavern that the black beauty had come back looking for me a little later. I figured my chances were better to stay on the boat so I did; not cool to mess with another man's woman.

That season I stayed with the boat almost to tie-up in early December. Thanksgiving dinner was served in the galley, and it is the truth, that was some of the best food I've ever eaten. Thirty-seven men on a boat on Lake Superior, sitting down for Thanksgiving dinner made for a memorable day replete with more food than you could normally imagine. U.S. Steel was paying us $2.60 an hour, plus lots of time and a half overtime when we were arriving in port or leaving port. That was the contract negotiated for us by the Steelworkers Union, and included in the contract was real, solid, good food and plenty of it for the men.

The reason I didn't finish the season is that the captain of the Darias was a pompous ass, and I was a rebel. There is no other way to put it. The bug-eyed merchant mariner liked to strut around with his white hard hat on, letting everyone know he was in charge, while we snickered at his fat belly, around which ran a gigantic belt for huge-waisted pants, hiked up to buckle the belt right in the middle of the ponderous paunch. The captain and three mates wore white hard hats, and all the rest of us wore yellow hard hats. But there was an egalitarian rebel seething in me, and one night, down in the blind tank, I painted my yellow hard hat white while my bunkmates stood with their arms folded defensively, shaking their heads at what would become of me, but my heart raced in the raw idealistic emotion that I was doing it for them. I left the authorities the dignity of being the only ones with their names stenciled onto the front of the hardhats, leaving mine just plain white. The next day I walked down the deck to the galley wearing my white hard hat. The deckhands and wipers looked at me respectfully but not without a twinge of fear of what might follow. When the captain noticed it later that day—and that was all I was doing it for—he visibly squirmed before he regained his rotund balance.

The porky bug-eyed coward never talked to me about it. He gave orders to his Bosn's mate, a tall congenial guy overall, to make the trip hell for me so I would pile off at first port. We were on our way up Lake Superior, to Duluth, riding high, as we carried no load on the return trip. The Bosn's mate came down to our quarters that evening and cordially invited me out of my quarters and instructed me to scrub the entire floor of that large area with…and he produced for me to accept, a toothbrush. Then he walked over to a bucket of grease and casually tipped it over with his boot so it ran all over the deck. That's what I had to clean up. Then the Bosn's mate, a veteran sailor who had seen it all in his day, softly advised me with a half wink that when I was done down there, let him know and he'd find more for me to do, but that he wouldn't be back down unless I called for him.

He climbed up the ladder and left me standing there in dirt and grease.

Well, it was past eight p.m., as he had caught me just as I was finishing my watch, and he wasn't likely to come back down that evening. In the morning we would be in Duluth. So the first thing I did was grab Pete from Pittsburgh, a shaved-head twenty-year-old muscular deckhand with zero body fat who had fashioned a pipe out of an elbow of metal from the engine room. We climbed up the stairs, looked around, and opened the door to the cargo hold and climbed down into the empty cavern that echoed every word, so we whispered and giggled as Pete produced some weed from his bag and we smoked up right there in the cargo hold.

My attitude properly adjusted, I returned to the clean-up area and began to scatter toilet paper all over the place, in the grease, on the floor, stuck to the bulkheads. Then paper towels ripped up. Then bars of soap rubbed all over the bulkheads. After about twenty minutes of that, my heart racing, I retired for the night, but not before I packed my duffel for an early exit the minute we hit port, which is exactly what I did. I was halfway home to Lakeside before old bug-eyes must've learned what I had done;

he probably vowed to keep me off the boats forever. Little did he know that this was my last trip on the boats, it was time to move on. I had $4,500 in the bank from my five months out there. There was a lot of time to think during those five months on the water, and now my plan was to take a trip around the world; I forwarded $2,000 to the Bank of New Zealand in Wellington, New Zealand, with the object of following my money.

But first I wanted to scrum around the states for a while, and after celebrating my twenty-third birthday with buddies in Minneapolis, the first thirty days of my new adventure was on a Greyhound bus. I paid for a thirty-day pass, which permitted me to ride the bus all night, sleeping much of the time, and get off in whatever city it stopped at in the morning. Charleston, West Virginia was just such a city. I stowed my pack at the Greyhound station and went for a walkabout. The hills in Charleston are awesome, rolling with such pitch it almost looked like a roller-coaster. I followed one street up a hill and came to the top where I saw some very old houses standing proudly in rows on either side of the street. One caught my eye. I couldn't help thinking it looked like a house from Lincoln's time, an old dark wood colonial. How would I know that? I truly don't know, although I do know that Lincoln's father Thomas died precisely one hundred years before I was born, January 17, 1851, for whatever that may be worth. I walked up to the door and rang the doorbell. A moment passed and then an old man, standing six feet two inches straight as a ramrod, opened the door, looked at me, and spoke.

"Yes? May I help you?" He asked me, crystal blue eyes peering at me through thick glasses.

"Hello, sir, I was just walking by and I wondered, how old is this house?"

"Well, it was built in 1810." I was right! Lincoln was a year old when this house was built. How did I know that?

"Would you like to step in?" He asked me further, showing me more hospitality than I had expected. Colonel Victor Brownland,

U.S. Army Retired, now 82, had been military attaché to General Stilwell in China, and had traveled the world during his own military career. He showed me around the house, pointing out beautiful artifacts such as an intricately carved black Chinese teak chest that had belonged to Gen. Stilwell. (I wondered but did not voice it, about the Chinese family who owned it before Gen. Stilwell copped it.) Then he took me out into the back yard, to the very back of the yard, where we stood together and looked at the rear of the house as he talked more about his life. He was clearly enjoying the company. When we returned to the house he gave me an apple to take with me, and as we approached the front door, by the stairwell that led upstairs, he whispered to me "The Mrs. doesn't come down for strangers anymore." But I bet she was listening to every word. I thanked the Colonel profusely; he smiled and waved as I reached the street, and I walked back down the way I had come up, tossing my apple up and down in my hand, thinking how grateful I am for everything I have.

I had one more stop in Charleston, as I knew a girl from Duluth, actually the big sister of a girl I had dated, who lived here now. Just to make a friendly connection, I located where she was and she invited me right over. She was engaged to an air force man, I think, and he was out of town. Rita was her name, and she definitely got most of the pulchritude in the family; she even had been Miss Zenith City for one year back home. When I arrived she was wearing a powder blue turtleneck, tight enough for onlookers to not be able to miss the bulge of her ample breasts. We sat at her table talking a while, she poured us each a glass of wine, and we sipped that for a while, then she went to a closet and brought back a bong; she packed it with her weed and offered it to me. I toked, and almost gagged because there, in Charleston, in those circles anyway, they put Scope mouthwash in the bong instead of water, thinking it would mask their breath. Rita laughed at me, smiling her big pearly whites at me as we got stoned together. Then she wanted to go lie down on the couch and I went with her. I sat on the floor next to the couch and then she offered me herself.

"You know, Nash, I always liked you when you were dating Rusty. I'll bet that you a good lover." Well, I sheepishly admitted my lack of experience.

"In that case I'd like to show you how I make love," she replied softly.

"I think if I had sex with an Aderlink, it should be with Rusty," I tried to let her down easy, while keeping my own hesitation under close guard.

"That's right," she cooed, "Rusty was your girlfriend." So it ended there. Soon afterward we said our goodbyes with a hug on her doorstep, and I left her there with her crazy Scope-filled bong. I got back on the bus that night still tasting that awful mouthwash and didn't get off again until I reached Boca Raton, Florida, where my sister Lila was living then. Lila had grown into a beautiful, brown-haired brown eyed sexy female who could wrap men's hearts around her pinky finger with a sideways glance of her dark mysterious eyes. Her latest catch was a tall dark-haired, smooth talking Texan named Clint who called her Babe. She had already been married and divorced and now was living with Clint about a half mile from the beach in Boca.

"Hey, Bro," she smiled when she saw me. Lila was one cool gal.

"Hey, Sis," I grinned.

"I want you to meet Clint," she gestured him over and he, like all her other puppies, followed orders and sat by her side.

"Hi Clint, take good care of my sister," I shook his hand. He definitely was handsome, in a movie star way, kind of a bashful Gary Cooper look. And he was drop-dead polite to my sister and to me. I liked him. We sat around and had a couple of beers and then Lila asked me if I had any reefer. I wasn't traveling with it on me. I didn't need to, because it was everywhere. Clint had some in his truck and he volunteered to go out and retrieve it.

"Isn't he a dreamboat?" Lila whispered to me after Clint left the room.

"I'd say, heck, you might want to hang on to this one."

"Let's not get carried away," she involuntarily shuddered. She was the first afflicted of the three of us kids, she called it "the family curse," and did everything in her power to not make the curse come true. The unspoken, the unseen, the unfortunately missing love from our childhood was stillborn, and none of us had a clue as to how to be loved, so that Lila, brilliantly acute of her own limitations, could not bear to expose her darkness to someone she cared about. For that reason she carried a heavy dose of thanatose. But we didn't talk about this when we visited, whether in Boca or Denver or Minneapolis. We chatted amiably about all sorts of nonsense, and all the while I sensed a tension between us. When we smoked pot the whole scene devolved to music and giggles. I was always the serious one, and my serious side was deepened by the pot, making me even more reflective. But it also made me more amiable. It was fun to hear my sister cackling and shrieking her laughter the way she did back home.

Clint took us out that night in his truck, a big shiny black Ford. His cowboy boots looked like he was born in them. I was wearing a red headband that night, just for fun, but when we arrived at the nightclub, a surly bouncer scowled at me and ordered me to "Remove your headgear!" He pointed a stubby finger at a sign posted by the door which read "No headgear permitted." But the rule and the bouncer struck me as funny and I stifled a chuckle. He saw that and got right into my face and repeated his demand into my nostrils. I reached up slowly so as not to upset him further and gently pulled my bandana off, still stifling an inner chuckle at the sheer absurdity of the whole situation. With that concession, we could enter, with the bouncer's glare palpable on my neck.

We all slept late the next morning. I awoke first, on my own internal clock, and grabbed my Indian blanket—red pattern faded to almost pink, worn from thousands of miles in my pack and many a moon wrapped up around me—and went for a walk on the beach. I walked about two blocks and saw a circle of people on the sand listening to some shaved head guy dressed like a spiritual teacher. I sat down by the circle and just listened, as the guru stared at the sand in front of him, humming something, and then lifted his shiny noggin and started making strange assertions. Upon hearing one particularly dubious claim, I told him no, that's not exactly true; he looked at me like an interloper who was messing with his followers, so I got up and left them to their own nirvana.

Next I came to a sand volleyball net, but there was only one guy there. It should be noted that while in school, all the teams we played on were champion teams for six years in a row, we always won every game. So now I asked the one guy there if he wanted to play one on one, each taking three hits to get the ball over. He agreed, and we went at it. That brought a bunch of people to watch us. I stood back, he served. I bumped it up, set it higher, and jumped up to spike it. Point for me. It went that way for about forty minutes, we both scored freely with only one defender. It was a lot of fun, though, and a great workout.

The sun was already about eleven o'clock high and the Boca Raton blue sky and blue Atlantic water shimmered in the morning heat. I walked about two miles up the beach, taking my time, letting my body rest after the volleyball in the sand. Ahead I spotted a shade tree up on a knoll from the beach. I stopped there and sat on my blanket and meditated "Truth, Understanding, Kindness, Peace." I did that for about fifteen minutes and then stopped and listened with my eyes closed. Full of the ideas I had been repeating, I concentrated on hearing the waves of the sea. Soon peace, kindness, understanding and truth were floating on the water. I sat silent, eyes closed, for about twenty minutes, watching my breath. Always aiming for that special moment of awareness that comes only at the exact point at which my breath out becomes my breath in. In my personal system, that falls between understanding and kindness. Pondering on virtues thereof brings inner rewards.

When I finally opened my eyes to the beautiful blue ocean, the soft white sand, the palm tree over my head, there—there running up the beach, look at that stride. It was a young woman runner, long straight blond hair, with very long legs which were carrying her so gracefully over the sand, I was impressed. I ran down from the knoll and intercepted her.

"Hi…I saw you running from where I'm sitting up there and had to tell you that you have a beautiful stride." I spoke as a runner to a runner, and I think she sensed that.

"Oh thank you," she smiled at me. "Where are you sitting up there?"

"Just over the edge of the knoll, under that palm tree, it's nice and shady."

"Let's go up there; I could use a rest in the shade." So we ran together up to the knoll and to my blanket, which I now spread out more fully. She sat down and stretched out her legs, propping herself up on her elbows. She looked very pretty lying there. I sat down beside her and we got to know a little bit about each other. She was a nursing student here, I was a traveling student from there. Before I knew it she was leaning over and kissing me. I kissed her back. We lay back and interlocked limbs and made out in the shade of that Florida morning palm tree. Then things started to heat up and she surprised me with her roaming hands. One thing led to another and then she was on top of me, riding me, fortunately for her, anyway, that I lasted a little longer than with the groupie from Albert Lea. After we were done she sat beside me and gently wiped me clean with a corner of my blanket; I was touched by her gentleness. She then pulled her running shorts and top back on, leaned over and kissed me, and ran off down the dune to the beach and disappeared slowly loping behind the palms. I sat there and asked myself, what just happened? I didn't even know her name.

CHAPTER SIX

Two days later I was back on the bus, this time headed for Port Aransas, Texas, where I had spent a couple of spring breaks while a student at UMD. The bus passed New Orleans and I thought hard and fast, do I want to jump off here? Mardi Gras was just about to begin. No, I'm going to Texas, dadgummint. And so I arrived in February 1974 in Port Aransas, Texas, which is on an island known as Mustang Island.

In the 1930s it was a hangout of the Chicago mobsters, since it was off the mainland, it afforded them better cover. That's back when driving was the only way to get there, and driving across that huge state took about 14 hours. The year-round settlement on Mustang Island by 1974 was about six hundred and the spring break population swelled it to thirty thousand. My intention was to stay a couple of weeks.

I found an old trailer for rent and called that my place until I found a little stone cottage for $20 per month. I talked myself into a job working on a labor gang, raking out cement for a retaining wall for one of the big new condo buildings shooting up. The only one who spoke English was me. My coworkers showed me how to make bean tacos. They ate beans for every meal. Somebody said they drove up from Mexico every morning and drove back every night. That was my first direct observation that Mexicans are hard workers.

One day one of the big loaders got a rock stuck in its track, and we had to find a way to clear it to move ahead. One guy came up with a rod, and another brought in a sledge hammer. For some reason I ended up being the one swinging the sledge hammer at the end of that rod which was held close to the head of the man who held it. Clank! Clank! Clank! He called out, "hold it!" I held back as he readjusted the rod; we were making progress. "Ok" he called. Clank! Clank! Then, just as I was seeing myself as a modern day John Henry, I started my swing, saw him move, tried to hold back, but my hammer grazed his head as it went on past its mark.

All work stopped. The fellow who had been holding the rod was now holding his head. I felt about an inch tall. Some John Henry. All I heard in my head was pride goes before a fall. I walked over to the injured man and apologized, he waved me off with "ah, just a scratch." I felt worse by the second and then decided I would just quit, this wasn't for me anyway. The foreman tried to talk me into staying, he said it was an honest accident, the guy would be fine, they'd take him to the hospital just to check, why don't I just stay? I couldn't, I told him. I was upset, almost in tears. He patted my shoulder and said ok, write down your address so we can send your paycheck to you. I complied with that, and walked off the lot, down the street to my stone cottage, into the bathroom, looked at myself in the mirror, and shaved my head in penitence. I told you I was serious. It's not every day that one hits a man in the head with a sledge hammer.

That night I walked into Moby Dick's, a hard-core bar at the end of the main drag, keeping my newly shaved head down. I took a seat at the bar, where I had been sitting for a couple of weeks, apart from the locals, who enjoyed themselves by themselves, studiously ignoring the outsider from Minnesota. Suddenly one of them said loudly enough for everyone in the bar to hear "He's as crazy as we are. Might as well let him in." Laughter all around, but it was said truly. From that point on I was invited, included, and welcomed into all their sundry parties and get-togethers. And what parties. In the laid back living room of the house of one cool cat, on the coffee table between two facing couches, sat a huge open bowl of fresh marijuana. A couple of corncob pipes lay beside it. Have a seat, take a toke, tell a joke, have fun. Jesse visited me for a while down there and he accompanied me to one party; we sat across from each other with the big bowl of weed between us and looked at each other, shaking our heads in silent laughter and wonder.

It didn't take me long to find another job, namely working the counter at a greasy spoon right on the main drag through PA. Dan Meed owned the place, which specialized in ham & cheese sandwiches, plus a fish and chips special for a buck to draw spring breakers. Dan stood about five eight, but seemed bigger, probably due to his unusual energy. He had been the drummer for a big swing band out west, and then he'd become a Hell's Angel. Now he ran this little dive on the Port Aransas drag, among other ventures, I assumed.

About that time one free afternoon I was on a run down the hard-packed beach, and I stopped to look around a hotel/condo development in front of which we had pitched our tent on the beach one spring break. While I poked around inside the compound, a gentleman walked up to me, sized me up and offered me a job as a security officer for his property. He told me I would be carrying a gun on the job, and I respectfully declined the offer. No guns for me. He said his name was Richard Stobb, and he built this property some years ago. He invited me to have dinner with him, but something about his manner told me not to accept. Mr. Stobb looked as if he had never worked a day in his life, soft, slightly slouching due to torpor, and although he lived right here in sunny south Texas on the Gulf, his puffy face was pallid as if he never went outside; his eyes were set close together and his nose was red. I said I needed to be going, and ran down to the beach and back to my stone cottage.

A few days later a car stopped outside my cottage and a young man got out and knocked on my door. "Mr. Stobb would like to see you," he said. Then he invited me to get in the car and he would drive me there right now. I found my curiosity rising and dubiously accepted, wondering how he knew where I lived. I sat in the back and said not a word. When we arrived at the property the driver led me inside to meet Mr. Stobb, who was wearing a purple silk robe like Hefner always wore, and smiled broadly over his paisley ascot when he saw me. "Welcome," he gushed. "A dear old friend of mine is coming for dinner tonight and I wanted you to meet him; won't you join us for dinner?" Ok, I nodded, what's to lose, there might be an important connection. These guys obviously had money.

It was still a couple of hours before dinner and Mr. Stobb gave me a tour of his house, which was quite lavishly decorated. Suddenly a young blonde man with wavy golden hair hanging down to his shoulders appeared in a doorway, stark naked, with his male appendage swollen like a donkey's. He looked silently at us and Mr. Stobb told him softly to leave us be, and just as suddenly the young Adonis donkey disappeared. I blew it off; let's see this through, my thoughts refocused.

When we got to the kitchen, which was stupendous, with broad stainless steel counters, cupboards, fridge, sinks and shining bronze handles on all of them, Mr. Stobb needed to finish preparing the meal, and asked me to help him; he handed me a big bowl of avocadoes and bid me to peel and mash them for guacamole. He glided about, taking care of this and that, as I stood at the counter mashing avocadoes.

He glided close behind me and leaned over and kissed me on my neck. I recoiled, repulsed, and sternly advised him not to try that again. Then he started popping pills. Valium, I think.

By the time Earnest, the friend, arrived, Mr. Stobb was practically passed out on his feet from the pills. We sat down to dinner with scorched fish, ill-prepared messy salad, lopsided cuts of bread and a huge bowl of guacamole, into which Mr. Stobb's head was nearing drooping. Earnest kept softly repeating,

"Elegant, elegant," Mr. Stobb slurred and drooped, and to the dismayed Earnest I excused myself to go to the bathroom. Once out of that room, I just kept walking, right out the door and back to my cottage. I never heard from Richard Stobb again.

Texans arrived first on spring break that year, then kids from Ohio, Iowa, Minnesota, Wisconsin, and Michigan. It was wall to wall oiled skin. They stood in line out the door and down the street for Dan's fish & chips special. We were, in Dan's drummer words, "shuckin' and jivin'," on high speed automatic pilot each day for about three hours before the rush finally died down. As a sign of the times then, one day I was working the register and we were going nuts. One college boy said how much for his fish & chips, I joked "that'll be one joint," to which he smiled, reached into his shirt pocket and placed a fat one on the register. I smiled, he smiled and all was well. At another particularly hectic moment, Dan looked up from his station at the grill and told me "when this is over I'll take you to Mexico." I just went back to taking money at the cash register, hand over fist. But I didn't forget.

Off work, I walked over to the Mainland Bar, which was named oddly since it was on Mustang Island. But anyway, it was locally infamous for harboring certain big name Chicago gangsters in the 1930s who liked the feeling of being off the mainland but still in it. The bar wasn't very big, with a tiny bar for about four people in one corner and a couple of pool tables below. I liked to shoot pool there. Eddie Edwards had installed a pool table in the playroom at home, and I knew a little about making cuts and banks.

One night, a gentleman from the Bahamas asked me ever so politely if I wouldn't mind playing him a game. Sure, I said, and racked the balls. He gently waived his right to break, I didn't sink anything, and it was his shot, stripes or solids. He chose the easiest, shortest play for the one, and had solids. He missed the next shot. I knew that most pool games are won about three feet up from the table, in players' heads. I just played it cool and sank four balls before missing. He made a couple and missed. Then I ran it down to three balls left for me but he had six up. So I started taking more difficult shots, in order to allow us to play the game to the last ball. That's the way I liked it, call me frugal, I like to play my money's worth, and my attempts at trickier shots did not go unnoticed by my gentleman opponent. Finally we got down to the eight ball alone on the table and I banked it in the opposite side pocket from where it had been. My Bahamas friend was gracious in defeat.

"You, sir, are a gentleman," he told me. I told him the same, and we parted ways with a cordial smiling hand shake.

It wasn't always that civil in the Mainland. Another night found me sitting on one of the four stools at the mini-bar and below, a mean drunk long-legged jeans and boots cowboy from San Angelo was playing pool with another, quieter fellow. To that point in my brief stay in Texas, I had already come to a general conclusion that San Angelo had its share of rednecks. Suddenly a fight broke out at the pool table, I looked over there and the cowboy was bashing his opponent over the head with the cue ball. It was an incredibly ugly sight, and impulsively I got up and bellowed "STOP IT" with my arms outstretched. The place went hush quiet, I lowered my arms, the cowboy arrested his arm in motion to hit the guy again when I yelled, and he looked at me with the cue ball still raised. I thought maybe I had a fight on my hands. But he put the cue ball down and stepped away from his victim. I walked out of the bar feeling all wrung out, and hoping that my action had maybe even saved that poor guy's life. What evil lurks in the hearts of men?

"You remembered." Dan grimaced a bit when I asked him about that side trip to Mexico. But he was a straight up cat and stood by his word. One day my job was at the other end of the counter, taking orders on a slow day, when a really cute girl walked up to the window and asked if we had trips to Mexico for sale. I said no, we don't sell those here. She looked over by the door, hesitated, and then back to me and tried it again. Nope, I said, no Mexico trips here. Finally it dawned on this slow-witted Duluth kid that she had been recruited by Dan to go with us, since he was taking his girlfriend Stacey; a perk I didn't expect and frankly wasn't all that comfortable with. Don't get me wrong, my date was very cute and sweet; I was the one with the hang-up.

The appointed day came and Dan picked me up at my stone cottage in a red Mustang; we drove to Corpus Christi to pick up the girls and we were off for Matamoros, my first-ever visit to Mexico. Cindy and I sat in the back seat, Dan drove what turned out to be Stacey's car, and Stacey sat in the passenger seat with her left hand on my right foot for the longest time. I felt like moving my foot but didn't want to upset her so I just let my foot become part of the floor. I wondered about her. She was a fun-loving big-haired redhead, a little too boisterous for my tastes, while Cindy, a sweet and kind-hearted brunette with a friendly smile, was nicer to be with, if Mr. Solitary were to be with anyone.

The first thing the ex-Hell's Angel did once over the border in Matamoros was to stop at a corner and flag down a local boy, from whom he bought, for ten dollars, a hefty grocery bag full of weed. We all went to a restaurant and had a big meal while the mariachis played their magical music, which I would come to very much love on later trips. Abruptly Cindy spoke to me in full earshot of the others.

"You're not very romantic, are you?" The effects of growing up with Ice were that noticeable, I thought. But I had a solution.

"A bottle of scotch, please," I flagged the waiter, and he promptly complied. By the time we all checked into the motel, Cindy and me in one room, Dan and Stacey in another, I was feeling the scotch. Then we rolled a doob out of the weed Dan gave us and we sat out on the deck of our room, stoned, a little drunk, talking. She was an interesting girl, intelligent, who liked to observe my thought patterns.

"Your mind is like a pond, and every time a new idea hits you it ripples through the pond like a stone just got tossed into it." I appreciated her insight, and her curiosity. Not to mention she was very pretty. We enjoyed a mellow nice night together, complete with scotch-induced lovemaking which was simply very sweet. The next morning we all met up for breakfast and loaded up the Mustang for the return trip to Corpus and Port Aransas. On our way out of town Dan had to stop and ditch most of the weed in the bag behind a bush since he hadn't found anyone to sell it to; he knew it was not a good idea to drive it across the border.

Within a few days I felt a burning sensation while I was relieving myself. Oh, no, I thought; when I was editor of the student paper I wrote an article about gonorrhea and by the second day of burning I knew that's what I had. I went to a local doctor and got 800ccs of penicillin in each butt. He told me to stay out of the sun for a couple of days. I went back to my bed and lay down feeling like my whole body was being poked by pins; a condition inherited from Eddie Edwards, a slight reaction to penicillin. I walked around with a bandana tied to my penis to stem the oozing of that awful yellow pus. When I went back to work at Dan's I told him about it and told him I needed to talk to Cindy and let her know. He loaned me his station wagon and I drove to Cindy's house in Corpus. We sat on the couch in the living room and I told her.

"Are you sure it was me?" she asked.

"Dead sure," I replied, knowing my scant history. And I strongly encouraged her to see her own doctor because from what I had read and reported, she might not be feeling any symptoms but if she didn't get it taken care of she could even die from it. Apparently her ex-husband, a former football player at Texas, caught it, didn't tell her and then got back with her for one last time. I couldn't believe that anyone would do that; what type of animal knowingly infects another with anything? She thanked me and I made her promise to see her doctor, we hugged goodbye and I drove back to Port Aransas that moonlit gulf coast breezy night, sweet Cindy very much on my mind.

It was becoming apparent to me that I would need to take care if I didn't want to become a lifer there. The owners of the six stone cottages where I stayed lived in a house in front of them all, and offered to sell me the whole property for twenty thousand dollars. A similar thing happened to Mike the shrimp boat builder, and he stayed, after he'd paid for the land upon which to build his shrimp boat, and live in the boat while he built it. He had started building in 1970, and it was 1974 now.

"So how's it going?" I queried.

"About the same as it's always gone," drawled Mike, a tall lean affable fellow with friendly eyeglasses over which he peered. "Very slowly," he added.

"About when do you think it'll be water-ready?"

"Ah, it'll never be ready," he whisked the idea away like a pestering fly.

"Never?"

"That's right, never," he shrugged. "I'll never finish it and I'll live in it for the next thirty years and then I think I'll retire." Mike saw himself more as a philosopher than a shrimper.

Such were the norms on Mustang Island, a truly beautiful place with great big dunes and a long wide hard beach facing the Gulf of Mexico. That's where I learned to body surf, in the big waves that roll in from Cancun.

The secret is in the timing. You swim out a ways from shore, watching the big waves as they crest, and swim into them, under the water, to come out on the draw on the other side and keep swimming out. Then, when you pick out a big roller to ride, you swim toward it just long enough and then drop quickly to the hard sand bottom, crouch and spring up with arms pointing up and blast out of the water at the top of the crest, arms to the sides, cup the crest in your armpits, enjoy the view and ride that wave one hundred feet or more before it drops you, crushes you onto the hard sand beach. My bones cracked each time Mother Gulf deposited my carcass onto that hard beach. But what a rush. Shake it off, go back for more.

Once I was walking down to the beach, through the dunes, and suddenly a cacophony of squawks drew my eyes upward and I beheld a huge tree whose round top was covered by hundreds of red winged blackbirds. It was an awesome sight for an old birdwatcher. My third grade teacher Miss O'Brien used to take us by twos along the sidewalks through the Lakeside neighborhoods, looking for birds. I turned and looked around, to see if anyone else could share this with me, alas no one, so I just turned and faced the red-winged hoard and feasted my eyes on a solitary splendor. Then silently I slowly raised my arms above my head, and the tree exploded in a blast of black and red as the birds took flight on my command. If I couldn't share it with anyone, so be it, I'm going to delight in my own amazing life.

The attractions of gulf and beach, pretty girls on break and laid back style kept me there almost four months. Since I'd been working my travel funds were untouched and after a celebratory walkabout around Port Aransas on my last night there I ended up playing pool at Moby Dick's, where I encountered a thick air at first. My primary pool playing partner there was Jim, a black guy, quiet and personable. Jim and I would play pool three or four times a week. That night as I entered Moby's, once through the front door I noticed all the blacks standing tightly together in the left corner of the room, and all the whites on the other side, and you could feel the tension hanging in the air between them like a wet curtain. I stood there for a moment catching the sense of what was happening, then walked over to Jim and offered my hand, asking if he wanted to play tonight. His buddies looked at me distrustfully. He hesitated, looked back at his friends, shook my hand with flashes in his eyes, first doubt, then recognition, then gratitude as he nodded "yes." We walked over to the pool table together and within a few minutes everything else fell into place.

That night I was offered a job at Moby Dick's as a "diplomat," but the next morning found me hitching to Corpus where I bought an airline ticket to San Diego. It had been a few years since I'd seen Ice and thought it was time for a visit, on my way to Hawaii. When she came to the door of her apartment on Balboa Avenue at first I barely recognized her. Gone were the slender vain semi- movie star dark-haired looks of yester year, and before me stood a roundly overweight, short gray-haired caricature of my mother. She wore a horizontally striped shirt with short sleeves out of which her fat arms protruded. It seemed like the gap between her two front teeth had grown. They were definitely worn down from grinding in her sleep all those years, working out the tensions of her doomed days. She invited me into her apartment without forcing a lot of gestures. We sat and chatted about nothing. I noticed she still smoked cigarettes, and she'd gained all that weight, not good.

Then she did a most amazing thing. She rose to her feet and asked me if I needed her to wash my clothes, they must be dirty from the road. She was right, of course, but coming from a woman who made me do all my own wash since I was thirteen, it was downright astounding. I let her wash and dry and fold my clothes. She was nice about it. Then she cooked me a dinner of ham, peas, au gratin potatoes, she always could cook. The tension somehow still was too great to sit together for very long, and I went for a long walkabout in San Diego that afternoon, and found myself a beach volleyball game to play in on Mission Beach.

The next day was a Monday and Ice had to go to work in the morning, except, get this, she called in sick to be with me. We chatted again about nothing, sat around, and then she took me to an early lunch and to the airport. At lunch she sat across the table from me and we talked. For my part of the conversation, I offered that I had put on my passport POET as my occupation. Her eyes clouded over.

"How did you get this way?"

"Reading." Which was partly true, but also traveling, writing, being me, which she did not understand and couldn't. She never knew me in the first place. After lunch she drove me to the airport, where we said goodbye, no touching, no hugs, no love spoken. That was the last time I ever saw my mother.

Flying to Hawaii is a whole other proposition; it is a long flight. But when I got there, I walked out of the airport with my pack on my back, watching all the tourist groups get the royal treatment from the grass skirts. I walked past them out to the main highway and stuck my thumb out and about the fifth car stopped for me. The driver was an Oahu native, an oversized Samoan chatty fellow named Norm, who invited me to spend my first night on Oahu at his family's home. I felt comfortable with him and couldn't turn down hospitality like that. As he drove up the side of the mountain, with Pearl Harbor behind us, he told me of the time he was five years old, riding in the back seat, his father driving, and then seeing the whole harbor in flames; the date was December 7, 1941. My large and generous host put me up with a bunk on his front screened-in porch. They lived in a local community on the north side of Oahu most tourists never hear about. Norm's thirteen-year-old daughter was given the assignment of delivering to me out on the porch the largest, highest piled platter of egg salad sandwiches I had ever seen. Now, I like egg salad sandwiches as well as anyone, but more than five or six and I'm toast. She smiled when I made such a small dent in the pile.

The next morning Norm drove me back over the mountain to Honolulu and dropped me right at Waikiki Beach. I found an apartment just a stone's throw from Waikiki in a neighborhood called the Jungle; I paid one hundred dollars up front for a month, and the first task at hand was to crank up the refrigerator to freeze out the biggest cockroaches I've ever seen. They were six inches long! Welcome to the tropics, I thought. Next I found myself a gig with a month-long lease on a pedicab for six hours a day, 2:00 p.m. to 8p.m. That cost me $90.50. So my routine was to spend my mornings on Waikiki, swimming, running, sunning. That's where I really learned to swim. Then, at 2:00 p.m. I picked up my pedicab, a covered two-seater behind a standard bicycle, like a bicycle rickshaw. The locals liked to laugh at me, a white guy doing coolie work, but I had the last laugh. My lease was paid off within four days. I would park first in front of the Honolulu Hilton, and wait for tourists. I charged five dollars to take them over to the International Marketplace and ten bucks roundtrip to the Diamondhead Crater. Every day when I had $50 cash in my pocket I would take my pedicab in early, stuff most of the money in my cupboard at home, and go out for a nice dinner in Honolulu. Plus pushing that cab all over the place kept my legs strong.

One morning on Waikiki I noticed a young black man, about my age, ripped, in phenomenal shape, running on the beach holding a stick like a relay baton. This guy knows track, I thought. I approached him.

"Hi…would you be interested in a race?" My impulse was to race him on the beach for 100 meters. Go figure that from the kid who was scared to compete.

"You want to race me?" He looked at me a bit oddly. "Here, on the beach?"

"Yeah, say from here down to that breakwall down there," pointing down the beach.

"Ok," he grinned and shrugged, and we lined up and got set, and off we went, in the deep sand, digging, digging, he was quick, he led me at first but I was at his shoulder when he turned to look, surprised to see me, as we finished. We both agreed to do it again. The same thing happened; he beat me by a foot. Third time? Same. He was all smiles and so was I; how many guys get to sprint all out against a worthy opponent on Waikiki Beach? The Jamaican's name was Martin.

All in all, it was a very nice month, but with a small bit of unforeseen news. My plan had been to find a merchant vessel to sail to Tahiti on my way to pick up my money in New Zealand. But in Honolulu I learned that Tahiti was a French possession (so much for seat-of-the-pants planning) and I needed a visa to enter it, and the only place to get the visa was back in San Francisco. Ok, plan B.

So it was that on July 4, 1974 I was inside the Diamondhead Crater with about 4,000 other hippy/traveler/ bohemian types all sitting in rows on the grass listening to a concert by Richie Havens and Dr. Hook and the Medicine Band. Richie Havens played the same guitar I had, a Guild D28. Sitting there on the grass, passing joints up and down the rows, I finally was buzzed enough to want to get up and move around. Now, inside Diamondhead Crater there is one tree near the big grassy area and I climbed it and found a cradle up there to watch the concert. And it was there that I was struck by a vision.

I saw myself at fifty years of age, with nothing to show for my life but a dusty old pack full of road stories. I resolved right then and there to go back and finish college. I climbed down from the tree, concert still going full steam, walked up the side of the crater, along the ridge of the crater, sometimes just a narrow path, where less audacious folks might not venture, but with eye-popping views of the ocean, which eventually led me halfway around to a spot where someone had attached a thick wire that led out of sight down the side of the crater. I tested the line, it held, and figuring that it had been put there for the purpose of climbing down, I put my faith in it and started down the line, and sure enough, it brought me all the way down to where I just needed to jump the last ten feet to the ground. I turned and looked back up at the wire, silently thankful. I really had so much to be thankful for, and among the best things was this golden silence of solitude. In fact, solitude by then had taken on almost a personal feeling.

Throughout my life it has sometimes seemed that I have had but one constant friend, and although at times he wasn't always welcome, the years have proven his assumption of truth to be true. The first time I saw him he was dark and penetrating and persistently melancholy and he set me to brooding so deeply that for a short time I resisted him. But finally, with the weight of a thousand oaks, he sat with me and I learned the somber lesson of his strength. I knew him when I clambered to the tops of my childhood trees; he strode beside me through checkered hallways of junior high. When he was with me, the truth of his thoughts resounded clearly, like the bells of a drowsy Sunday morning; and when he was away, the rambunctious world tried its best to make me forget him. But he always returned. I have known him forever, and I will remember him long after this world has forgotten my face.

This companion has been my strength when even the masterful sun could not muster a wink; he has shown me the beauty of rain even as it caused me discomfort in a leaking tent. In his eyes are all the answers, every refrain to every song, every result of every poll contrived by the insipient wisdom of the human race. In his heart is the only solace to a hundred broken hearts. While we grew together in a troubled youth, I often felt so childishly confused that I blamed him for the unrest which picked at my still-forming consciousness. I often ran from him, seeking the diversionary, frolicking nature of all the other children; and always, through silence and steady reassurance, he proved himself to be my most reliable guide. With his perspective I have managed to find my way surely to the present moment; and in his silence I have seen into the slightest shades of tomorrow.

When the sureness of young manhood tilted my head with promises of fulfillment, my friend stood behind me and allowed the world its sense of playfulness; and when the circular games refused my most heartfelt pleadings, he was there again, softly whispering the truth of all folly to me. Without his voice I would never have been able to discern the suggestions of the true world; without his hand I would have leaned too far, and never would have stood upright. Together we have watched as clouds of fury and indignation collided, and one by one we have sidestepped the wreckage of so many misunderstandings. I have never been able to explain the folly or the misleading hopes which have sprouted like weeds at my heart's doorstep, and he has never tried.

Though my destiny is known to none, perhaps his melancholy touch will suggest a clue; perhaps the active remembrance of his persistent message will grant me the fulfillment I have so long sought. But then perhaps he'll leave me to learn as I always have; and when the light of my life finally shows its face to my perception, his autumn hand will turn my mind to greet it. My friend is Solitude, and he is with me nearly always. Just as others have feared his presence, I have learned to welcome him, for through his strength I have found my own. And with his companionship I have learned to be happy, for even with no one but him, I am never alone.

The trick, as Emerson pointed out, is "to keep with perfect sweetness the independence of solitude[2]," when one is in the midst of a group of people; the multi-sensory diversions of persons is all too often distracting from the goal, as would turn out to be more often true than not throughout my life. But ever persisting, my willful detachment from society allows me to more happily deal with other persons. Sometimes I felt invisible, that I could make myself invisible, much the same as Roy Ellison, who published his "Invisible Man" the year I was born.

After nearly seven months in mild temperatures, on July 6, 1974 I arrived in Anchorage, Alaska, and quickly learned I wasn't prepared for an Alaskan trek. Hitchhike from there to the lower 48? First you have to travel four hundred miles to the northeast before you come to the road that heads south. It was light almost all the time. I asked the desk clerk at the seedy motel I stayed at, how do they get used to it? He just pointed to the clock, which read three a.m. but you could see out the window that it was still mid afternoon light. Well, I spent exactly one day in Alaska that time and flew the next day to Tacoma, and then to Minneapolis.

I found myself returning to Duluth with a twenty-six-state, seven month journey under my belt. Still twenty-three, my pack had now been through fourteen countries and forty states, and I was, no question about it, Dr. Philip Saragoza, never the same again.

Remember that dark-eyed old flame who told me I "threw it all away"? Well, truth be told, she was in my head up in that Diamondhead Crater tree along with the rest of my visions. I picked some lilacs and went up to UMD to look for her, and to my surprise she was coming out the door as I approached the stairs. An omen? I said hi, she looked at the lilacs and then she told me she had found someone else, a real friend, she said, and walked away. I turned away slowly, tossed the already wilting lilacs in the garbage and began to wonder again why I had returned. At any rate, it didn't take very long before the fact landed with clear remembrance how much I had outgrown UMD and, it really felt this way, my scenic northern hometown by the lake, with its own peculiar safe charm.

From some chord deep within me, something told me I would not live out my life there. It was nice to grow up there, but there were not enough people to talk to about what interested me, and the career opportunities simply were not there; any time someone got a reasonably good job, they hung onto it until they retired, since slim pickins' were just outside their doors.

CHAPTER SEVEN

The University of Minnesota-Duluth had been my hangout for four years, but now that I came back from my seven month journey and enrolled back at UMD to finish my degree, it took about three days to fully realize I had made a mistake. I got a job as a cashier in the school bookstore and made plans to move to Minneapolis after that quarter. That fateful quarter in the Fall of 1974. It is true that one moment of one's life, one decision, can affect the rest of the life. Almost every day, a young woman named Betty stopped by my cash register in the bookstore and asked me when we could have lunch together. I wasn't really interested but she kept stopping by and asking, so one day she wore me down and I said yes and we agreed the next day we'd have a brown bag lunch out on the grass terrace outside the school.

There we were, on the terrace, eating our lunches, sitting on the grass, when she started really talking to me.

"What are you thinking about in that head of yours?" she asked pointedly. She could see I had a lot of experiences and a heavy mind, but then I asked her something.

"Why do you want to know?"

"Well, I just want to learn what makes you tick."

"Good luck with that; I'm still figuring it out myself."

She took a liking to me and wanted to see me again.

I vaguely remembered her from high school, she went to Central and I went to East. She was very short, about five feet tall, brown hair, with a cute round face, but she wore way too much makeup; I thought if I ever kissed her I'd slide off. That was before I had figured out that too much makeup is a cover for insecurities. We went out a couple of times, and she started getting serious. This young woman moved quickly.

"Just give me a couple of kids and you can go wherever you want." I thought that sounded a little strange, but what did I know about women? I was renting a room in a home just a block away from campus. Jesse was working on the boats then. But he got off and needed a place to stay, so I told Betty about him and she let him stay in her tiny house's basement. That lasted about three weeks, when something told me if an Edwards would be living in her house, it should be me, not Jesse. So Jesse and I switched rooms, he went to the home where I was renting a room, and after knowing her for all of two months, I moved into Betty's house, not in the basement. She cooked me homemade meals, with fresh bread, and I thought wow, this is nice. It was the first time a female had been so domestically good to me since my Grandmother.

It turned out after I moved in that she was not yet actually divorced from her first husband, who she married when she was nineteen. The thought weighed on my mind that I did not belong there, but she seemed so vulnerable, and not understanding that I could not solve her problems, I became involved. In her senior year in high school, she still sat on her mom's lap while her mom tied her shoes every day. Betty Botan never spent a day living on her own; she went from her mom's lap to her first marriage, and before that one was in the can, I was staying with her. But when the fall quarter ended, I needed to get out of Duluth once and for all, and transferred to the "Main U" as it was called in Duluth.

I moved into a boarding house in Dinkytown, next to the University campus, and almost every weekend Betty would drive down from Duluth to stay with me in a motel. She said she was afraid to drive at night because her eyesight wasn't the best and she couldn't see. I thought she was a little nuts to drive, then. She brought me homemade loafs of bread and granola. Shortly after winter quarter ended, she transferred her job to the Twin Cities, moved to Minneapolis and we got an apartment together. "Marry the wife of your youth," flashed through my head periodically. In those days I wrote a letter to her father, a Finnish union boss in Duluth, telling him my intentions were to marry her. It seemed to me the right thing to do. So one day I asked her with a gold band hidden at the bottom of a glass of red wine, and when she got to the bottom of the glass, she gasped yes. When I graduated with my degree in Journalism, I drove her out to Denver, where Lila was living now, and a former teammate from track flew out to be my best man.

On the way out Betty and I tented in a park right smack below Mount Rushmore; during the night I heard someone snooping around the campground, and they stopped right outside our tent checking it out. When the intruder left, I quietly zipped out of the tent and followed him down to the parking lot, where he got into a truck and drove off, but not before I memorized his license plate. In the morning I went down to the owner's quarters and told him about the guy and gave him the license plate number. He was so impressed by my actions he wanted to sell the place to me.

"I've been looking for someone honest to sell this campground to, all sixty acres of it." And then he proceeded to offer it to me for sixty thousand dollars. I turned him down gratefully, since I didn't think I want to live out there. But ever since, I have occasionally allowed myself to wonder, what would sixty acres in the front yard of Mount Rushmore be worth today? Not to mention, what would a twenty thousand dollar investment in the middle of Port Aransas be worth today?

When we arrived in Boulder, where Lila was staying in a house owned by a Denver narcotics detective, Lila was frantic. She told me some drug lords in Denver had found out the identity of her detective landlord, and she was afraid they would come and shoot the house up. Jim, the burly narc, joked with her, saying the shooters would be aiming at him. That didn't help.

So Lila got one of her doctor friends from the emergency room where she worked to give up their cabin in the mountains for us, so we drove up to Vail to find it. Lila had been there before, and this time she brought her twenty-foot pet boa constrictor with her. Lila lived largely. Elsie, the boa constrictor, got loose that first night and Lila couldn't find her. She told my fearful fiancé that everything would be fine, Elsie would find someplace warm to rest, like our bed (she joked) but wouldn't hurt us. Betty's short legs trembled with fear for about two hours before she finally fell off to fitful sleep.

We awoke the next morning to a beautiful Vail vista, and I went out to cut up some firewood with a chainsaw first, then an axe. Before I got two minutes into sawing, Betty ran out on the porch waving her arms and yelling to me that I might get hurt with that thing. I hollered over the chainsaw that I'd be fine, go back inside.

Twice already on this trip I was witness to the fear in her. I never did understand fear.

Don't people realize that fear is the opposite of love? That fear brings negative consequences? That there really is something to the power of positive thinking? And therefore also negative thinking? To the extent that I am master of my own fate, it well behooves me to think, speak and act positively in all matters. To do otherwise would indicate blindness.

We drove back to Boulder after a couple of beautiful mountain days, and Lila told us not to stay at her place just yet, and so we took a room at the Boulderado Hotel until the heat blew over. Tall ceilings, bare light bulbs hanging from them, lighting a threadbare rug in front of a sagging bed—that was our honeymoon suite. We only stayed there one night and then, on September 19, 1975, the four of us, Lila, me, Betty and my track buddy Natch drove up to Ptarmigan Mountain outside of Boulder, in Lila's yellow beetle car. I picked the date because it was my Dad's birthday, so every anniversary we celebrated would be in remembrance of him.

We were met up on the mountain by a Justice of the Peace, and as the sun began to set over the Rocky Mountains, I played and sang a song written for Betty on my guitar, and then we exchanged vows that I had written two nights before, the Justice spoke a few words and declared us husband and wife. As we drove back down the mountain to Boulder, my new bride, a second timer herself, turned to me and said "See, the ceremony didn't mean anything." I chose to run through that red flag too. Natch passed me a lit doob from the front seat, and given my bride's unenthusiastic comment about the ceremony, I took a hit, and as I held my breath my bride again turned to me and said "My husband," apparently not approving what I was doing. Lila and Natch and I smoked it.

When we got back to Minneapolis I was hopped up to go to graduate school. That two quarters and a summer session at the "Main U" convinced me of the difference between a university and a college, and I loved the university. But Betty, whose first husband was allegedly a lazy perpetual student, didn't like my plan.

"You're the kind of person who will always be in school," she sneered at me in her own snickering style of putdowns. So, having no experience whatever with negotiating with women, I went out and bought a banjo with my tuition money to please her. I took a job in a cube correcting computerized test scores in a suburban company and lasted about five months, until one time we were visiting her relatives in Duluth, and I went out to a sawmill with one of her brothers-in-law, Fred, who built his own beautiful canoe with his own hands. On the way back Fred and I stopped to hang around a beaver hut, and that is when the north woods beckoned something in me back to Duluth. Like a homing pigeon, I flew the cube and pieced together employment as a grave-digger and a janitor and then a community organizer and moved my wife back to Duluth, which made her happy.

This is not to chronicle the entire nine years we were together, but some light ought to be shed on them. For example, when we ended up back in Duluth we had our share of good times, but her idea of a real party was to gather at a sibling's or parent's house and sit around and talk AD nauseum about the same old mundane things they always talked about. I learned that I had married an intelligent woman but not an intellectual, as I had eventually figured out I was, since most of my life was lived between my ears. I never saw that as a better-than situation, it was just a difference.

When the whole Botan clan got together, I couldn't sit for long listening to the blabber so I just sat in another room reading or away from them in a park, thinking on my own. I do understand that my presence was not easy for them, but thanks to Ice, I was a loner, and couldn't help myself. One thing I didn't like about Betty was that she always thought it was her job to "knock me down a few pegs." In other words, my big ideas didn't sit well with her, and for good reason, she hadn't been out of Duluth traveling as I had and she hadn't read any of the books I had read. So she wanted me to be stripped down to her level, as many, many insecure people routinely do.

Career options being what they were in Duluth, and still are today, I took a job at McDonald's as an assistant manager. After eighteen months of marriage our constant bickering had given me an upset colon, and she had her first affair on me while I worked or stayed at home. I wrote her a poem about my love and she embroidered it, framed it and hung it over our bed, and I thought we were good from then.

Twenty two months, four days and three and a half hours I worked for McDonald's. They did teach me how to run a business, and I learned a couple of jokes I would tell for years, but overall it was not my work. One day I was staging buns, in other words, placing them on a rack to toast them, and Henry David Thoreau was suddenly speaking through my arms.

"Most men lead lives of quiet desperation[3]."

At that, I took off my apron, told the other manager on duty he had it by himself for the rest of the night, and walked out. I took my golden arches ties and vest and burned them in a ceremonial fire I built down by the lake. I went home and told Betty, with whom I had now a beautiful baby son, and she called her dad, the union boss, and he got me a job driving a city bus as a Teamster. Hanging around the old bus barn was a lot like being on the boats, with the same ilk of men, language and attitudes. It was coming up contract time, and the drivers were all talking with multiple F-bombs about their union negotiating more money for them. I thought, wait a minute, I drive a bus, nothing fancy, and I was making $13.92 an hour, which was real good money in 1979. I turned to one of them and offered my opinion.

"We make pretty good money now, don't you think?

"You ever say those words around here again and I'll tear your head off." The surly driver took offense easily. I knew right then and there, this would be a temporary gig.

It turned out to be, because after six months I had finally yammered Betty into going to Madison with me to get my Ph.D. so I could teach, read, write, and learn for a living. First came a two year Master's program, where I got a teaching assistantship to help with the bills. Actually, the union there had negotiated a pretty cushy deal for the graduate assistants so we were not hurting. Betty's little sister Narbi came for a visit, when I overheard Betty telling her she had never been happier.

Now we had three-year-old Ted and a brand new beautiful baby girl who we named Mandy. Narbi, the sister, couldn't understand how anyone could be happy outside of Duluth. She was a real piece of work. When the new Radisson Hotel was built in downtown Duluth, it had a revolving restaurant on the top floor, so patrons could eat their dinners with a slowly constantly changing view. It took forty-seven minutes for one complete revolution. Narbo told her family that she was afraid to eat there, because she didn't think she could finish her meal before the restaurant whipped around. The crazy thing about Narbi was that she always acted like she knew a lot, but her mouth consistently betrayed her.

With a three year old and a six-month old, I learned the hard way about the so-called "frozen father" syndrome. Betty's maternal instincts kicked in powerfully, that was a big reason I married her, I knew she would be a nurturing mother, the opposite of Ice. My kids would grow up knowing they were loved. The dark side of that maternal instinct was that I lost my partner. All she wanted to do was be with our kids; she wouldn't go on dates, or do anything with me.

Except drive to Duluth, which we did several times a year from Madison, including one Christmas, 1979, where, as usual, the entire clan was gathered at the father's house for Christmas Eve. I was doing all right interacting with them, I actually liked some of them by then, and then I was referred into a spare room to take a call. It was Lila calling from San Diego. She had gone out to dinner with our mother who complained of nausea at the table, Lila accompanied her to the restroom, where she puked into the toilet bowl, stood up, grabbed her head, said "my head" and dropped dead of a massive aneurism onto the bathroom tile floor right in front of my sister on Christmas Eve. She was fifty-seven.

The family respected my privacy and let me sit alone in that room for a while. I was grateful that I had picked up the phone just last month at Thanksgiving to talk to Ice for the first time in five years; we talked about thirty minutes, and the conversation ended with a vaguely relieved notion that somehow the hatchet had finally been buried. Now she was dead. One of the brothers came into the room and let me know that they had all agreed to pool enough money for airfare if I needed to go to San Diego. That touched me deeply but there was nothing for me to do there. Ice had set the terms; Lila was to have her cremated and dump her ashes in the Pacific Ocean, no memorial service. The whole ordeal took an untold effect on my sister, who on the exterior at least was cool and efficient as ever.

Back in Madison, we went back to the normal not doing anything together routine, so I buried myself in my studies. My favorite place to study was in the bowels of the library, in a cage, away from the world, in virtual silence. My reading was done under a bare light bulb above a small metal desk in virtually total silence, three levels below ground. Once, in my teaching assistant role, I subbed for my professor who needed to go out of town. My topic for the class was the coming "information revolution," which, my talk proceeded, would occur at the intersection of the arcs of computer companies and the phone companies. That was 1980; it hadn't happened yet.

As my Master's degree program began to come to an end, I negotiated a three-year research assistantship with an eminent legislative specialist; actually he had been LBJ's assistant secretary of HEW, the man who walked the Great Society programs through Congress. He was going to take me on as his last advisee before he retired and teach me everything he knew about legislation; my head spun with expectations, and I was all set to earn my doctorate in political science. At the end of the last semester, a communication history professor, the one whose class I taught, invited me to a party at his apartment for all the graduate assistants. As usual, my wife turned down the opportunity to go with me and stayed home.

The party was fun, my professor had sprung for booze and food and a bunch of us had a great time conversing academia and listening to eclectic music. I drank too much scotch and wound up sitting on the bed in the bedroom, feeling under the weather. One of the older undergraduate students, her name was Mary Serena Burns, who was going into the graduate studies program, came to me in the bedroom and talked to me.

"Are you all right?" she asked.

"Yeah, I just had too much to drink," I explained.

"Do you want to have lunch sometime?"

"I'm married."

"We could just be friends."

"I'm married."

"OK, well, see you around then." I definitely did not expect it, but just like that she had gotten into my head. I was lonely, with a wife at home who ignored me to take care of our kids. And now this attractive woman liked me. The next day, on campus, I called her to see if maybe we could do something just as friends. She picked me up in her car that afternoon and drove me to her apartment, where she and her two girls lived. They were off at school, and Mary Serena made me a nice lunch. Then she walked over to her bed, which was a box spring and mattress on the floor, and she sat on the edge and asked me to come over. I did, and she proceeded to undo my pants and go down on me. My head spun, my wife had only done that to me once, before we were married, now she thought it was "dirty." I let Mary Serena have her way with me and I was off balance. For the next four days I went to her and we frolicked, we went out to lunch, for walks in the arboretum, and I went home every night dropping no hints; Betty and I were hardly ever even touching anymore, but finally my conscience was killing me and I told Mary Serena I had to leave, I had to go back to my family. She was gracious about it. I was sick about it.

Back at our married student housing apartment, I walked in the door, closed it behind me and had a stiff lump in my throat. Betty took one look at me.

"Is it another woman?" She was good at first instincts. Or, in retrospect, maybe she just noticed her own limitations in others, as so many do.

"Yes, it was, but it's over. I'm sorry. It's over." She didn't say anything, blinked and left the room and went into the bedroom. I sighed a big breath of tentative relief and sat down on the couch, trying to figure out how I could make it up to her. Within an hour, though, her true colors showed up. When she had fooled around behind my back, I wrote her a poem. But now, in response to my fall from grace, she came out and demanded that I move out immediately. Wiping tears away from my eyes I scanned the newspaper ads for apartments. I moved to a little hole in the wall near campus with an old mattress on the floor where I caught the crabs; I had to shave my pubic hair. Betty wasted no time. She moved lock stock and barrel into a truck and moved my kids back to Duluth, leaving me with two apartments to deal with. It was sultry August, and when I returned to our former apartment to get the rest of my things, the place was crawling with cockroaches. I pressed my lips together, breathed slowly and took care of business in the bluest of blue funks.

The next four months saw me hitchhiking at thirty years of age, since Betty had the car, between Madison and Duluth, Madison and Minneapolis, Minneapolis and Duluth. When in Minneapolis I stayed with my old friend Jack Lourdes, who had become the state champion in the half-mile at East High, which earned him a four-year full ride athletic scholarship at Wisconsin. While still at East, in his senior year, I was a junior, and often handed off to him in relays which he would anchor. In those days, we called him the Duke, because he didn't lose to anyone. Standing about 5 feet 9 inches and weighing about 160 pounds, the Duke actually sang his way around the track during a half-mile race, "Catch me if you can." In his senior year at East, he won at state with a time that still stands as one of the three or four fastest times in Minnesota high school history.

Now the Duke was waiting on tables at the Carlton Celebrity Room, and staying on the third floor of a big old house at Twenty-third St. and Pleasant Ave. in south Minneapolis. I crashed on a mattress out by the front entrance, where I was witness to his way with the ladies. His bedroom was down the hall in the back, and once, while he was ushering one girl down the back stairs, another one came up the front stairs for round two. I stood in awe, but not envy. That lifestyle eventually earned him a lifetime with herpes.

While in Minneapolis I received assurances from the University of Minnesota that they would accept me for their doctoral program, thinking maybe Betty would be more comfortable three hours away from her mom instead of seven hours to Madison. But she would not budge, once she got back to Duluth, she never left again. So it was that I gave up my Ph.D. dream and went back once again to Duluth, where I got back in with Betty and the kids, and immediately moved them from the dingy central hillside apartment she had moved into. My kids would not grow up on the central hillside; if they had to grow up in Duluth, it would be on the east end; that was my commitment to them.

I found a nice four-level town home on East Second Street for starters. One night Lila, who also was living in Duluth at that time, called me and told me she thought the CBS affiliate TV station needed reporters, because she watched the news last night and the anchorman read the entire newscast himself. The next morning I walked into the station manager's office and asked him if they needed reporters; I had a Master's degree in Journalism, which must be good for something. He sent me out into the parking lot with a cameraman and had me do a standup right there. I was stiff as a cigar store Indian, but they hired me, and for the next couple of years it was "Nash Edwards, Scene 3 News." Unfortunately there seemed to be a sort of silent cartel in Duluth among station owners to not pay their people very well. One day my news director told me that seventy percent of the station's employees were on food stamps. All the reporters except me spent their extra time editing their resume tapes, angling for bigger, better paying markets. I knew I couldn't go anywhere because my wife wouldn't go. But it was a fun job, and I learned a lot, and met a number of influential people, especially as I covered politics and the 1982 elections.

One day I noticed an advertisement for a development director for the public TV station in Duluth. I got the job and enjoyed a raise from $9,000 a year to $16,000 a year. Within four months I had already generated enough sponsorship dollars to offset my salary, and they started using my voiceovers for public interest announcements. Then I ran into, for the first time in my experience, jealousy at the workplace. One of the long-timers at the station had been the only voice on the PSAs and now he had to share that with me, it only made sense to add some variety, but his little ego couldn't take it. So he started telling little fibs to the station manager about me until one day the manager called me into his office and let me in on the secret that a whole list of accusations against me had been lodged. I got out of that cesspool as soon as I could, and found another job.

My new employer, the Arrowhead Regional Development Commission, told me I had beaten out four hundred other applicants for the job. In the first six months on that job I produced the annual report, organized and staffed three different local government councils of mayors, state legislators and county commissioners, and handled everything that had been given to me to do. My six month probationary period was coming to an end, and I was confident that my performance would make it a rubber stamp decision to keep me. But when I walked into my supervisor's office and took a seat, he informed me that they were letting me go. I learned from another co-worker there that they had basically lied to me when they hired me, telling me that I had beaten out four hundred applicants. They never mentioned the other one, who wanted to take six months in Europe first, and that's why I was hired, to keep the fires burning until he returned. I was told by several people afterward that I could have sued them for wrongful termination, but my heart was not into fighting them.

Speaking of fighting, at home about that time, things were coming to a head. Two years after my infidelity, Betty still occasionally brought up her name, as if she were unable to forget it and wanted to kick me forever for it. Maybe whatever love she once might have had for me died that day. Something made time stand still for her on that moment. But at this time, I wanted my partner back. I read in the newspaper that the Duluth Playhouse was holding auditions for the musical, Brigadoon. I told Betty about it.

"Why don't you try out and maybe you'll get a part," I started.

"What about the kids?" was the expected response.

"I'm their dad, I love them too, I'll come home, feed them, put them to bed." My reasoning was that if she got even a bit part, she might find herself again, and if she found herself, maybe I could get my partner back. I eventually talked her into it, she got a bit part in the chorus line, and started going to rehearsals. Then she started staying out late. One night she waltzed in at 2:30 a.m.

"I'm sure rehearsal didn't last that long."

"Well, you know how theater people are, we all went out and talked."

"Well, please don't do that to me again." I looked intently at her. She nodded in agreement. For the next few nights she was home before midnight, which would have given her time to rehearse and spend some social time with the cast afterward. Maybe she was finding herself, my hope was real.

One night, the time was 3:15 a.m., I knew because that's what the alarm clock next to our bed displayed. I had been asleep on my side, so when I awoke that's the first thing I saw. I turned over onto my back and looked at my wife, who was lying on her side, propping up her head with her hand, staring at me. I took one look at her and turned my head back to stare up at the ceiling.

"What?" I dreaded the answer.

"I think we should split up," she calmly said. The terms had turned on me. I had gotten her out of the house to find herself, only she found herself in the arms of another man. The next day, on my way out the front door for the second time in our marriage, I turned to her as she was sitting on a chair in the corner.

"Just tell me how many times you cheated on me."

"You don't want to know." She pulled her knees up to her face.

"You owe me that much."

"Four." Her face was white as a sheet. I shook my head in seething silence and walked out. Ted was five, Mandy was two and a half, and my heart was shattered as I once again moved out to a crappy little apartment. Two weeks later she moved Shotgun Sam from the chorus line into my bedroom and hung his clothes in my closet and told our kids they had a new dad now. I consoled myself with the opinion that she had traded down, probably deliberately, so she could rule the roost. One dark thought persisted in the back of my memory—"just give me a couple of kids and you can go anywhere you want to." Had she just been using me? Had she expected me to stay as long as I did?

Everyone I consulted told me the same thing: get out of Duluth. But I couldn't leave my kids, I wouldn't leave them just to her to raise, my Edwards kids would not become little Shotgun Sams if I had anything to say about it. My anger fought with my broken heart; back and forth they heaved and drifted.

After a month of living in my new little apartment, just three blocks from my kids, I arrived home to find a bulletin pasted onto the stairway: "Unfit for human habitation." Imagine the level of depression that arrived with that announcement. Divorced. No Ph.D. No car. Unemployed. Part-time dad. Apartment "unfit for human habitation." I rebounded to a big old apartment down on First Street near downtown; for two hundred dollars a month I took the corner space on the top floor of an old stone building with the front moniker of St. Elmo, who was, I learned, the Patron Saint of forlorn sailors. Fitting, my dark mood figured. There, I bought an answering machine to hook up to my phone, and then got depressed over nobody ever calling. To fit my overall mood, I walked down to the lake and picked up old worn planks and bricks and carried them up one trip at a time to build myself a bookshelf out of flotsam.

Other than that, I just went back to my old standby, and strapped on my running shoes, and ran like a madman. After three or four months it seemed that my feet were under me again, until one day, preparing to go out, stopping at a mirror on the wall, looking at myself, suddenly tears erupted out of nowhere. My life was a rollercoaster.

I walked the streets of downtown Duluth aimlessly. One former East High student, who graduated a couple of years ahead of me, befriended me about that time, and let me come over to his pad to listen to music. I had been with Betty for nine years, separated from the world as she had refused ever to go out, and now I had no idea what to do for entertainment. My friend Steve told me Grandma's saloon down on Canal Park had good chili, sometimes he went down there for a bowl and a beer. I asked him what's a good time to go down there. He said, how about right now? So I went. That began a several year association between me and Grandma's; I played on volleyball leagues there, ran four Marathons there, and shared laughs over beers at the bar many, many times.

I even bought my duplex there, sight unseen, from a kung fu artist who had rehabbed an old brick grocery store with cocaine money. I had heard about Mickey's place and jumped at the chance. Mickey was a 1968 Central grad who read Friedrich Nietzsche as an eighteen year old and then spent nine years traveling back and forth to Hong Kong, studying Kung Fu from a Chinese man who spoke no English. Mickey could kill a man with one blow, and walked solidly, the way most assured people do, but his way was somehow more natural, animal-like. From the exterior his building appeared old brick and worn out doors, then you stepped inside to a fourteen-foot-high tin imprinted ceiling front room, where the grocer's cash register once stood. Then a big left through a tall narrow doorway into the baddest

Manhattan-style bachelor pad in Duluth for sure. Deep grays and black highlights. How about an eight-foot-high copper hooded, five sided, eight foot diameter fireplace, with a carved wooden bench all around it?

The next years would be all about being there for Ted and Mandy, putting my life on hold for them. But I was to find out my life couldn't be held down, back or on hold.

That decade 1983–1993 also was a period of growth for me, at least professionally, intellectually and physically. Retrospect teaches that another aspect of my life, the emotional, was attenuated and unhealed after the deep sorrows of becoming a part-time dad. Maybe even from losing Eddie Edwards. Maybe even from being beaten by my mother. But the 1980s were by and large good to me. I gave up TV for three years. In its place I joined Book of the Month Club, subscribed to Newsweek, the Economist, and the Nation. I listened to the radio or played my guitar. I ran seventeen miles a day, down on the sand dunes of Park Point, all the way to Wisconsin Point and back. I built a business and generated national attention for my hometown.

But my emotional side dragged behind me like a shadow. I came to terms with solitude, and again found it a good friend. Various new women entered and exited my life with less and less intensity of desire on my part, and the peace and quiet I enjoyed at home left little else to want. The Buddhists don't call it the Golden Silence for nothing. Why should I give up, I thought, my freedom for home-cooked meals? Why can't I learn to cook? I was not comfortable with younger women, pretty and appealing, since they would want children, and I couldn't see supplanting my Ted and Mandy with new ones. For the longest time it seemed that all the good women were attached. And one had to be careful who one took to bed, since each bedded one would want to have lunch the next day. Anyway, I was not interested in just falling into the arms of the next sweetheart, as many of the other "walking wounded" guys did; I wanted to give myself some time to regain my balance, and then I got so balanced I didn't need or want a woman.

In fact, in 1988 I felt so untethered in Duluth I put myself forward as a candidate for the Minnesota House of Representatives. It was a possible way to an exciting career based right there in Duluth. I lost, but the point was to offer my services, to stand up and be accounted for, and to be willing to roll up my sleeves in the service of my hometown, seeking, as Lincoln said of his own first campaign, to gain the esteem of my community.

My second try at that seat was more successful, earning the DFL endorsement in 1990, but certain elements of the local party withheld their support of my candidacy because I still was an outsider to them; I hadn't paid any dues in the rank and file. Still, with my twelve and ten year old kids helping me paint lawn signs, and one friend pounding them for me, I ran to thousands of doors and wound up with forty two percent of the vote. Even the old-school downtown Republicans told me afterward that the next election was mine; and then I was taught a little about the dark side of politics. One woman from Duluth had worked her way through the rank and file to be vice-chair of the State DFL Party; she sat with the legislator who drew the new lines after the Census of 1990, and had me drawn out of my natural home district by three blocks, then she had the DFL lines pushed out the north shore into the townships, where it was said that one could put a baboon on the DFL ticket and they'd vote for it; and finally, she put her husband forth as candidate in 1992 and he won the seat, and for all I know, still holds it today. If I had…no, I never allowed myself the figments of what if I had fought back? I stood up to be counted. That was enough for me.

Ultimately I found my emotional life being healed through the love of my children. They made me complete again. Against long odds, in the end it appears my efforts succeeded in being the best Dad I could be while they were growing up. I even did my part in ending the cycle of doom in our bloodline, what Lila called the Curse, as my kids grew up being loved on all sides.

CHAPTER EIGHT

Those chains of love that kept me in a town I had long ago outgrown were the prime source of joy in my life. I lived for Friday nights and Saturdays, when the kids would be with me. Betty had wanted every other weekend, but the first thing I did was go to the library and read all about part-time dads, and learned that it was more important to see a small child like little Mandy more frequently than for a longer time. That way when I dropped them off back at mom's house, I could say "See you next Friday!" They would look forward to it too. But when I took them back each Saturday night, I kept up a good face until they went into their house, then I drove around the corner and stopped my car because I couldn't see through my tears.

Betty had asked me if she could keep the "Monkey Ward's" card, because all the other credit cards we owned were in my name; I told her that I didn't want to her to screw me; she swore she wouldn't, so I let her keep it. A couple of months later I received a bill in the mail from Ward's, for a diamond ring! Absolutely not one second lapsed before I dove into my car and screamed out to Lakeside to confront her about it.

"You actually expect to have me pay for your diamond ring for your third marriage? I was furious. She faltered under my withering eye and accepted the bill from my outstretched hand. But in a corner of my eye I noticed five-year-old Ted looking at us with eyes as big as apples, and I resolved right there, on the spot, never to let my kids see me angry again.

Betty was from a Baptist background, and she liked to be thought of as righteous. But again, her true colors showed when she banned me, literally banned me from the church where I had grown up and been in Boy Scouts. Now I was never to set foot in that church again, or, she threatened, she would take the kids up the hill to the covenant (much more conservative) church. So I stayed away. For seven months.

Then one Sunday morning I woke up somehow unsettled. For some unknown reason. I was drawn to my boyhood church that morning, where I waited until everyone entered and the service started before I slipped unnoticed into the back row like a dark intruder. At the end of the service I was turning to leave but the pastor saw me and walked back to say hello.

"You heard about Betty?" he asked.

"No, what's up?"

"Well, she's in the hospital, they don't know if the baby will live." I thanked him for the information and found myself rushing to the hospital; somehow I still cared about her, and burst into a room of strangers standing around her bed. I took one look at them and knew they were Sam's family. I looked at her and asked her if she was all right. She answered yes, but they were worried about the baby, their baby, conceived while I was still her husband. I left the room, uncomfortable with the others there. Later it turned out that the baby, a girl, was born with all her bones broken, and was sentenced at birth to life in a wheelchair. When I heard that I had to sit down, shaking, thinking my God, is this how it works? Why must the child suffer for the mother's sins? I couldn't shake that idea so I went for a ten mile run. Those always helped to clear my head.

It later came to be my understanding that Betty was controlled by her fear, specifically her fear that I would take the kids away from her. Fear being an irrational emotion, it was not surprising that she might think I would actually take the kids. She never did understand that I had married her largely to be a good mother to my children. But the fear made things tough, as she came off as wanting to carve me out of their lives. She refused to meet me once a month just to discuss how the kids were doing. She signed Ted up for school at the neighborhood parochial school without consulting me. She told her new husband to sign on Ted's report card where it said "father." I received a copy of that in the mail, sent to me by the school at my request since nothing came from their mom to me. I looked at the signature, not my signature, in the father's space, and immediately ran out my door, jumped into my car and raced to Lakeside to their house, where I pounded on the front door until Betty opened it, and then I stepped in uninvited and addressed Shotgun Sam, who was sitting his corpulent butt on my couch.

"If I ever see your signature where mine belongs again, I will come looking for you." I was seething.

"Is that a threat?" He choked a semi-nonchalant reply.

"That's a promise." At that point I realized I was standing in the middle of their house, I looked at Betty, shook my head and left. The reader may be entertained to know what harvest that seed produced. She went to court and got a restraining order, which was fine with me, now for the next year she had to drive the kids to my place every week and pick them up. I had to laugh. When I became the assistant coach for Ted's Little League team, she wouldn't let me pick him up or take him home. She would drop him off before practice or games and leave, and come back to get him later. Even when Ted was the star of the game, striking out the biggest hitter on the opposing side and then hitting a home run to win the game, Dad/Coach was not allowed to take him out for congratulatory ice cream. A little extreme, if you ask me.

But Friday nights and Saturdays belonged to me. Friday nights we would walk over to Fitger's and eat pizza and wander around, or I'd take them with me down to Grandma's if I had a volleyball game, where they sat and watched. Saturday mornings

I would make dollar pancakes for them; Mandy was fussy and wanted hers real light brown. No problem, anything for my kids. Once I overheard Ted whisper to Mandy that he thought I was an angel because I was so nice. It is impossible to put into words how that made me feel.

Saturdays became our greatest day. I took them each week out to Lester Park, where we hiked up the trails, Ted leading the way and Mandy riding "upstairs" on my shoulders. This is the park where I had come of age, riding my bike to the deeps in eighth grade, walking the trails carpeted by huge white pine needles. The first time out there with my kids I picked up some short logs that had been left by the trail by the park workers, and carried them back into the woods a little way from the trail, and built a "Fort" for us.

Every Saturday would find us out there; Ted lit his first campfire at the Fort, and for years that was our special place. I invented a sovereign nation called Funland, and taught the kids that we were all citizens of Funland. We spoke Funnish, and we had fun. Ted got the title of Wizard of Time and Imagination, and Mandy became the Secretary of Pennies and Munchies. I was el Presidente de Funland. Funland existed inside a bubble of love, and the bubble stretched when we were separated, so we were always inside it. When I got back home from dropping them off, I called them.

"See?" I excitedly said. "The bubble stretches, we're all still in it, can you feel the love?" And they said yes. I called them about the Bubble stretching from Alaska, from Minneapolis, from New York. Each time the bubble stretched that far, so we were, simply put, always in love. And we named my home Headquarters, so when they came for their weekly visit, it was to HQ. We didn't always go to Lester Park; once we walked up Chester Creek, and I encouraged the kids to grade it…what we were doing we named the "Lester-Chester Bester-Tester." We all voted for Lester.

Among the things I had taught them was that when we were at the Fort, in Funland, we were invisible to human beings. Clearly they couldn't see us in the Fort from the trail because of the pile of branches and logs that formed the front wall of the three-sided fire pit. The three of us Funlanders each sat on our own log as the fire burned, and they wondered in the intricate flames and sparks that floated into the early darkness of late Sabado afternoons. One year as dusk fell around us with light snowflakes floating down to rest on our shoulders, Ted, waving a wand of a stick with one end burning, burst out "I love this place!" I taught them to count to ten in Spanish, and also the days of the week, so they knew Saturday was Sabado.

One day when we were walking out of the park on the trail, I spotted a couple walking toward us. Quickly I turned to the kids and told them to grab my hands and close their eyes and count backwards from ten and we'd be invisible to the others. They did, and thankfully the couple said nothing to us as they passed; I looked down at The Wizard and Secretary, whose faces were beaming like cats who just ate the goldfish.

Running out of job options in Duluth, I finally spent my last six hundred dollars on a full page AD in the Chamber of Commerce magazine and started my own PR and advertising company. For two and a half years I ran that business from a Macintosh 128k computer. I produced TV commercials, logos, newspaper ads, and a sports motivational video that ended up being shown to public school fourth graders statewide. The Wizard had a starring role in it; the Secretary had a cameo.

One day I went for a walk in a late-season blizzard. We had those in Duluth two or three times a year. The radio announcements told everybody to stay inside, it was nasty out there. That was my cue to gear up with my Gortex pants, my parka, my Air Force bunny boots, the kind they wore in the Korean War, super warm and light, and head out into the natural environment. I walked from HQ all the way down to Canal Park, where I was walking on top of snow drifts that came up to the second story of buildings.

This is the power of Lake Superior. The wind from the lake blew the snow so hard it packed drifts twenty feet high, upon which my bunny boots walked, until they reached a point where the wind had scooped out an area next to a building on my right, and I looked down there and saw the top of someone's car parked on the street about twelve feet below me. I looked up and found myself in a white-out. But this was Canal Park; I knew every inch of it from running seventeen miles a day down there, over the lift bridge to the Point.

But right now I couldn't see a thing. All white. Blowing. Ice crystals cutting into my cheeks. I crouched my way down to the lift bridge, which was partially visible when I reached it, and began to walk across it on the harbor side, to stay away from the front brunt of the wind off the lake. I crouched, because of the intensely strong winds, and then suddenly one gust actually blew me off both of my feet and I instinctively grabbed to my left and caught the cable there, by which I saved myself from almost certain death, being blown into the icy water in a blizzard with no one around. I super-crouched holding onto the cable to the other side of the bridge, I was intending to stop in for a fun surprise at a friend's house down on Park Point. But when I got off the bridge, I stepped into a four foot drift of snow, and was extricating myself from that, when a huge burst of lake wind knocked me off my feet and back into the drift.

Whew! I said to myself, this is how people die out here. I looked back at the bridge I had just walked across and couldn't see it. Every inch of space around me was white. Well, the novelty of me showing up at my buddy's house in a blizzard quickly took a back seat in my plans.

I picked my way carefully back across the bridge, got back on dry land, so to speak, and maneuvered my way over the drifts all the way back to the new Fitger's Brewery renovation. I shook off the snow, and walked into Chi-Chi's Mexican restaurant there, and found a couple of people sitting at the bar, which was surprisingly open. I sat down next to a large fellow I didn't know, ordered a Corona, and he began to speak to me.

"Hey, it looks like you've been out in this mess." He opened with the weather.

"Yeah, I like to walk in the blizzards."

"That's really super to do to keep you fit."

"I agree, I've always tried to be in good shape."

"You want a job?"

"What kind of job?"

"Well, what are your specialties?"

"I write, draw, plan, promote and deliver more than promised." He looked at me with a quizzical smile under his slim moustache. Then he went about explaining that he, Nick Jurry, had been brought back to Duluth, where he had been a graduate of Central before going to New York and Chicago to be a big impresario, to be the executive producer of an all—school, all-class high school reunion for Duluth. He needed a PR person and offered me a $25,000 retainer on the spot. I actually had been thinking of picking up another paying account for my business, and after he talked the manager of Fitger's Restaurant to fire up the grills for filet mignon and we pigged out all by ourselves in an empty room, I accepted on the spot.

Nick smiled his snazzy smile under his slim moustache. I had a moustache too but never had thought of trimming it down that way. He was about 5'7", and weighed at least 260 pounds, his fingers fat and dimpled, bejeweled with rings of all colors. His wavy black hair was slicked back tightly and he gave the permanent impression that he was about to go hidy hidy hee, hidy hidy ho. He would be my cheerful boss for a year.

Nick Jurry was a mastermind about promotion but lacked interest in the business end, that's why he brought Bob with him from Chicago. Bob was a no-nonsense chain smoker who wore tinted aviator glasses and managed the books for Nick. Then there was Aurora. I never could read her; she was a bleached blonde okay looking slightly frumpy fifty-something, and while working around her for over a year I never did figure out what it was that she did. Sometimes the demons encouraged me to imagine the connection might be Bob, or maybe she had the goods on Nick, but I quickly put those behind me as soon as they crept in.

Nick was all about the Big Show. His grandiose ideas were impressive and I learned quite a bit from him. For example, in preparing the promotional slide show to hook people into the all-school all class reunion, he demanded the musical score to be the music from the Superman movies. It built excitement, he said, and the power of the images on the screen, when envisioned at the same time the rising music is heard, makes the message so much more indelible. Nick's life in big cities showed sometimes.

Nick was hired by the Reunion Committee because of his big ideas, and for entertainment of the troops when they descended in hordes on Duluth, he chose the Everly Brothers, Miss America, the Oak Ridge Boys and George Burns. Some of the more conservative members of the Committee balked at the expenditures the stars commanded, but the show went on. As the PR guy, one of my assignments was to drive to the airport and pick up George Burns. That was a hoot. I had seen him so many times on TV in the 50s and 60s, now he was ninety, all five feet of him, and still carried a huge stogie in his mouth. He sat in the back seat while I drove to the hotel, and on the way he regaled me with stories about his seven ugly sisters.

When we arrived at the Radisson, remember, that's the one with the revolving restaurant, I "introduced" Mr. Burns to some Committee members, and then Miss America arrived, to a general rustle of interest. I still have the photo of me, Miss America and George Burns; at first I stood next to him but quickly learned the old pro preferred to stand next to a tall woman and certainly not between two tall people. He asked me to show him his room, and I replied sure, although this will be the first time I see the presidential suite myself. He waved his cigar at me and said "Let's go." We rode up the elevator together. I opened the door to his room for him, he walked in and starting looking around as if he'd done that a million times, I looked the opposite direction, found the bathroom and reported its location to the special Occupant. He nodded vigorously, "This will be fine." On the way down the elevator after taking my leave, I couldn't help wondering what it would feel like to be ninety years old and still working.

The next morning my assignment continued with picking Mr. Burns up and chauffeuring him down to the Arena-Auditorium, where the Big Show would go on. He introduced me to his piano player, a congenial white-haired fellow, and then learned that they had been together as an act for sixty years. I stood there and just smiled. Ray, the piano player, told me I was welcome to visit them in Los Angeles if I was ever out that way. Then George motioned his cigar toward a stool behind the curtain.

"See that stool over there?"

"Yes."

"Drag it over here where it's just inside the curtain, so if you sat on it and leaned forward you would see the audience." Which I did.

"Now," he continued, "That's your seat for the show tonight." And so I was on stage with George Burns for his whole show in Duluth. I took mental notes from a master. Oh, the little soft shoe of a ninety-year-old that raised rounds of applause from the audience. After the show George confided in me that the secret to being famous is outlasting everyone else. I made a mental note. That week I was also chosen to be the date for Miss America for the Oak Ridge Boys concert. Dinner first, then we met the band members, then the show, every minute chaperoned by a nice but firm representative from Miss America corporate. It was nearing the end of Miss America's term and she looked a little weary, and even confessed to me.

"When my reign is over, the first thing I'm going to do is get in my car and drive."

"Drive where?"

"As far as I can without talking to anyone."

I came to understand the heavy demands on a Miss America. This pretty young lady was worn out.

When it was all tabulated and scored by Bob, we had 117 class parties for 10,000 people over a seventeen day period. I came away from that year with a good feeling that a lot of people had a good time. Nick packed up his show, himself looking a little peaked from his intense work schedule. Bob and I had a smiling goodbye. Aurora huffed past me saying that she would see to it that I never worked in that town again. What? I wondered which planet she had been visiting.

At any rate now my $25,000 retainer dried up and I went for a 3 a.m. walk down to Chester Creek and lay on the rocks above the rushing river, looking up at the stars. Ok, I said to the universe, what's next? I have to stay here for the kids, so what's next here? I lifted my hands and prayed to God to show me the way. Truth, Understanding, Kindness, Peace. I ought to say here that no time in my life has been clouded more than a moment by doubt, and that I consider a gift from somewhere.

CHAPTER NINE

A week later I noticed a small advertisement in the newspaper for an Executive Director of the John Beargrease Sled Dog Marathon. I clipped it out and set it aside for a week before I called the number. I really didn't know much about what I was getting into but I went for the interview held in the back yard of a key volunteer and the new president of the all volunteer board. We went back and forth a while, then we negotiated terms, and they hired me, telling me, now go out and find $50,000 so we can pay the purse and hold the race, but the first $5,000 raised had to be sent to the previous year's winner in Alaska, who patiently waited.

It was July 1987 and my challenge was to find the money and the promotion and the media coverage for a little regional sled dog race and do it all by Race Week in January. The Beargrease actually had a historical validity, based on the travels by dogsled of one John Beargrease in the late nineteenth century. My contacts around town from having been a reporter still had juice, so the first place I went was to the newspaper, and talked to the promotional manager. To start a grassroots Friends of the Beargrease campaign, he gave up a series of twelve full page ads and donated his graphic artist's time to design a really cool image around my theme of "Let your minds turn to mush."

As musher entries came in, the bank account grew, and then one day we got a musher entry from Alaska who was bringing a team of standard poodles to race against the huskies. I used my reporting chops to put out a story on the AP wire about "Poodles to challenge Sergeant Preston's huskies in Minnesota sled dog race."

Well, the poodle team drew ABC World News Tonight, which did a two and a half minute story on it. Friends of the Beargrease collectively covered the $30,000 purse. The banquets were a big success. I ended the last night with a winds at your back poem. One lady told me after the banquet that she felt they had found the right person in me, all was well. But if anyone is wondering, what happened to the poodles? They dropped out early and the musher finished the race with seven huskies.

From my time with Nick, the big-idea man, plus my own outside of Duluth mentality, plans were laid to build the race into the best known race in the world after Alaska's Iditarod. To help me accomplish this I hired a young lady, an East graduate, who knew me from some other ventures. Maggie Brether was her name, and she had been a paralegal among other things, and between me and her we accomplished a lot. She looked out for me too. After Race Week the second year around, with an increased purse, a bigger field, second year in a row of ABC World News Tonight, Maggie tossed a brochure on my desk and told me I needed to take a break. Are you kidding me?

I hadn't had a vacation in years. And so my real love affair with Mexico began at the Hacienda Hotel in Mazatlan, Sinaloa.

It was eighty degrees on the front porch of the Hotel Hacienda, which was situated across the street from the ocean, with a four-mile long malecon. My bag had not arrived yet from the airport and I had to wait a couple of hours on the porch in my Minnesota jeans, and I began to sweat. By the time my bag arrived I was really hot, and carried my bag up to my room, emptied it out on the bed, picked out shorts and a T shirt to wear, and headed for a Mexican walkabout.

What is it about Mexico that so appeals to me? I was amazed and delighted to find a whole different culture right next door to the U.S. And the old stereotype of the Mexican lazing under a sombrero quickly gave way to the reality of an incredibly industrious people. Not to mention, how many 80-degree days did we get in Duluth in the summer, let alone in February? Then there's the music. I don't know why, but music moves me, inside, all kinds of music, but this homespun blend of horn and guitar and vigorous singing got to me.

And then there's the language. My experience with German had taught me the value of learning other languages, since the world looks just a little different from each linguistic angle. Spanish, made easy to learn by the Spanish government in the New World colonizing days, is muy facil a aprender. Very easy to learn. I found Spanish to be more romantic than German or English, which are by varying degrees exact. In Spanish, a lyrical note is added, so that when we in English say a woman delivers a baby, in Spanish they say she gives a light, "dara una luz."

Is this a key stroke into the Catholic nature of this nation melted from Indian and Aztec and Spanish? To give a light when one has a baby lends itself to further questions, such as, is the light in a baby divine? I personally cannot think of a more divine human form than a baby. Our light from birth grows for years, possibly all our lives, although that requires a good deal of attention. Most folks' light grows for some years, then begins to dim, until at the end of their lives it just goes out. It seems to me that growing our light increases our vibrations, and thereby gives us a higher existence, so the attention required is well worth the effort, in one man's opinion.

But to the Catholic point. A baby born is a light, so what is the mother? The source of light, the giver of light, a light herself, born of her mother. And the mother of Christ is revered by Catholics, and many others, for her gift of light to the world. But still, light given is light given, and each time a baby is born a new light is added. As for the Mexican people, their innate spiritual beauty is their simple belief, their faith.

Mexico had an emotional effect on me. That first trip to Mazatlan made me feel more at home than I did at home in Duluth. Life is fun on vacation, sure, but more than hours in the sun at the resort, more than a break from work and cold weather, this was a rediscovery of my own true self, heretofore buried beneath the bonds of love and obligation to my children. I felt alive walking those Mazatlan streets, poking into cantinas, finding cool out of the way restaurants or taking in the lights and sights in the Zona Dorada where all the gringos stay. But I preferred to walk in the colonias, the neighborhoods, what other Americans called ugly, dirty squalor. What I saw were women constantly sweeping their doorsteps and the dirt floors in their houses, the men with hoses spraying the streets to keep the dust down in the hot Mexican sun.

I played hoops in the street with some little kids, and wandered through mazes of narrow streets, up and down hills, and everywhere rubble and peeling paint and broken hand-made bricks and dirt. Low-roofed houses, stone on stone, doors standing ajar or non-existent, open-air windows. And everywhere life surged, little kids playing soccer, teenagers smirking, ancient ones making change, drop-dead beautiful brown-skinned chicas tittering on corners, street-wise adolescent youths, families doting on each other everywhere.

Many who lived in the city of Mazatlan had jobs in the Golden Zone, the Zona Dorada. Every day they would take the bus the four miles up the malecon to work in the glitzy resorts, and then bus back to their modest but very alive colonias. The acute contrast was not lost on me, that the money-laden gringos provided the ching for the industry there, but it was a symbiotic relationship for all the local jobs it supplied. Nothing could be more natural, in the end, but for people in sunny places to make some money off people who don't live in warm zones.

Which gets to another question that bugged me back then, namely is there something about living in colder climates that contributes to the inhabitants being more aggressive than those in southern climates? Otherwise how could one explain the imperial, conquistadoring, colonizing of southern nations by northern ones? Does it have something to do with the hot tropical sun, which does seem to slow one down when laboring under it? Seems this question may still be open.

On Friday nights the chicas came out in force to dance their cares away. Many of them owned three dresses—one for work, one for church and one for Friday night. The Friday night dresses were the special ones, the fancy ones, the ones that accentuated the natural beauty of those brown-eyed black-haired girls. They would get back on the buses, or take a taxi back to the Zona Dorada discos, or to Senior Frog's, which catered to gringos but the chicas commanded the dance floor. I spent a night dancing with one of them, and was invited by her to sit with them over on the Mexican side of the dance floor. The perspective was interesting, listening to my hostesses talk about the gringos over across the dance floor, while this gringo sat with them, danced with them, laughed with them and left with them.

We all hired a taxi and went downtown to the local disco. Bam bam bambam, the beat was intense. Sweat ran down my back as I boogied to the beat. Tropical release, primal, bam, bam. Such pleasure those young women took in dancing and clapping and hooting to loud music. It is one of the few escapes from the utter poverty in which they toil and live. But I was betting that few of them, if any, knew they were poor, since the colonias were so alive, pulsating, vibrant. This gets close to the notion that being rich or poor is not a material question, but an internal one.

I found myself wondering at my fellow Americans in Mazatlan. They mostly appeared to be satisfied with spending their entire vacation in the Golden Zone; they considered the actual city to be dirty and dangerous. It was the same in Europe twenty years earlier, me in the streets while they motored by in air-conditioned tour buses or on the Eurorail. Maybe the difference is that most

Americans who travel to foreign countries are those who can easily afford to, who perhaps never really felt the pinch of hunger or were ever near the edge of utter necessity. They express fear of being mugged and being treated badly, while my experience reaffirms my long-standing observation that if one travels close to the people they will be close to him. Once I even overheard a Mexican say to his friend when I walked by that I dressed like an American but something about me appeared Mexican. They said the same thing about me in Germany twenty years earlier. Maybe I'm just comfortable in foreign places; maybe it was just my general happiness to be out of Duluth, even for a week.

All good things must come to an end, and as I stood on the stairs of the jet before entering it to fly home, I couldn't restrain a feeling that I wasn't yet quite ready to leave this beautiful place. Five hours later I drove my jeep through two-foot snow drifts getting back to HQ.

One year at the Beargrease office we took a call from a specialty insurance agent in Texas, who asked me if we had snow insurance for our Race Week yet. I laughed away from the phone, then turned back to the receiver.

"Sir, may I ask, have you ever been in Duluth in January?"

"Well, uh, no. I suppose there's a lot of snow there?"

"Pretty generally, yes."

"Well, what if it didn't snow one year, then what would you do?"

"I'd still take my chances on having snow in January in Duluth." He finally gave up and went on to his next call, and I went on with mine. Little by little I was becoming a salesman; as the person responsible for raising the budget, I needed to sell in a number of ways. First, Friends of the Beargrease: firmly established by year three of my five as $35,000 to $40,000 annually. Then bib sponsors: the mushers were required to wear numbered bibs over their Carharts and Gortex during the race, and local sponsors bought exposure on the top of the bibs for $500. More mushers entering meant more entry fees and more bib sponsors. Throw in some corporate sponsors and that's pretty much the mix.

The other link was TV coverage, and after three years of hounding a guy at ESPN, he finally gave us an hour if we produced the show. Sponsors wound up getting mega signage exposure during six hours on ESPN. That's a lot of eyeballs in anybody's ballpark.

CHAPTER TEN

Finding the biggest sponsors took a little extra mileage. I accomplished that by observing the old adage given to me while still in my teens by Mr. Aderlink, father of aforesaid Rita and Rusty. He leaned over as if to impart an esoteric secret and just above whispering said "OPM."

"OPM?" I asked, bewildered.

"Other People's Money."

"Other People's Money?"

"Always try to use other people's money to get your projects done." He stood back, looking satisfied. I nodded and thanked him for his wisdom. So years later I needed to go to New York for a sports sponsorship conference and I needed to take my dog, a half-Siberian husky, quarter Malamute and quarter Arctic Wolf, to draw attention to my booth, which he did indeed, I used OPM to get there, by way of a vote of the board authorizing it. In Chicago on Board OPM the following summer at another sponsorship conference, I found a representative of a major company and gave her a brochure that I had written and designed, and that contact turned into a four year, $400,000 sponsorship, including a pair of fifth row first base line Cubs tickets at Wrigley Field, for the Wizard's thirteenth birthday, but also including funding for the ESPN project and financial support of an international friendship exchange between the U.S. (Minnesota) and the U.S.S.R.

Completely on sponsor OPM, I flew with two mushers to Frankfurt, Germany, and rented a car and drove down the autobahn, with a sentimental stop at the Heidelberger Schloss, and south to the Black Forest, die Schwartzwald. We were there for an international sled dog symposium in the lovely little town of Todtmoss. We spent four days there, where I boned up on my German, then we drove back to Frankfurt, dropped off one of the mushers who flew home and I flew with John, the other musher, to Moscow, U.S.S.R.

The year was 1989; it was still Gorbachev in charge, and rapidly opening up.

A little background, perhaps, is in order here. The international friendship exchange that was John's idea and I sold to the big sponsor, called for two representatives from the U.S. and two representatives of the U.S.S.R. to visit the other, including one musher from each nation to race in a race in the participating nation.

By way of adequate foresight and a vote of the Board, I was the other American sent, representing, as it were. Ten days we stayed in Russia, including an overnight flight on Aeroflot with a big black long haired dog to Petrozavodsk, formerly a city in Finland, and a sister city to Duluth. The public signs there were both in Finnish and in Russian. John and I, escorted by Mr. Vladlyin Korochent, who would be the musher designated to visit the U.S. and race the Beargrease, together met with city fathers and talked about joint ventures. That was a hot topic in the Soviet Union then, joint ventures. I still have my copy in Russian of a joint venture John and I hammered out with some Soviet investniks crouched over typewriters, of which nothing further ever came.

Our hosts, being Soviet, had our schedule pretty booked. One day we were driven out of Moscow about an hour to the farm of the Russian author Gorky. It was very natural, with stout Russian babushkas hauling carts and goats waiting in the yard to be milked. We also toured the Soviet state television station, where John and I appeared on a nationally broadcast popular travel show with Vladylin. We were on to talk about our Friendship

Exchange but Vladlyin insisted on telling about his Siberian trek, I could tell he was straying from the subject, so I touched his arm and said "Prastiti, Tavarisch" (excuse me, comrade) to bring him back.

After the show we were treated to cafeteria-style lunch Moscow-style. I saw pale green beans, oily hunks of bologna, "fruit juices" that were in soiled glasses half full of water with hunks of what appeared to be used slices of fruits. One of their favorites was their "black bread," a dark rye that tasted either like it had been made with sourdough, or else it was rancid. I couldn't stomach it. About the only edible thing on the menu were the hot dogs, warm, not hot, no bun.

As we ate our lunch I asked Nikita, the Russian blond young woman who hosted the travel show we had just been on, if she accepted commercials on the program, expecting her to say no, but she said yes. So I asked, how much for a :60 spot aired to 250 million Soviet viewers. She looked up for a moment.

"$30,000," she affirmed. (For a :60 aired to 250 million viewers? I wondered, that was awesomely cheap.)

"And how much would two :60s be?" I probed.

"That would be $60,000," she looked as if I should have known that. "But if we buy more than one, don't we get a discount?"

"No discounts!" She was firm on that one.

"Then let me ask you, Nikita, would you rather have $30,000 or $60,000?" Suddenly a light bulb went on in her head, and she understood what I was driving at, one for $30,000, two for $45,000, three for $60,000.

"Oh, yes, we will do discounts," she brightly advised me. I came away from that meeting wondering how Russians would ever catch up after being denied any kind of innovative thinking for seventy years by the heel of totalitarian rulers.

Another aspect of that very thing was evident in Mr. Gorbachev's effort to curb the national drinking habit, namely to close one-third of the State stores. After several days of prescribed tours for us, I protested, asking for a day off, just to wander on our own. They granted us Sunday. John was a pretty serious Christian and he used his day to look up several churches which were just opening back up after the Soviet heel had been lifted. I went for a walkabout down Leninski Prospekt from the sports hotel where we were staying, all the way down toward the Kremlin.

On the way I marveled at the sheer mammoth size of their buildings. Wider, thicker, maybe not as tall as Western skyscrapers, but definitely relaying a broad, strong people. Most of the storefronts revealed a depressingly spare amount of goods for sale. A whole shoe store with four pairs displayed. A department store with three scarves on two of the counters toward the window. I crossed the incredibly wide street and entered a small deli, where, again, to my amazement, the same sordid sour pale greasy fare was offered as I had seen at my hotel, and at the TV station.

I crossed back over the Prospekt and continued walking down the rows of thick empty buildings until I came to some windows that were full of people, a coffeehouse it looked like, so I ducked inside. American music was playing, "My name is Luca; I live on the second floor." There was hardly any place to sit, but I ambled up to the Turkish-style coffee bar, which means heating the coffee on hot sand. By then I already had learned to ask for my coffee "biz sucre pejouste," without sugar, please, otherwise my cup would be two-thirds sugar. I took my java and found a spot with my back to the wall where I could survey the whole roomful of young people; this must be just around the corner from Moscow University, I thought. Now one young woman is walking up to me, pointing her finger at me.

"Amerikanski?"

"Da," I nodded, "I'm American." She walked right up to me and shook my hand firmly.

"My name is Olga, I am part-time student at the University."

"Very nice to meet you, Olga."

We tossed a few English and my smattering of Russian words back and forth and then ran out of vocabulary, so Olga turned and waved her friends over to join us. One of her friends from high school, Eduard, had studied German, and I had just been brushing up in the Black Forest, so for the rest of our conversation it was German from me to Eduard, who translated it to Russian for his friends, who asked me questions through him in Russian, which he put to me in German. It was very fun. Now one of the older ones, a sort of slouching James Dean type, named Michel, asked me do I trink? Da, da, I smiled, I trink.

So Michel got up and led us out of the coffeehouse and down the street where black market money changers were hot at it in the alleys and then we came to a line of people, fifty deep, outside one of the remaining State liquor stores. The customers were carrying empty bushel baskets, cloth bags, plastic bags, coats with pockets, pants with deep pockets, anything to carry the load for the week. Michel bought three one-liter unlabeled bottles of "Pivo," beer, and tucked them inside his coat and quickly led us to a restaurant, where I began to wonder what is he doing? But his desired spot was on benches in the foyer, still outside the doorway to the restaurant. There we all waited for Michel to open one bottle with the cap of the other bottle, pop, and then he passed the bottle all the way down to me, telling Eduard to tell me the Americanski guest trinks first. I raised the bottle with a smile and down the hatch went the worst beer I ever tasted. Wheeee! Keep a straight face. Don't insult your hosts.

After the second or third trink it didn't matter anymore. In Russia they call this the national disease, alcoholism. The rural drinking tradition, as sociologists put it. It was an entertaining afternoon and evening running with those young Russians on Perestroika Soviet streets. Toward the end of our time together, Michel offered Olga to me for the night; I was not sure she was his to grant, and anyway, I said in my country, sex must be for love, or at least affection due to time spent together, so I respectfully declined, noticing Olga's eyes warm to my unexpected words.

One of the perks of being one of two Americans representing our country was a great seat at the Moscow Circus, an immensely entertaining evening of trapezes, porpoises, flying players, very well done, multi-level, full of surprises, perfectly timed and lit. The Russian people are a deeply talented, driven, loyal, strong-hearted fun-loving lot. If only their government could catch up to them. This gets close to the notion expressed by Thoreau, who wrote that poets are the legislators of the future, which, if true, means the poets, at least, are always ahead of the government.

The year after that, I used more Board OPM to accept an invitation to fly up to the Iditarod in Alaska, where I helped out at the Wasilla restart, then was flown in a little two-seater into the interior. Now, for those who haven't had the opportunity to fly over Alaska at a low altitude, I will just say the land is magnificently captivating. Big. The biggest. We flew past two mountain ranges and over hundreds of miles of wind-swept icy tundra to the Rohn Roadhouse, which really was a trapper's cabin at the confluence of the Rohn and Post Rivers, mountain peaks all around. My Eskimo pilot Floyd put her down on a packed-snow runway cut into an ongoing forest on each side. I stepped down with my bag and he looked at me.

"You got a firearm?"

"Nope. Think I need one?"

"Ya never know in these remote parts," he looked around, "but you should be fine. You'll have a lot of mushers around." I watched him take off in the pale March sky and suddenly I felt the enormity of interior Alaska around me. Silence. Just take a moment and be silent. What do you hear? Nothing. The kind of nothing that crushes your ears. Long pristine moments passed; then I heard a wolf's low howl in the afternoon low light and began to look for my cabin, which reportedly was down at the end of the runway and there's a trail that goes in from there. The

Rohn road-house was an appointed checkpoint on the Iditarod Trail, and frequently was used by the mushers as a mandatory twenty-four hour layover to rest the dogs. Not even a quarter mile into the woods, there was the cabin, with smoke coming out of the chimney, so I was preceded by someone.

That someone was a red-haired attractive young woods woman named Pet. She was a regular volunteer at the race, and had worked at several different checkpoints, and this year pulled Rohn duty. So there we were, in a 12 x 25 foot cabin with a couple of bunks in the back and a cast iron stove toward the front that heated up the whole cabin. Pet and I split duties in preparing for the teams to arrive; she sorted out the cabin and carried the firewood in, and I carried bales of straw from their drop point to various spots around the forested surroundings. That evening arrived early, being that far north, and we enjoyed a long conversation over hot chocolate and marshmallows. The next morning was a continuation of the previous prep day, but I split & stacked wood this time, since we would need a lot to keep the stove going for days.

The leader of the race arrived the next afternoon with fourteen dogs still in harness. She took care of her dogs, set them out on the straw, started a cooker fire, heated up their food, which consisted of steaming hunks of beaver meat tossed and caught in mid-flight by hungry teeth. She went to each one, taking off their booties and putting salve on their paws, then putting new booties on them. Only when she had fully comforted her dogs did she walk to the cabin, stiff and sore herself. Sharon was famous, having won the Iditarod three times and the Beargrease when she ran it, and the coolest caregiver to dogs I've ever seen. One year at the Iditarod I worked the McGrath checkpoint, which was on the great Yukon River, which makes the Mississippi look like a trout stream.

Sharon drove her team off the frozen Yukon and checked in, then drove her team of about fourteen dogs down the airstrip, then sharply called out "Haw" and the lead dog immediately turned a hard left, leading the rest of the team into the woods where she was going to bed them down for the night. It was so impressive to see the team follow her verbal orders, I'll never forget it. It was in McGrath that I sat with a couple of mushers who were discussing the price of a good lead dog, $10,000. The story went that Sharon originally was from Boston, but moved to Colorado, where she fell in love with huskies, and packed thirteen of them and herself into a Volkswagen Beetle and drove all the way to Old Joe's in Alaska. Old Joe was the patriarch of the Iditarod, and trained twenty-dog sled dog teams that he then leased out to city mushers for $20,000 a team.

Now the second, third and fourth place teams arrived, followed in ten minutes by three more, and pretty soon the cabin was getting hot and crowded. The mushers strung their wet socks and clothes over lines strung down one side of the cabin and stood around to dry their butts near the stove. Finally I got up, put on my parka, grabbed my sleeping bag, went out and found a yet-unbroken couple of straw bales, and went to sleep there on top of them, in lightly falling snow, at about minus 15 degrees. Tightly wound into my sleeping bag, parka and all, I was toasty.

The day after that, as the assumed "visiting dignitary," I was flown out to Nome, on the Bering Sea, for the official finish of the race. At that time and I suppose yet still there were not many hotels in Nome. The Silverado and the Golden Nugget each had their sordid histories of gunfights and Russian intrigues. I must admit my surprise to see so many beautiful Russian women wearing black sable coats in Nome, Alaska. I wondered if they had any relations in Amsterdam who utilize red lights. Otherwise, I chose the Nugget and was swashbuckling down Front Street in my knee-high fringed mukluks that had already been to New York and Moscow. My partner in crime at that point was Pete, a veterinarian who volunteered on both the Minnesota and Alaskan races. Race vets had total control over which dogs stay in the race and which ones must be dropped. Pete and I swung into the Nugget Inn, a low slung bar on the Bering Sea. He'd been working at the White Mountain checkpoint, maybe seventy miles out from Nome. In walked a white guy wearing Indian gear, and Pete recognized him immediately as the fellow who lives down by the river in the otherwise Indian village.

"Hey, partner, when did you get here?"

"Just tied the team up now."

"The team? You mean to tell me you just drove your dog team seventy miles for a beer?"

"Yep. And for the finish."

"Well, then pull up a seat! And the party was on. We had absolutely nothing else to do but hang out there and wait for the winners.

After the 1991 Beargrease paid out a $75,000 purse and had generated six hours of ESPN coverage, our biggest sponsor reneged and I had to put some big ideas together quickly. At that time there were two major competitor dog food companies, and one was French. I knew that the French liked to do business in person, so a plan began to hatch to get myself to France for their stage race, the Alpirod, to try to put together a dual crown sponsorship package with points combined between the Alpirod and the Beargrease, with TV coverage on ESPN and its sister station in Europe.

With fully authorized Board OPM I flew to Paris, hopped on a train to Geneva, rented a car and drove into the mountainous village in Italy where the next stage would be held. There I was greeted warmly by my hosts, I brought them Beargrease gifts, and they showered me with hospitality. A stage race is a little different from a marathon. This is more like the Tour d' France, where the competitors finish each day and restart the next morning, so the host communities can put on a big celebration. I hung mostly with the French dog food people, drank wine with them, which can be helpful in generating relationships. We traveled out of Italy, into France, back into Italy, back into France, stopping each night at a different village festivity. I was feeling a very good connection with my gracious hosts. It would be a wonderful branding opportunity for them.

After five stages the time had come to finish my schmoozing and leave them to their event. We exchanged business cards and more gifts, had cheerful goodbyes, and I drove off for a week's vacation, starting out with skiing the French Alps at 14,000 feet, in Puy St. Vincent, France. I rented a pair of skis and rode the chair lift as high as it would go, then a T-bar into the last stand of trees, and then a rope pull the last thirty meters, out of the trees, now above the trees, heavy winds, look right or left, you see snowy mountain peaks. All the signs up there are black. I didn't know what that meant anyway, so I picked one called La Draille, which I later learned was "The Dragon." Now, I was and am not a good skier. I was and am strong, and capable of many things. I kept my balance shifting my weight from side to side for about fifteen minutes, when I needed to stop to catch my breath. My quads were screaming. Pretty thin air up there. Another twenty minutes keeping my speed down, I reached the full-scale resort at mid-mountain, the village still way down below. Decision time. Continue all the way down, ride all the way back, or head back for the hardest part again. I chose down.

After about six full runs I was ready to hang it up. I got into my car and drove southeast, out of the mountains, into the rolling country, all the way to the medieval city of Narbonne. This was a walled city, original from the middle ages, with the modern city still encircled by its history. From there I drove south, through Barcelona, to Valencia, an imposing Spanish city with remarkable architecture, where I stopped for twenty minutes to buy groceries in a Mercado and returned to my rental car to discover that I had been robbed. The streets were crawling with different types of people, locals, and some Moroccans; whoever robbed me took my camera, my airline ticket, most of my Alpirod gifts. From all my travels I did know to keep my passport and money on me at all times. I had to place a call to Maggie at the Beargrease office to get a new ticket authorized. Then I stopped in a small town called Denia, named for the ancient goddess Diana. There I rented a condo for a week and caught up on my reading, among other things.

I read Socrates' exposition on the immortality of the soul and I felt the great reach of time. Two thousand four hundred years ago such wisdom and achievement, and today I am touched by it. The masses of my countrymen watch the Simpsons, while the few study their own souls. Probably I could not improve on the height achieved by Plato and Aristotle in the matter of soul-awareness; maybe the course of human evolution is more a matter of broadening the understanding to include more people. The few have always known; must the many always remain in darkness? I knew in my heart then that a grace of sorts enables the flow of life, marking the need for reverence. Each entry into my personal journals ended with a written thank you to God for all that I had been given. When I was down on my luck, I said "I allow myself to be swept through the door on winds of change." Courage overruled anxiety or fear.

What else could I think? Growing up as I did, being thrust into the world on my own at twenty-one, working my way up to a Master's degree, father of two great kids, what else could I be but grateful? An attitude of gratitude permeated my consciousness. I was and am grateful for every thing in my life, including music. If "music soothes the savage beast," am I then a beast? Is my beast, that urge within me, more refined than soul? Or does music simply seek its goal? It seems the spirit, high and pure, responds to harmony with clear and absolute discovery. And the beast, the urge that coincides is pleased to take melodic rides. Music, the undulating waves of sound that first caress, then put me down; the harmony of life goes round and round.

At the end of my week I drove back to Barcelona, spent a day and night in that awesomely unique city, then took a train overnight to Paris and flew home from there with four bottles of wine given to me by my French friend, Dom, a veterinarian who had worked on my race and the Iditarod. I looked him up while in Paris and he took me out to dinner in a 700-year-old restaurant, we had to duck to enter the front door which gave testament to shorter people back then.

By the time I got back to my Beargrease office in Duluth the president of the board was waiting for me. I was brimming with information and contacts and plans for our big new French dog food dual crown and I started telling him about it but he interrupted me.

"Nash, we want you to resign."

"And the dog food people were talking six figures, and they insisted on multiple years…" I didn't hear him at first.

"Nash, we want you to resign." That time I heard him.

"Why?"

"We have a laundry list of complaints."

"Can I see the list? Who's been complaining?"

"No, you can't see it, and I can't tell you who."

"Well I want to come to the next board meeting and address those complaints one by one!" I was feeling like my legs were being cut out from under me. In five years I had put the race on the international map and was on the brink of a big new deal.

"You can if you want but we want you to resign today." At that point I cleaned out my desk, carried the box out and went home to HQ. That was the second time in my professional life when I was the victim of petty jealousy. I discovered later that the all-volunteer board of directors included a couple of hard-core veteran volunteers who didn't like me being Mr. Beargrease, getting all the media exposure. I went to the next board meeting and offered to answer any and all questions any of them had, but met with stony fearful silence. Now I was feeling like I got the short end of the stick, and went back to HQ to figure out how much in back commissions they owed me according to my contract.

For years I had been plowing my commissions back into the race to keep it building. The number was $26,000 and I took that to the office to meet with a couple of board members and their brand-new executive director. I told them they owed me $26,000 but I didn't want to hurt the Beargrease so I would settle for $15,000. My replacement answered that they didn't have the budget for that. I turned to her and pointedly reminded her that I wasn't there to talk about budget, I was there to talk about what the board owed me, and I would settle for $15,000. The board members knew I had them by the shorts and so for the next two and a half years I would get checks in the mail from the Beargrease until they paid me off.

CHAPTER ELEVEN

By that time I had finally gotten out of Duluth for good. I met with the Wizard and Secretary and asked them how they would feel if they visited El Presidente in the Twin Cities, and with their blessing I sold HQ and moved to St. Paul, thinking I would find a job in advertising or public relations somewhere. Strangely enough, I sold HQ just as I bought it, to a guy in a bar who bought it from me sight unseen. I was riding the winds of change with no firm prospects, a vague idea of landing a PR or AD agency job but my willingness to dare resulted eventually in my being hired by the Minnesota Timberwolves of the NBA, as a corporate sales manager whose only duty was to sell sponsorships. Over the next six years I would generate nearly seven million in sponsorships for them, and travel a good deal more on OPM. The position necessitated an annual trip to New York to meet with potential sponsors.

Usually the New York trips were packaged around a game against the Knicks, so very early on I witnessed how grueling the NBA life is; one hour after the final buzzer, the players had to be on the bus to go to the airport and fly to the next city, where at 10:00 a.m. they had shootaround, and then at 6 or 7 p.m. play the next game. For eighty two games over six months. Ok, if they paid me five million guaranteed I might try it.

One December day in 1994, I took a call at my Timberwolves desk from non other than Betty, the mother of my children. She called to inform me that Lila had passed away that morning. My sister had ended her vast travels years before, saying to me "I am moving back to Duluth to die," before anything arose to indicate such an event. But that was part of Lila's thanatose, having watched Eddie Edwards die when she was 22, having watched her mother drop dead in front of her when she was 30, and all those years working in emergency rooms with all that blood and carnage; my sister carried an adolescent sullen attitude about our family to a gloomy adult interpretation of her world. The honest truth is that I feel she could have brought disease upon herself with all her negative thinking. I have seen in my own life the power of positive thinking, so who's to say there is no power in negative thinking?

Lila was, nevertheless, the mistress of her destiny; she scripted and assembled a multi-media presentation of her life for her own memorial service and set every last one of her matters to order before her time came. True to her rebel spirit, the slide show ran with the music of Jim Morrison, "Break on through to the other side." I had taken to driving up to Duluth to stay with her over the past three months; she just made one ground rule—no talk about anything in the past. So I would never really know what she had against me. The last time I saw Lila I barely recognized her. "Love ya, Bro." "Love ya, Sis." Breast cancer is a bitch.

After her memorial service, Jesse and I walked to my car; he had her ashes to distribute up the North Shore, by Lila's wishes. He had grown into a rather large man, about 6'4" and a beefy 260 pounds. Looking down at his big brother he dramatically intoned "And then there were two." He drove north out of town; my kids went with their mom somewhere, and all the others drove off to their own groups. I sat alone in my car, across the street from the funeral home, everyone gone but me, feeling very, very alone. A heavy snow began to fall.

My car drove out to Lester Park and I hiked to the Fort, started a fire in the falling snow, lit a joint, and smoked one more time with Lila, my tears falling into the fire at the loss of my beautiful talented estranged sister. She died one week before her forty-sixth birthday. Yes, you read that right: I lit a joint. Forty four years old and still imbibing, albeit with countless efforts over the years to chuck it, to flush it, to dump it in the garbage, to get it into the rear view mirror, all futile.

This was my private life; nobody knew. I got so good at masking the effects nobody could tell if I were stoned or not. But I pretty much kept it away from my work life; MJ was my recreation, she was just difficult to get away from, like some women I have known. But at least it wasn't like the old days, all the time. By now she was limited to weekends, or a couple times a month, and many months often went by without seeing her at all.

My Timberwolves OPM took me to New York twice, Seattle, Salt Lake City, Denver and Chicago twice. Sometimes after a game, one or two players would get on the staff/sponsor bus, and after his first game against the Chicago Bulls, nineteen-year old Kevin Garnett sat right behind me jumping up and down on his seat, he was so excited, repeating over and over, "I played Michael Jordan! I played Michael Jordan!"

Of course, Garnett went on to have a Hall of Fame career because he ended up being a league MVP, 15-time All-Star and a champion with the Boston Celtics.

During that time working with the Timberwolves I broke a pattern in the office, taking my vacation during the season. When the season schedule came out, I would check to see when the team would be on the road for at least a week, and that's the week I would book for a Mexico vacation. I went to Ixtapa-Zihuatanejo, Playa Del Carmen, and Acapulco before I ever discovered Puerto Vallarta.

One day my travel agent across the street from the Timberwolves called me asking me questions.

"Nash, have you ever been to Acapulco?"

"No, I haven't."

"Well, how does $92 round trip sound?"

"Leaving when?"

"Anytime before Dec. 25."

"Book me." And that's how I got to Acapulco; when I arrived, I picked out a van at the airport and shared costs with three other travelers, who all got dropped off at big hotels along the Costera Aleman, Acapulco's main drag, and only I was left.

"Where you want to go, man?"

"Nada especial," I said, I just need a room limpia and barato (clean and cheap.) The young man driving the van then took me back to the main drag and took a left back into the neighborhoods. Three blocks from the busy Costera, he found me a small room upstairs on the back veranda of little Hotel Las Estrellas. It was sufficient for my solo adventure; it was spartanly furnished with two tic-tac old kitchen tables, one with partly wooden chairs and the other with white plastic ones, protected from the sun by the next door Hotel Josvy. A soft breeze cooled the 80s temperature even at nine in the evening, and sitting there alone just listening, I heard a maid rinsing a bucket downstairs, and the faint music from yet another neighborhood hotel. I paid seventeen dollars a night to stay there, and first thing every morning I was awakened first by roosters and then by women sweeping. Mexican birds chirped in Spanish in the trees, lovely flowering foliage was all around me.

That first night in Acapulco I went for a walkabout on the busy main Costera; in my back pocket I carried twenty crisp new one dollar bills, which I would give to the little ones who tried to sell me chiclets. The very next morning I took a city bus to the end of the run before it continued up the hill to the old cliff divers' hangouts. I got off at a little beach called Playa Caleta where a servicio named Sylvester got me a chair right down in front of the water, and for the rest of the day he was at my beck and call, for water, for cerveza, for chicken tacos with guacamole. The entire afternoon lolling on this pretty little beach cost me sixty pesos, and with my tip to Sylvester, it totaled about $7.75

U.S. My general rule of traveling was and still is to fear no one, expect fantastic bargains, enjoy meeting others and don't be afraid to ask for help; in any case, an honest approach with a question is likely to get an honest answer, especially if you see a little bit of yourself in them.

That evening found me still hanging around Old Acapulco; it was very pretty. I found a little off the beaten track cantina and found myself a seat at a very small half-circular bar. Conversation was heard by all. Ernesto, a polite young man, took a seat in the corner across from me.

"Are you American?" He probed.

"Si," I replied.

"Habla Espanol?"

"Un pocito."

"De donde eres?"

"Yo estoy de Minnesota."

"Bueno, Senor, bienvenida a Acapulco!" Ernesto grinned at me and clearly was impressed by my minimal command of his language. We chatted over a cerveza while he waited for a friend, and what a friend! Dolores showed up in a frilly bright blue print dress that accented her brown sugar skin. She was gorgeous. She pulled up a chair right next to me, the only one left at the tiny bar. Ernesto talked to her from his corner seat, telling her that he just met this gentleman who speaks Spanish. At first Dolores flatly denied such a possibility, then she turned to me and asked me in her native tongue.

"Where did you learn your Spanish?"

"Most of it I learned during the one semester I audited a Spanish class in graduate school." After I had managed to tell her that in a moderately proficient attempt in her language, and after she had probed me assiduously she finally eased up and turned to Ernesto.

"El habla solamente Espanol de la playa. El es un playero." I knew she had me there. Most of my Spanish was for getting to, around, behind, and on the beach, playa. They talked Spanish to themselves for a minute or two, then the bartender, whom I had befriended upon my arrival, proposed that the Senor from Minnesota understands more Espanol than he shows. Finally Dolores was convinced that I was a man of valor, and upon that notion she took a cotton to me. So it turned out that Ernesto and Dolores met before going to night class.

"What kind of night class are you two going to?" Never hurts to ask.

"English," they both chimed in. So the long and short of it is that they invited me to come to their class with them that night and I took them up on it, and was introduced to Roberto, the instructor, whose parents were Mexican but he grew up in El Paso so he was bilingual.

"Now Senor Edwards, you shall be our instructor in English tonight." He took me by surprise. The class was small, eight or ten students. He went on to explain to me all I had to do was ask them questions in English and they had to answer me in English. So that's what I did, tossing each student an English softball, then slightly harder balls, some got it right, others flubbed and restarted. Fun was had by all.

After class we all went down the stairs to one of Acapulco Viejo's prettiest pedestrian flowered and treed walkways. We found a spot where we could all sit, and over beers they peppered me with Spanish questions and completely overpowered my slim knowledge, which they found to be a great diversion. Dolores sat near me the whole time, and her deep dark eyes looked up into mine on several sultry occasions.

The next noon found me back in Plaza Alvarez, sitting on a stone fence under the shade of a large tree near the cathedral, the holy place of old Acapulco. I walked over there and watched from outside the door, I could not enter due to my near-absolute inability to wear long pants in shorts weather. Anyway, just as at the Vatican in Rome, these poor peasant women shawled in black clutching their beads, bent over from hard labor, faces looking upward at the image of the cross. Something deep within me resonated with them, I knew not what.

Just then, jolting me into the present moment were shouts of small children, no, they're singing, where are they? I looked around and there, just beyond the cathedral, there they come, marching in twos, each holding a flag, all appearing to be about six years old. It was Mexican Flag Day, and the blue uniformed schoolchildren were doing their part to commemorate the auspicious occasion. The little feet in sandals trooping by me as their owners sang a patriotic song, all watched over by the eagle eyes of the teachers, reminded me how much the Mexicans value family. It was just nice to sit there and soak it in; my inner stores long ago may have been depleted, but for the eternally wonderful mystical truth of my life, I always get what I need. Even when it's gotten vicariously through wonderful families whose names I shall never know.

CHAPTER TWELVE

Eventually due to the readings and ponderings and unforeseen turns to my life, there was no question that my path was clearly on "the road less traveled," as Robert Frost said. I lived alone, most people lived with another. I saw the world as my back yard; they saw it as a universe away. They watched television, I read books. Many wouldn't ever even think of going solo to a movie or a concert or a play. That difference alone created a disparity between respective views of our society. Research was out in the 1970s showing that people who watched six or seven hours of television per day actually thought it was more dangerous outside than it really was.

In the same sense, I had long harbored the notion that whenever I met another person who had never hitch-hiked, never traveled alone, never learned how to overcome fear, my conversation would probably be limited to whatever they wanted to talk about; for some reason, total strangers bent my ear with their life stories. But many times I met one who really caught my attention for a while; there are so many interesting people.

Along the way there was one lady I spent a few years hanging around in very much a fairy tale come true. Back in eleventh grade, before my summer on the railroad, I was in the student council and there was a dark-eyed, black-haired beauty also on the council, from her twelfth grade homeroom. Mila Bernstein was a Jewish girl, seemingly untouchable to non-Jews, but her smile was so sweet, her eyes so deep, I found myself riding my bike up to her house and sitting across the street just to see if I could catch a glimpse, and at times I did.

Now fast forward thirty years, and I drove to Duluth with the Duke who was going to his thirtieth reunion, and for the first time I crashed it, thinking a lot of my old sports buddies were in that class and I hadn't seen any of them all that time. And they were, but I couldn't help noticing one pretty woman whose name I didn't know.

I walked over to her, said hello, and leaned forward to read her name tag: Mila Bernstein. I stood straight back up and introduced myself. She remembered me. We danced. Outside, by her car, we stood and talked. She was getting a divorce from her husband.

Back in the Twin Cities the next week, we met for lunch, and one thing led to another and before anyone knew it, four years of fun, love, and a healthy relationship had passed. During that time I took an interest in finding out everything I could about Judaism. I read the 4,000 year-old history of the Jews and wondered how they ever survived to today if not by Providence. I went to Temple for Yom Kippur, Purim, and other holidays. I read some mystical Kabbalah. Reading Torah appealed greatly to my way of thinking, very logical, very concise, and offering me gems of wisdom hidden within the pages.

Yes, my God is the God of Abraham and Isaac and Moses. That is the God I have looked to all my life. One thing Mila said to me once made my head turn; she said it was clear that I would never be a Christian. In her terms, Christians were barking up the wrong tree. And up to that time, I had been right with her on picking holes in Christianity. It was so easy, with their history of bloodshed, war, political hijinks and big name preachers living lies. Not to mention so many so-called Christians not walking the talk; and there were philosophers on public television saying all the Biblical stories were just that—stories.

Mila and I took a couple of trips together, one to Mazatlan and one to Costa Rica, where the Secretary was for six months going to school. Mandy was living with a local family, and when we got there, we took them to dinner in their town, Heredia. Heredia was the capital city of Costa Rica before San Jose. Mandy was studying at the university there, and one day we went to her class with her, and we sat in back observing as the esteemed professor, formerly the Costa Rican ambassador to the United Nations, and I watched in awe of the young people there, including my own Secretary of Pennies and Munchies from Duluth, taking copious notes in Spanish. Due to the grammatical structure of Spanish, I had to listen closely, as the important verb was usually at the end of each sentence. I got about sixty percent of what he was saying, talking about the Middle East peace plan, at least the plan of the moment in that sorry situation.

We rented a van with a local driver to take us to the Pacific Ocean side of Costa Rica, passing through some of the most beautiful country any of us had ever seen; and we passed a sign near a small town in the hills, proclaiming "The Best Weather in the World." I didn't doubt it for a minute, far enough south for year-round warmth, and up in the hills so it wasn't too hot, and cool for sleeping at night. We passed through Quepos, a popular fishing spot, and drove a little further down the road to a lovely little hotel overlooking the Pacific. Our driver bid us goodbye and said he'd be back in three days.

We hiked up the road to the national park named Manuel Antonio, where we found the most beautiful beaches ever. One problem there was that it was so hot and humid, on our little walk up the hill looking for monkeys in the morning, our clothes were soaked with sweat by 9:30 a.m. We came down the hill and found a little jungle restaurant and sat down to order lunch. We three—Mandy, Mila and I—were sitting there and suddenly on the corrugated metal roof we heard "bam bum, bam" like an army was jumping onto the roof. Then the monkeys showed up, all around us, on the rafters, at the table, and our server stuck out his arm with a banana in his hand. One monkey jumped up on his arm, and with the server's other hand he peeled the banana and the monkey grabbed it and ate it right there on his arm.

We also tried the canopy ride there, where we learned it was Costa Rican technology, now copied in Mexico. We hiked up a river bed path, and one by one we got strapped into a harness, held onto the handles over our heads, and then swooped through the jungle at high speeds for about a quarter mile, then slowed down for the finish; definitely worth the price of admission. Back in San Jose, travel expert Mandy advised us to not carry our packs on our back, but in front of us; otherwise the local thieves would zip our packs open and rob us without our ever noticing it.

Later, Mila and I took a walk around San Jose and found a big old hotel that was painted pink, called the "Rio." The bar was packed with people; we found a couple of seats in the corner away from the bar and ordered a beer for each of us. From that vantage point, I saw beautiful young Latinas sitting with grey haired, beer-gutted unshaven Gringos; the girls were stroking the Gringos' skinny legs and smiling at them, and then they disappeared up the stairs in the hotel. Hookers. Too bad, I thought, such incredibly lovely ladies, and that's all they could find for work? Mila and I finished our beers and it was so busy in there, we didn't want to wait for the server to come back, so I walked up to the bar, couldn't wedge myself in anywhere, and went all the way around the semi-circle bar looking for a spot to order, and finally got the attention of the bartender. I got the beers but the most interesting thing about my walk around the bar was that I was propositioned no fewer than three times. There were plenty of hookers and swingers in there; not my cup of tea.

In the end Mila called our relationship off, mainly because I wasn't Jewish, but also because her old friends were all fairly wealthy, and she missed hanging out in those circles. If I had big money I don't think it could have solved the ethnic difference, even though she once told me that I knew more about her religion than she did. At any rate, it was a wonderful four years and I am grateful to her for her warmth, generosity and kindness.

From Judaism I turned my curiosity to Eckankar, the New Age religion founded in California (where else?)in the early

1970s. Their world headquarters is in a Minneapolis suburb, and I went to a service, where I learned the power of chanting. They chant their holy word for God, "Hu." Hundreds of voices united… "Huuuuuuuuuu." I could see how they could draw souls in with that. Just as with the Gregorian chants, Native American spirit songs, Buddhist repetitions, any constant verbalization of a concept is going to lend it at least perceived power. But I read a little farther into what Eckankar calls their scriptures and learned that they believe they can spirit-travel to a spiritual city on Venus, in their dreams, guided by a blue man named Harold. Hu, indeed.

After September 11, 2001 I went out and picked up a Koran to read. I wondered what in the world would motivate men to fly airplanes into buildings in the name of God? And sure enough, right there in the first few Suras, there are exhortations to kill the unbelievers, destroy the crusaders. But then for the rest of that holy book, it's all about peace, kindness, hospitality to strangers, and love. Those Jihadists are a perfect example of a little knowledge being a dangerous thing. They read only the first part, thinking they have God's will at their backs, and then run around murdering innocents and brainwashing illiterate youths to blow themselves up with a promise of having 72 virgins in Paradise. If that sounds like lunacy, well…

By that time, on a more mundane note, I had also gotten myself into an annual trip to Puerto Vallarta for Christmas and New Year's Eve. The reasoning went like this: I was in sales, in the United States of America, which collectively starts to stop working the holidays by Dec. 21 at the latest. In other words, it was a difficult time to get any business done. "Call me after the first of the year," began by Dec. 15. In the meantime, my Christmas time with my kids was limited to a few hours on Christmas day, and the whole week was emotionally bleak. So my solution was to take anywhere from seven to twelve days, starting Dec. 23, returning Jan. 2 through the 6th and spend them in what had become my favorite neighborhood in the world, the Zona Romantica of Puerto Vallarta.

The Malecon in PV is shorter than in Mazatlan, and a steady string of good restaurants face the ocean, as street artists draw crowds of onlookers, right after they pick their favorite treat from dozens of carts of sweets, there is even a little amphitheater built right into the sidewalk. Every night a different act consisting of one or two people juggling, doing magic tricks, telling jokes that made all the kids laugh; I usually bought a frozen strawberry yogurt.

From there, hike up the hills to a street that takes you to Gringo Gulch, where you can see the lovely pink bridge that arches over the street, a grand gesture by Richard Burton, whose house was at one end of the bridge, while Elizabeth Taylor's house was at the other side. Hiking down from there you'll eventually come to a river, the Rio Cuale, which divides the city into north and south. Depending on how high up the hill you are, the river may be swift, may have women kneeling and doing their wash, or the river may be languishing as it nears the ocean. To the south of the Rio Cuale you will find the "Romantic Zone."

What do I love about this neighborhood? The climate, the people, the ocean and oh so eclectic Playa de los Muertos; the food, the music, the hills, the cobblestone streets, the Amapas neighborhood which reminds me of Perpignan. The Malecon at night. Red Snapper broiled with garlic. Tacos from the corner street vendors. Art crawls. Dancing. Yes, the dancing. There is a place in PV where you can either watch middle-aged people dance like fools or be one yourself, and the beauty of it is that the dance floor is too small so people dance right where they stand, by themselves but not alone. On New Year's Eve the place is packed, and over the years going there for the same week, I got to know others who did the same, and they became my PV friends.

Darcy was the ringleader of the San Diego bunch; she was a buxom blonde real estate investor and she got down to PV two or three times a winter. Darcy and Pam and Dancing Jerry, Pam's husband, Kirk and Wendy, all from San Diego, and a whole slew of others from Vancouver, Colorado, Calgary, and other places hung together on the beach and then partied together at night. The first time I went there I noticed them as a pretty tight group that knew how to have fun. The second year, they were there again, and I said hello. The third year, finally I asked their names, and from then on, over fourteen consecutive Christmases and New Year's Eves, I was included in their circle. That meant I got an invite to an annual private boat ride paid for by Gig, the San Diego construction company owner. I also was invited to go along for a day trip to a little pueblo down the coast, bringing two boatloads of Christmas presents for the school children there. It was a big event at the school when Darcy showed up wearing her Santa hat and all of us lugging in bags of treasures for them.

Then we all had lunch at the beach restaurant, while little brown-eyed girls brought wild flowers for Darcy's blonde hair. I will never forget the time I accompanied them on that day trip one year when I was not drinking any alcohol; I had decided to take a year off. So at lunch on the beach that day, we all ate and laughed, and I watched my friends as they drank and drank, and got louder and louder, and then to my amazement they all began to slump in their chairs and their faces began to droop. This is what it looks like to get drunk? I was happy not to be sharing that with them. The pure fact was that I never could drink like they could; they were veterans of a Mission Beach bar in San Diego, and could drink like fish. Kirk and Wendy offered me this tip: Take five aspirin and drink three glasses of water before going to bed after drinking, to avoid a hangover. How about not drinking too much, I thought.

Those PV breaks gave me time to do some extra reading. One year I read the Trial of Socrates, and marveled at his wisdom from 400 years B.C. After I read that, I looked Socrates up and discovered that he never wrote anything. All that is known about him or his ideas is from Plato and Xenophon. Another trip found me reading the sayings of Confucius, from a full century before

Socrates. Confucius taught culture, conduct, faithfulness and truth. Here is an example:

> "There may be men who act without understanding why. I do not. To listen much, pick out the good and follow it; to see much and ponder it: this comes to understanding[4]."

Or another saying: "Without a sense of courtesy, attentions grow into fussiness, heed turns into fearfulness, courage becomes unruliness, uprightness turns to harshness[5]." That one made me reflect on my trashing the floor on the ore boat that time the captain told the Bosn's mate to make it tough on me. If I had exercised a little courtesy my courage may not have become what was indeed, in retrospect, unruliness.

The sum total of all my reading, as it would to anyone who led a an adult life pretty much away from the humdrum and issues of daily family living, gave me a perspective on life and the world which was not shared with many. I did feel a connection with the ancient philosophers, also the Transcendentalists such as Emerson, Thoreau, and George Ripley. Emerson's Essay on Self Reliance was a mainstay in my personal library, with lines like this burned into my memory:

> "Whoso would be a man must be a nonconformist. He who would gather immortal palms must not be hindered by the name of goodness, but explore whether it be goodness[6]."

One of these years, I thought, maybe I should finally get around to reading the Bible as I have read all my other books, cover to cover, and even more important, open-mindedly. Then life got in the way and I put that off for another few years while I read a lot of philosophy and history and various literatures.

CHAPTER THIRTEEN

One thing about living alone most of your life, you tend to see yourself not as others see you, but as your thoughts proceed. In this sense it was necessary to learn to first tolerate, then understand, then exhibit kindness when any other person saw me as an arrogant, conceited, thinks his poop doesn't stink kind of guy. I do understand why they think it. I am definitely confident, in control of myself, not accepting the norms of others on face value alone. I do not like to be told what to do. I make my own choices, albeit not always wisely. I am focused on my goals and determined to accomplish them. I know what I like and what I don't like, but remain open to any new venture. I often choose not to join in with profane folks. My posture is straight. Perhaps it's just my innate strength—my upbringing made me strong—that rubs some people the wrong way; misery and weakness do love company. And I am comfortable alone. Solitude is a great teacher.

This is why Epictetus bothered me so much. The Stoic Greek freed slave philosopher wrote from quite a different angle.

> "You are impatient and hard to please. If alone, you call it solitude;...and when in the company of many, you should not have called it a wearisome crowd and tumult, but an assembly and a tribunal; and thus accepted all with contentment[7]."

Precisely. Which makes me a human mistake-prone little bug in the grand scheme, and (perish the thought) maybe I need to be knocked down a couple of rungs…um, no. I must refuse to go to such extremes to find my way. Epictetus again:

> "Knowest thou what a speck thou art in comparison with the Universe? That is, with respect to the body; since with respect to Reason, thou art not inferior to the Gods, nor less than they. For the greatness of Reason is not measured by length or by height, but by the resolves of the mind[8]."

The greatness of Reason is measured by the resolves of the mind. Now, that makes sense to me. Increase your will power and watch the results. This is also where I find myself refusing to give up any power to any mere idea.

Whether from an unnatural lone perspective or from an attempted compassionate observance, my observations have included that most people I've met along this journey are anxious about something, jealous or envious about something, or even worse, their conversations are either about what they saw on TV or what they think about another person. Where are the original thinkers? Has my country been completely narcotized by the "plug in drug," TV? Since I finally gave up TV, I have seen my time enhanced and expanded beyond expectation. To that point, I recently read about a scientific study that showed a lot of screen time, whether watching TV or being glued to a computer screen playing games or surfing the net, causes a lack of attention span in the viewer. Duh.

I respect the scientific method as much as anyone, but for heaven's sake, wouldn't that be obvious to any alert observer? It is a total shame that parents allow their children to be diagnosed with ADHD, without stopping to consider what all that screen time is doing to the kids' attention spans. The worst part about this is that they then allow their children to be drugged, to make them settle down. How about just spending some quality time with them, how about teaching them at a young age to love to read, or making them spend time outdoors?

But back to solitude, great teacher and friend that it has been to me, has also cost me personally, as my true friendships are few and my bed is empty but for me. Does this impel me to become more sociable, more like the others, more vulnerable? What began as self-containment under Ice has become what I am in adulthood—a very private, quiet, reflective man. I attempt to improve myself through reading, and to a great extent that suffices. And my skills when with others have grown over the years. But to know sustaining emotional love in an intimate way, that remains perhaps for another day.

My experiences with observing others were in abundance on my travels around the U.S. One driving trip I took in my late forties with my German Shepherd, Norman, was to the Ozarks, just for a look around. The first two days were dismal rain all day, and by the time we reached Arkansas, we passed tiny towns in small hollows between ever-larger hills, and found ourselves sailing right past Dogpatch, Arkansas, which appeared to be nothing more than a broken-down hillbilly theme park below the sidewinding road as the hills really began to rise. A guy in Branson, home of all the entertainers who live off of blue-haired fans, told me to make a stop in Jasper, a supposed artist colony over the hills on Scenic 7 just a piece south of Dogpatch, so we did.

That was my first encounter with rural Arkansas community layouts, and I was mildly astonished by the smallness of the streets, blocks and buildings, almost like toy towns nestled in the hills. Norman and I walked around in the grey drizzle and covered the whole downtown in minutes. I ate a biscuit and sausage at a tiny table in a tiny café with my back to another tiny table, at which sat an older, very large man with drooping jowls and a beaten-up oversized nose, who also turned out to be hard of hearing. Our brief shouting conversation consisted of him telling me that the road south from there was some of the most picturesque country in the U.S. Good thing I bought some picture postcards because we soon found the road to be locked in by a dense fog which precluded viewing any of the fabulous views. It was all I could do to see the shoulders of the road.

Through the foggy hours we continued in and out of fog, up and down through the sidewindiest road we'd seen yet, and passed Ozark hollow tiny towns like Ben Hur, Tilly, Rupert and Crabtree until we gassed up in Clinton, which had the miniest of mini-downtowns. I'm talking about one-way streets that run about eighty yards, then turn into another one-way diminutive street with closely packed mini buildings. Maybe they needed to conserve space in the hollows, I thought, but Clinton isn't really crammed into its space, it's just that the town is laid out small.

From Clinton we took Scenic 9 back north to Mountain Home, and large sections of that area were visible, the rain pattern leaving us faster than we followed it. During that roll through the Ozarks, from Pelzer to Clinton to Mountain Home, we saw more trailer homes than ever before. Very few people in the northern Arkansas hills live in houses, and some of the trailer setups on their slanty junk-strewn roadside lots filled my head with stereotypes of real down-home hillbillies.

Some of the trailers were so small I couldn't believe whole families lived in them, and at least one had wet blankets draping over its sagging roof, as if blankets would keep out the rain. I saw barefoot children playing in their thimble-sized yards and I wondered about their education, and of that of their parents. I was surprised to see in that whole hundred-mile stretch of Ozarks not one tavern in any of those tiny-towns, but I did catch a glimpse of a working still up a hill as we rolled by. For a time my curiosity was piqued by a sign placed strategically at a particularly hairpin turn: *Don't miss Booger Hollow…Pop 7 including .one coon dog.*

By the time we reached Mountain Home, it was still lightly drizzling, but Norman and I both needed to stretch our legs, so we went for a long walk on the outskirts of town in a (what else) trailer park. I stopped at the first motel we came across on the main strip through town. The desk clerk at the Mountain Home Motel was a stooping, weathered woman of about seventy years with poor red hair and hardly any youth left showing, until she talked, then she was a graciously garrulous provider of information, including that we would be safe there because the richest man in Mountain Home owned the Dairy Queen across the road and he had the police cruise by it several times a night. Doris also gave me her recommendation of the seafood restaurant in the little strip-mall next to the motel, but assured me I didn't have to eat seafood, they served other kinds of food too. Once I got Norman situated in our room, I drove down the strip looking for whatever mischief I could find.

I stopped at a nondescript place called the Back Forty because there were so many cars parked in the lot. It turned out to be the first bar I had found since Branson, and I learned inside that all the surrounding counties are dry, hence no taverns spotting the countryside the way you'd find them in, say, Wisconsin. It was a restaurant too, and I tried out their not-so-hot chili and a pretty good big burger while seated at the bar, always a good bet for catching the local gossip.

Gert, the stout square-faced woman behind the bar, quickly introduced me to Skinny, who wasn't; quiet, elderly Curt, who was, and George the realtor who soon proved to be the most talkative and, perhaps a related fact, the drunkest of the bunch. I don't remember how many times he told me his wife was German or how he had the biggest, best dog in Mountain Home, while I bit my tongue thinking of the real holder of that title snoozing in our motel room. I learned long ago to let folks have their say and that way they'll like you. Anyway, it's funny to think of how many people must think their dog is the best. George was drunk enough to think he was being funny when he snorted at Gert that he thought her hair looked better before. She defensively touched her new short curlie top and said well, she likes it better now.

George wasn't the only one in a fun-loving mood because Skinny laughed with him. Skinny was a fiftyish man with a full white beard, wearing a tie-died T shirt and a dirty red mesh baseball cap whose crown carried the dubious message "Get stoned in Mountain Home." Actually, Gert was also wearing a tie-dyed T shirt; at one point Skinny suggested they swap shirts but Gert looked suspiciously at him, knowing her shirt wouldn't fit over Skinny's ponderous belly.

Now George was slurring in my ear that Mountain Home is a nice place, I should move there. Then he started leering at Gabriella, the black-haired forty-something part Navajo waitress in tight jeans and a neat red top as she worked the tables. "I'd like ta frush her pansa a blub," he slurred, leaning off his stool, his energies dissipating in her direction. Suddenly he straightened back up as if jerked by a puppeteer's string and earnestly drawled "Ya know, mah whaf is Gzjerman." After he tottered out boasting that his brother in law is a member of the local constabulary and he'd never once gotten a deedubbyaeye, I seized the opportunity to tell Gert I thought her hair looked nice. She liked that.

The next morning Norman and I awoke to a blue sky, hurray. Now all roads led to Hannibal, Missouri, the boyhood home of Mark Twain. We took 62 out of Mountain Home, through Henderson to Salem, where we turned north on 9 to get to Thayer, Missouri, and then Scenic 19 into the Mark Twain National Forest. Scenic 19 is nothing short of a rollercoaster road, swooping down and back up on shoulderless pavement through the woods, up and down, up and down. It's the kind of road that leaves your stomach at the top of the last hill and it doesn't catch up with you until almost the top of the next hill. A little practice teaches you go let off on the gas just before cresting each hill so as not to take flight into the next gully.

That night we camped at the Silver Mines campground outside of Fredricktown, Missouri. There I read more of the Dalai Lama's book about the art of happiness. The crux of the first few pages was that it all depends on my attitude I choose and that with my inner discipline I can train my mind to consistently choose a positive outlook. Given my lifelong tendency to do just that, I heartily agreed, not without my usual sense of wonder that more people don't get it.

When we found Sam Clemens' boyhood home in Hannibal, with its whitewashed fence where Tom Sawyer connived to get his buddies to paint it for him, and Judge Thatcher's big white house, where yellow-haired Becky Thatcher looked out her bedroom window at the boy playing across the street, the books came to life. Just at the corner not two hundred feet away is Grant's Drug Store, where Tom witnessed a man being murdered in the Adventures of Huckleberry Finn. And there's Old Man River, two blocks from Sam's house, clearly the focus of any boy's attention; no wonder he took to the river as a steamboat captain. No wonder I worked the ore boats on the Great Lakes after watching them from the maple branches of my Lakeside home.

Our trip wasn't finished when we lit out from Hannibal, which incidentally showed a great contrast to any of the other towns we'd been through, namely a disproportionate number of bars, even three on one short block, lending the impression of a depressing locale. Maybe, I mused, everyone is bummed that Clemens was the last Hannibalite to hit the big time. A lone old grizzled black man sat dolefully on his porch in the rising afternoon heat and I could just imagine how hot it gets around there in the summertime.

Cruising north through Davenport, then Clinton, I witnessed a sharp contrast. Davenport has a pretty Central Park, where the locals like to take their summer evening strolls. Clinton, Iowa is a foul-smelling town with a huge petrochemical plant on the river, and any part of town is vulnerable to the smell, depending on which way the wind blows. My heart ached for the people who actually lived there and breathed that polluted air every day of the year. We couldn't get out of there fast enough and soon afterward found the Great River Road, along the Mississippi all the way to St. Paul.

But first a night in Bellevue, Iowa. This is a scenic river town of about 1,800 people with a history going back to U.S. Grant and his brother staying there from time to time when doing business with the local boot maker. The Grants had a leather goods business across the river in Galena, Illinois.

Another slice of the town's history is posted on a marker in the riverside park. It seems one W. W. Brown and his wild bunch of woodchoppers were caught stealing horses back in the town's early days, and the townsfolk organized a posse to confront them at the two-story log Brown House on the riverfront. Gunfire broke out as the posse approached and when the smoke cleared, several of each side lay dead, including Brown, and the remaining rascals were seized. The next morning they were given a public whipping and sent down the river on a raft, told never to return. The date: March 1840, pretty much one hundred forty years to the day before Norman and I discovered this lovely historical spot.

We stopped not far from that marker, in front of a pretty little hotel, the Riverview, and Norman and I went into the bar full of happy hour locals to ask about a room upstairs. The bartender was the owner, and said sure, my dog could stay in the room with me. Norman always gave off a good vibration. There's something about a one-man dog to make a six-legged household, a sentient being as loyal and watchful as any, to make a man know a special kind of love. I loved that dog and he loved me. And everybody he met loved him, including the bartender, Bill. I signed up, paid for a night, and then went back outside to give the big guy a well-deserved walk. When we returned we went up to the room, I got him settled in, then went downstairs to the bar for a cool one.

This group was as eclectic as any I'd seen yet. Before I sat on the stool I picked out, one bushy-haired fellow in army fatigues said "Nice haircut." (I kept my hair cropped very short) I looked at him, surprised to be spoken to already, and was about to say thanks, when he hurried to say "No offense intended, of course." No problem, I assured him, thanks, it's getting a little shaggy. "I certainly didn't mean any offense," he repeated. Before the evening was done I would hear him say that a few more times. This was a very gentle and slightly over sensitive soul.

Most of the others around the bar were in varying stages of intoxication, some speaking louder than others, but one gentleman caught my eye in particular, as he was ignored by everyone else to whom he spoke. He kept repeating the same things to each one he approached, and they in turn rolled their eyes and turned away from him. The fact that he was about a dozen sheets to the wind may have had something to do with it. The guy was positively tilting. He was a slightly built man in his late fifties or sixties, plainly dressed, with thick sandy hair parted on the left and large round-rimmed glasses that made his face appear to be narrower than it actually was. He had put quarters in the jukebox and was asking everyone if they liked the songs he had chosen. In absence of replies he seemed contented to lean back in his shoes and announce to the whole room that this was great music, some of the greatest ever.

He spotted fresh meat in me on the other side of the bar, and tilted over to regale me with his routine. I allowed myself to be engaged, for the sheer experience of seeing what may come next. His name was Roger but most people around there called him Pogey, which he confided that he didn't really like. He was a retired brick tender from Iowa City who had spent forty years on the same job. "I was on a treadmill carrying bricks for forty years," he reported. "Now with my pension I make $40,000 a year and I don't have to work." He was clearly proud of that and I assured him that he certainly deserved it. That's when the alcohol in him began to make him repeat himself. On a treadmill. On a treadmill. On a treadmill. Man, I thought, what a life. How dull must that have been! What could be left of any spark of creativity or joyousness after spending four decades carrying bricks?

Roger had heard that I had my dog with me and he started in about Alsatians being the best. "They're from France, you know." He drummed. Whenever he made a statement of fact or an assertion he had a habit of drumming his fingers either in the air or on the bar and tweeting a little whistle. That seemed to buck up his confidence and then he really took off.

"My family's from France, I always wanted to go back there, to Alsace-Lorraine, it's in France, you know. Alsatians are the best, they're black, they go about a hundred twenty pounds. Alsatians. They're the best. I never had one. I have horses. I have the best trained horses in Jackson County (drum roll)."

"Horses?" I cut in. "What kind of horses do you have?"

"Well," he stepped back an inch or two and feebly twiddled his fingers in the air. "Actually I have mules." For an instant he looked sheepish but then he brightened and drummed on the bar. "They're the best trained mules in Jackson County!" Bill the bartender heard the drum roll.

"You ready for another one, Pog?"

"Yeah," Roger unsteadily looked at his half-full regular's mug as he confirmed that he would have one more (his third one more) but apparently Bill wasn't worried, since Roger lives close enough to walk home, in fact right behind the hotel, across the alley. Now Roger turned back to me and abruptly stated that he was about to turn sixty-eight. I congratulated him on his youthful appearance and it was as if I started the broken record again.

"I was on a treadmill for forty years…" He repeated it a couple of times, as if he were still trying, after six years of retirement, to fully grasp the raw fact of his menial existence. "Alsatians are the best, they're black, they go about a hundred twenty pounds…"

His enthusiasm for that line of advice trailed off as he looked down, deeply down into his beer.

"I'm gonna go to my fiftieth reunion," he slurred, looking up at me. I quickly replied that he would really enjoy that, but then endured a new conversational treadmill about how he was never in a clique, they didn't really like him, he was going to wear his cowboy hat and boots, he had horses… Soon after that I took my leave of him and went up to my room for the night. I wanted to share his pain but couldn't do it all night. I went to bed slowly shaking my head in quiet humble gratitude for being allowed to have such a varied and wonderful life, and to be continually reminded of it at virtually every turn.

CHAPTER FOURTEEN

"I want to meet you." I pointed my finger at her and walked toward her as we walked in opposite directions around Lake Calhoun, one of the lakes in Minneapolis.

"Well, you'd better keep up then." She never broke stride. So I spun on my heel and walked alongside her for the rest of the way around the lake, a distance of 3.1 miles, I knew from running it so many times. She was a voluptuous black woman who obviously took care of herself. Her prominent cheekbones gave indication of some Cherokee blood, and added to her beauty.

Mardou was a single mother of an eight year old girl, whose Venezuelan father had abandoned his child after the mother divorced him. But Mardou said several things that indicated some spiritual depth and high morals. I found myself respecting her and wanted to see her again.

We dated for a couple of years, during which time she invited herself to meet my kids, by then both living in the Cities, and invited me to accompany her to her church, where at first it seemed to me that they were talking in foreign languages. I had been away from church so long, and this particular church was different, mainly due to the unique pastor, who was from the Caribbean and spoke with a lilting accent that made it tricky to understand him at first. But it wasn't just the pastor's accent; it was the words he used, Father God, Lord Jesus Christ. Everything was couched in terms of the Savior. Then one Sunday after service, a friend of Mardou's smiled at me and said to her "first in the hearing, then in the spirit." She looked as if she knew something I didn't.

Mardou wanted to get married but I couldn't see it. She didn't read books, wasn't interested in sports, and actually said country music hurt her ears. Naturally her daughter took after her mom, so when I bought the girl a year's subscription to National Geographic, a gift many kids love, I was read the riot act.

"Why don't you buy something she'll like?" Mardou asked me.

"Like what?" I replied.

"Well how about one of those celebrity magazines?" Great idea, I thought, that way she would just look at the photos and work up some half-baked dream that she wants to be famous too. My interest was in helping her to be ready for college; her mom never went past high school. As the National Geographic's magazines showed up, they stayed in shrink wrap; nobody even wanted to open them to see what wonders might lie inside. But there I relearned that my way of looking at the world was not in sync with many others.

Why should she read books? "What good is all that information in your head?" Mardou actually asked me that. How is one to answer such a question? "The only book I need to read is this one," she stated emphatically, as she patted her Bible. Never mind that her pastor always talked about improving all your skills, but Mardou turned out to lack the one thing I absolutely need in a partner—intellectual curiosity. Without the impulse to learn, we slowly begin to die. This reminds me of those unfortunate souls who say their high school years were their best, and everything has been downhill from there.

Nevertheless, due to her basic sweetness and, admittedly, some pretty hot brown sugar, I continued to see her, to accompany her to church, and even to go with her to her church's summer picnic. I felt like an outsider, a foreigner, among all those wonderfully nice Christian people. And slowly, almost imperceptibly, I found my mind growing receptive to what the pastor was preaching, he preached kind of a common sense approach without the religion. He taught that it was all about a personal relationship with Christ. Forget the rest that you've heard, he said, this word will make you free. I was stunned to have copious tears run down my face at sermons. Over a period of a couple of years Mardou eventually took her leave of me and I kept going by myself to hear that word, to the point at which I finally went out and bought a Bible. I had dozens of books on my shelf, some of which dealt with histories of the Bible, interpretations of the Bible, refutations of the Bible, New Age Bibles, alternative Bibles, but not yet a Holy Bible itself. Now I had one.

The world I live in is quite different from the environment in the church. On the History channel, when I still had a TV, I saw shows that put up scriptures in old English type, and then the narrator told the audience some other stories that were not in the Bible, and put up quotes from those stories in the same type and style as the scriptures, almost as if to make those stories part of the gospel too. One of the narrators was a female professor who had written a book I had already read, about how people in the second and third centuries had put other stories into the Bible, and how they made Jesus the man into Jesus the Christ. The implication was, in that book, and on that History channel show, that Jesus was just a man, nothing more.

Another book I read became a national best seller, talking about human evolution, and how it is not complete, but the next stage is for humans to become what the author termed "multi-sensory" people. The crux of that message was, in my estimation, right on, namely that for the full run of history to modern days, people operated on the perception of external power. "Authentic power" was the author's term for where we are headed[9]. In other words, we have a soul, and it is that soul in us which is immortal, and we all would be better off if everyone operated on the basis of being first a soul, next a body. That was the instinct I recognized when I was seventeen. But the most the author would grant Jesus was the title of "Teacher," and "one of the most evolved of our species," writing about Jesus in the same way as he wrote about Gandhi. Somehow, somewhere inside of me, I disagreed with that, and that was before I ever opened the pages of the Bible. Certainly Gandhi had been a great man, a large soul, a founder of modern India who led by moral example. But it was never said of him that he rose from the dead. I knew in my heart that that was the crux for me; to believe that Jesus rose from the dead is the basis for all Christian faith. I wasn't there yet, due to my lack of reading the Bible and also due to the influences around me.

My oldest friend from back in Lakeside, the Duke, told me I was going backward if I started believing in Christ. "They're just stories!" he asserted. One thing I had observed over time in the Duke was that he read the newspaper every day, and then parroted back what he read, as his own ideas, regardless of whether or not I had read the paper too. Usually I would just let him go, it wouldn't hurt anyone. He watched the public TV shows with the old academic philosopher who told his viewers that all the Biblical stories were just stories. So the Duke said they were just stories. He had been reading some Buddhism, some of the stuff I had read decades ago, and was buying into that hook, line and sinker, just as he told me I was doing with Christianity.

Admittedly, Buddhist thinking is very logical and makes a lot of sense about just living the right way, peacefully, compassionately. Consider this quotation from the Dalai Llama:

> "Whether people are beautiful and friendly or unattractive and disruptive, ultimately they are human beings, just like oneself. Like oneself, they want happiness and do not want suffering. Furthermore, their right to overcome suffering and be happy is equal to one's own. Now, when you recognize that all beings are equal in both their desire for happiness and their right to obtain it, you automatically feel empathy and closeness for them. Through accustoming your mind to this sense of universal altruism, you develop a

> feeling of responsibility for others: the wish to help them actively overcome their problems[10]."

Perhaps a simpler way to say this: "Love your neighbor as yourself." I respected and still do respect the Buddhist system of thought, which is frankly what it is. But the Duke admitted to me in a rare moment of candor that he chanted in front of his little iconic bowl until he was "blue in the face," and then the next morning he felt drained. I couldn't help thinking that it was no wonder he felt drained, as he was doing nothing to invite the Divine spirit fully into him; he assumed he already had it in him, and all he had to do was "summon it up." I told him that's not possible without reverence and humility, as I knew long before I ever picked up a Bible; my life had always been one of profound gratitude to my Maker. Another time when I brought that up to him, he explained that it was because he was new at the practice that he felt drained. It did no good to try to tell him my fulfillment from learning about Christ was almost immediate and did not "drain" me. He accused me of thinking God is "out there" somewhere, but that I could not accept. I do not think the Divine is "out there" somewhere. I know a spark of it is in me; but to be alive in me, to engage with it, it needs me to acknowledge it, to welcome it and be humbly grateful for it.

But humility was never the Duke's forte. He had been a champion runner. Any success I had in track was totally overshadowed by his accomplishments. We called him the Duke because he was. The Duke was a wounded soul who had come up under an abusive father, and he ran his heart out to keep his balance. Humility had no role to play in his life. It couldn't, as he challenged the best in the country in college, and that ally of super self confidence stood by him all through his adult life.

But the Duke was certainly not alone in his assessment. Once I was visiting another friend, who was being visited by yet another old friend who I previously had not met; Herman's old friend Frank was a wiz at electronics, very scientific and rational, balding, but still with straggly hair down almost to his shoulders, grizzly unshaven face prominently punctuated by dark furtive eyes. During our casual conversation he dropped a couple of profanities, the likes of which I had not heard since my time on the ore boats, and which included what Christians would call blasphemy. I'm not sure why I did, but I called him on it, and began to defend Christ to him.

The most amazing thing then happened—Frank became agitated, almost brittle in his talk, and clearly uncomfortable in earshot of the name Lord Jesus Christ. It was as if some unclean spirit inhabited him and it hurt his ears to hear any talk of Jesus. Short of that, however, I tried to compassionately understand him, and maybe, I thought, he had had a bad experience somewhere along the line with some Christians who didn't walk the walk. That's like throwing the baby out with the bathwater, but at least it may explain Frank's unease.

On top of all that, the society I lived in had become secular in tone, and there were plenty of my fellow countrymen who wanted to completely eliminate religion from the public sphere. Never mind that the author of our Declaration of Independence referred to man's "unalienable rights endowed by their Creator," or that Thomas Jefferson's own monogram on his personal seal read "Rebellion to tyrants is obedience to God." Or, how about our sixteenth President, Abraham Lincoln, who said in his second inaugural address:

> "With malice toward none; with charity for all; with firmness in the right, as God gives us to see the right, let us strive on to finish the work we are in; to bind up the nation's wounds[11]..."

But what do we have in our modern society that Jefferson and Lincoln did not have in theirs? Light bulbs, airplanes, cars, radios, TVs, personal computers, cell phones, space stations, the world wide web, you name it, our technological advances have far outstripped our spiritual advances. Nowadays one is more likely to hear Jesus' or God's name as a cuss word than in reverence in the general street. My modern counterparts appear to think that science has made us free of what used to be called Providence.

The old "God is dead" idea grew from Nietzsche's strenuous postulations, such as "the Bible…is perhaps the greatest audacity and "sin against the Spirit" which literary Europe has upon its conscience[12]." Something in Nietzsche's soul was severely agitated; to understand him is to know the society he lived in. There were no "personal relationships" with God then, just pronouncements from above. He saw humans as good, moral on their own, capable of great things on their own, while he saw Christianity as the purveyor of a morality that made people think they were low and unworthy. He wrote as if he never read the whole Bible, even though his father and grandfather were clergymen. I could not wonder, as I read him, if only he had spent half as much time reading the Bible as he did feverishly writing his own opinions in Alpine attics, his end may possibly have been other than going mad as he did.

The way theology is shared is a big part of the problem. Take a look at the first half of the American nineteen century, and read the Transcendentalist George Ripley:

> "But what are our prevailing systems of theology? What claim do they present, as now organized, upon the attention of the philosopher or the lover of nature? It is hard to imagine a study more dry, more repulsive, more perplexing, and more totally unsatisfactory to a scientific mind, than theology[13]…"

Add to notions like that our modern scientific marvels and it is understandable how modern humans may adopt a hubris regarding religion. Why bother with God, they reason, when we can split atoms, learn all about how the universe began in chemical and geological terms, and even clone species. Evolution, they say, is all we need to understand. Atheists, humanists, Pagans, agnostics, they claim one or the other title to show their minds are liberated, and their hubris shows plainly.

Some say "there are many ways to God," meaning they choose to ignore what the Bible says—the path is narrow. Of course, what we think about, we become. But still the atheists beat their drums, as if to buck up their own courage to dare their destiny with such audacity. As Benjamin Franklin noted, any fool can criticize, condemn, and complain and most fools do. And just try to call them fools; it only serves as fuel for their insatiable fire to burn Christian ideals to the ground. Better to show them compassion, to lend them love, in spite of themselves. The evangelist's heart yearns to restore lost souls to the light of all light. But they call me fool; I remember to mind my own plot to ponder such words as these: "Our own heart, and not other men's opinions, forms our true honor[14]." And so be it with those who disagree with me, may they keep their own honor, true to the chords they hear from their own minds' core; I find myself involuntarily pausing to pray for all to find a way to open their hearts.

In this environment I took a job for six months selling long term care insurance to farmers and rural folks down in southeastern Minnesota. The method was to visit first with existing clients and get them to tell us about others in the township, so we would know where to work "smartly." One fellow I met actually had been some sort of township official, and he knew everyone; he pointed to one particular name on the plat map and told me to skip that one, the owner was in his nineties and obviously too old. So for a week I drove up and down that gravel road, each time passing by the ninety-year-old's place, but one day I felt an urge to drive up that driveway.

Seated on the front porch of an alpine style house were two old folks, enjoying a sunny afternoon. I drove up, stopped my car and got out. They greeted me and I greeted them, introduced myself and told them that I sell long term care insurance, but I suspect they probably are too old for that. They laughed and agreed. Then for some reason I started to talk to them about all my studying of religions and philosophies and "isms," but had recently been wondering about the Bible. The old man, with a full head of white hair, wearing an old but clean pressed blue work shirt, the collar a bit ragged, looked at his wife, and she looked back at him, saying "Should we show him the book?" He replied, "You're younger, you go get it." He was ninety-three, she was eighty-three. So she got up and went into the house for a moment, and came back carrying a huge tome of a book, and gently handed it to me over the railing. I held it in my hands, all 1,156 pages of it.

This quiet and unassuming man, sitting there on the porch of a house he had built himself, had become a Christian pastor at age twenty-one, and over his lifetime had preached, studied, taught in seminaries, and written several books, including this one, the compilation of a lifetime of study. He published it when he was eighty-eight. It was a book of theology, historical and Biblical. I gently turned the pages in quiet awe as I realized what he had accomplished here. He wrote it out longhand on yellow legal paper and his wife typed it up. I told him I would go home and buy the book on Amazon.com, and I did. The end result of the meeting with him was that he inspired me to finally take care of my own destiny and write my own book.

So I went home and bought his book, but also decided it was time for me to sit down with an open, seeking mind and read the Bible for myself. I did, cover to cover. Then I sat there and said to myself, hmm, that was heavy. I had seen how the prophet Isaiah predicted the life of Christ:

"He was wounded for our transgressions, crushed for our iniquities, upon him was the punishment that made us whole, and by his bruises we are healed[15]."

So I turned back to Genesis 1 and started it all over again, but when I reached the part in Acts 10 where Peter was telling a group of people:

> "We are witnesses to all that he did both in Judea and in Jerusalem. They put him to death by hanging him on a tree; but God raised him on the third day and allowed him to appear, not to all the people but t*o us who were chosen by God as witnesses, and who ate and drank with him after he rose from the dead16."* (My italics)

I fell on my knees in a moment of sheer terror and awe. Witnesses, I thought. Eye-witnesses. Why would they say that if it were not true? Why would they risk their lives, and give their lives (Peter by being crucified upside down, Paul by being decapitated) if it were not true? I had accepted without hesitation the veracity of Socrates' thoughts, although he never wrote anything.

I had accepted without hesitation all that I had read in history, philosophy, science, but never once had I been willing to look seriously at the divinity of Christ. Still on my knees, I fell forward prostrate on my belly, my face on the floor, my arms outstretched, my heart pounding, my tears flowing, my body trembling and my soul leaping with joy at having finally found the truth.

And then the most amazing thing happened. All of a sudden I began running into books and essays that verified my newfound faith. The Transcendentalist George Ripley who previously was shown to think theology was stuffy and boring, also wrote this:

> "Man's heart is formed for religion, and in the Bible he finds it. Man's soul was formed to drink in religious truth, and in the Bible it gushes up from everlasting fountains. While everything else has changed or passed away, the essential truths of the Bible have remained the same. The permanence of the Bible, then, is a strong proof that

> religious ideas are congenial with the human mind, and are indestructible and everlasting in their character[17]."

Jump ahead to the 20th Century and consider what G.K. Chesterton had to say about that. "The Christian ideal has not been tried and found wanting; it has been found difficult and left untried[18]."

Still, I heard nothing but criticism from my oldest friend, the Duke, and ran into many others who thought me foolish to believe in "old myths and stories." Some proclaimed their atheism proudly, asserting that God is a figment of man's imagination, and that in this modern day of science and progress, we need to think critically and rationally.

G.K. Chesterton again: "There are arguments for atheism, and they do not depend, and never did depend, on science. They are arguable enough, as far as they go, upon a general survey of life; only it happens to be a superficial survey of life[19]."

I was baptized in the name of my Lord Jesus Christ on June 28, 2008 and have known nothing but a fountain of internal joy and peace since.

And my Furnace Room Friend? Since the age of five I had known the comfort of that mystical arm around my shoulders; now I suspected it had been my guardian angel all along. That mystical sweet thread that ran through my entire life was a gift from God to me, a companion, an assuror, the promised Holy Spirit. Now, I can hear the atheists say my Furnace Room Friend was nothing more than a physical result of having my back warmed by the furnace. But I was there, they were not, and I know what it was. And my beloved Grandmother appearing to me in that dream three nights after she died, telling me I was born to write a book about my father? For decades the kernel nestled in the back of my mind, but now I had to face the old fact with a new perspective: From whence was she speaking to me then if not Heaven? If any human being ever deserved to go to Heaven, she did. So just who did she mean when she said "You were born to write a book about your Father?" Admittedly this notion had been sneaking into my consciousness forever, never certain, always open-ended.

In a cumulative moment of light and higher vibrations I finally realized it was not my Dad, Eddie Edwards, that she meant, but my Father in Heaven, God Almighty. So this journey leads home to God, in spite of me, in spite of my pride, my arrogance, my base human hubris, in spite of my many sins. I raise my hands and shout *Thank you Lord, Praise Jehovah on highest, and Praise my Lord and Savior Jesus Christ!*

ON TRUTH

I do not believe it was by mistake that my four ideals, to which I dedicated my life in my twenty-second summer, began with Truth. My journey led me to the truth that has made me free. To anyone who would deny me this truth, I am in total agreement with Chesterton: "Great truths can only be forgotten and can never be falsified[20]."

As Emerson said in his essay on the Over-Soul,

> "We know the truth when we see it, let scoffer and skeptic say what they choose. Foolish people ask you, when you have spoken what they do not wish to hear, ' How do you know it is truth, and not an error of your own?' We know truth as we see it, from opinion, as we know we are awake when we are awake."
>
> "For the soul's communication of truth is the highest event in nature[21]..."

Now, truth also matters in mundane everyday life, too. Tell the truth. Uphold the truth. Share the truth. Expect the truth. We live in this modern world where even truth is said to be relative; "It depends on what it looks like from where you sit," runs the popular adage. This mistake comes partly from misunderstanding Einstein's proof of physical relativity; if the physical world may be understood in terms of particles or waves that can be scientifically explained, that does not negate the spiritual basis of all creation. Certainly there is a place for science, but that's not all. To put it in

Einstein's own words, "Science without religion is lame, religion without science is blind[22]."

The same sort of misunderstanding rose with Social Darwinism, which was unsuccessfully tried in the late Nineteenth Century. Spencer and his followers thought the scientific theory of evolution could be applied to human organization, but it failed due to the egregious error they made. Without a general acceptance of certain absolute truths, we have social anarchy. With only a "survival of the fittest" theme, how could people love each other altruistically?

> "We hold these truths to be self-evident, that all men are created equal, that they are endowed by their Creator with certain inalienable rights, that among these are life, liberty and the pursuit of happiness[23]."

Jefferson's immortal words included "that among these," which tells us there are more self-evident truths than the three specifically named in our Declaration of Independence. Without a personal commitment to always tell the truth, we short-change our own persons. Without discernment we have deception. And there can be no greater folly than self-deception based on pride in one's knowledge, as had one troubled soul, Friedrich Nietzsche. After all, one philosophical truism that most thinking people recognize, namely that the beginning of wisdom is one's recognition of one's own ignorance, tells us something of our innate abilities.

Why not ponder this: "Wisdom cries out in the street; in the squares she raises her voice. At the busiest corner she cries out; at the entrance of the city she speaks: "How long, O simple ones, will you love being simple? How long will scoffers delight in their scoffing and fools hate knowledge[24]?" Or how about "The fear of the Lord is the beginning of wisdom, and the knowledge of the Holy One is insight[25]."

And still the atheists persist. Sir Francis Bacon, in his Essay on Atheism, suggests that

> "It is true, that a little philosophy brings man's mind to atheism; but depth in philosophy brings men's minds about to religion."

Bacon goes on in that essay to itemize the causes of atheism, namely, first, many divisions in religion introduce atheism (more so even today); secondly, scandal among priests (some things never change); thirdly, a custom of profane scoffing in holy matters (even more prevalent, perhaps, today than in 1625); and lastly, times of great learning and peace, for "troubles and adversities do more bow men's minds to religion[26]."

But reason, they cry, we need to depend on reason, not some childlike faith. Chesterton: "Reason itself is a matter of faith. It is an act of faith to assert that our thoughts have any relation to reality at all[27]." But they still cry, all paths lead to God. Chesterton: "Impartiality is a pompous name for indifference, which is an elegant name for ignorance[28]." And still they cry, these are new times, why depend on old ideas? Chesterton: "Men invent new ideals because they dare not attempt old ideals. They look forward with enthusiasm because they are afraid to look back[29]."

Many modern Americans take their spiritual food from the East, mainly because, as I understand from my own reading, it allows them to exercise their spiritual ideas with their open minds, but also permits such spiritual work to be done without the active resonance of the heart. It is possible, I'm sure, that much deep concentrated and sustained spiritual mind-work can unlock the key to the heart, but this seems backward to me. Again, it's the heart that counts. The heart not only beats. Here's Confucius:

> "To put the world right in order, we must first put the nation in order; to put the nation in order we must first put the family in order, to put the family in order we must

first cultivate our personal life; we must first set our hearts right[30]."

The Truth that makes me joyfully free is that Jesus is my personal Savior, and that God is my Father, as I am, quite assuredly, a child of God. I may rest in God's grace and persevere with God's favor, as long as I internalize and am willing to verbalize "I accept Lord Jesus Christ as my savior, I bow at His feet, and freely of my own will follow Him" And frankly, gentle reader, this all comes to me seemingly undeserved, only God knew what I needed. To know this quiet strong strength in my soul, this armor of divinity, this valor is mine, and can also be yours.

We must all die sometime; what happens to us then is very much at question here. I for one choose to follow the truth as it appears to me, based on decades of reading, pondering, writing, comparing, observing, stretching, researching, exploring faiths, philosophies and histories, and which cumulatively add up to my rock-solid faith in the eye-witness reports written down at great risk and peril of the writers' own lives. My fundamental assumption in all this is simply that I believe the eye-witness reports that one man named Jesus foretold three times how he would be killed and buried, and after three days rise from the dead, and then HE DID IT! And was seen by hundreds for days afterward! And his followers were totally transformed from dejection to joy. Why? I follow the truth as the Holy Bible tells it.

I have seen the rest, been at the rest, read about the rest, chanted with the rest, and no story shows up truer than the story of Jesus Christ, no other story even remotely claims to have accomplished what Christ accomplished. So what is the deal, exactly, with otherwise rational people flatly denying this truth? Is it because they sense it may be right, and they may have hell to pay? Consider a paraphrase of the old wager: if I'm right, my path is righteous and golden, and if I'm wrong, my path is at least righteous. So what is it that holds people back from this appealing truth? Is it that they, like myself at one point, wish so much to get it right, after all it's a big decision, and one thing we hate to do is err on the side of over-exuberance? The last thing we want to do is make a mistake about our own immortality options. But then caution runs both sides of the river. A rational person does not play dice with eternity. If, as I did, anyone should feel their own hubris within, their own chip on the shoulder, their own arrogance, their own pride, their own self-centeredness, perhaps they need a dose of this absolute truth: Jesus is Lord.

> Truth is the first step on my ladder to higher ground.
> Truth is the secret door to harmonious sound.
> Truth is the leap to joy in the earshot of perfection.
> Truth is the laughter of light in the right direction.
> Truth is my deepest strongest most supreme song
> Truth is where my soul does quite happily belong.
> Truth is what the entity known as "I" does display.
> Truth is that ineffable fiber holding our wills at bay
> Even when the will to power lurks and grovels
> Truth is my first ideal because I want it that way.

ON UNDERSTANDING

In my twenty-second summer, my second ideal to pursue in a mantra of my own, fooling no one but myself if I dared to reorganize my mind's arrangement to the truest fork in the road ahead, to Understanding. Why was this important to me as it was and still is? By way of a manner of speaking, such as to derive any benefit to one's self or soul? My humble guess is that you would want the same. Choices are to be made, including to protect and ensure oneself.

Benjamin Franklin, a man of many talents, wrote down for posterity his considered opinions. To promote understanding is a virtuous act, for it results in a positive reception from a healthy and aware receptor. Franklin saw it as a matter of building a bridge to your receptor's position and bring them slowly over to the side of understanding.

Many appear to be governed by their all-too-often auto-pilot egos. There are, in fact upon direct observation, many unhealthy and or unaware persons. Picture them at their screen of choice and watch them go blank, crashing in comfort with pillows properly placed for the ache of the day, loaning their brains to the plug–in drug photons beaming at them. Occasionally rubbing their finger against a user-friendly communication device and becoming totally absorbed. This is what I would call unaware. With deeper understanding it may be also seen more aware of certain aspect of life, if not totally consumed by being endlessly entertained.

But persons who watch television seven hours a day are unhealthy and, for at least seven hours are unaware of their actual surroundings, so that they fear their exterior world more than reality would inspire. They are sleep-walking. If you, gentle reader, find a grain of truth in this fact about television, really, think about getting rid of it. And just like shaving your head, you will find you have a surprising amount of time on your hands afterward.

Without the benefit of having a significant other to love, my emotions yet flow in a positive direction, freely given, if not to humans then to God from my heart. But when the person who is thinking and aware ties the mind to the agape impulse, clearly seeing the distinction between the two, the person is generating personal power. The act of understanding is, at its highest, a divine gift, for which I for one am actively grateful. Just cock your head a little to the side and see the other's side, step into their shoes, listen to what they say, trusting in the simple absolute truth of your faith, and walk them back into full light.

"Trying to understand is like straining through muddy water. Be still and allow the mind to settle[31]."

There is an argument, a good one in my grateful opinion, that all of creation, without national borders, was indeed created by the God of Abraham, Isaac, Jacob, Moses and Lord Jesus Christ. To my way of thinking, that is an absolute truth, and I wish it to be understood that I firmly plant my feet in Christ, I walk in Christ, I breathe and laugh in Christ, and I do feel my own power increasing. There is in fact power in His name.

And still the atheists persist. And I give them credit for their persistence, like a wart on my foot. I remember Chesterton: "If there were no God there would be no atheists[32]." "To one who has faith," wrote Thomas Aquinas, "no explanation is necessary. To one without faith, no explanation is possible[33]." So we devolve into necessity to peacefully coexist, hence the need for understanding.

But there was more that this journey gained out of actively promoting and seeking understanding, than simple peaceful coexistence. Who can deny this will to brotherly love, to agape? To the feeling that we are all brothers and sisters of the planet, no matter what color or language, so that we can live in a community of happiness and children are raised by a village again? Understanding love took me in my own hubris decades to come around to a mature perspective, thanks in part to Ice. And thanks in part to my guardian Furnace Room Friend, which is a truth for me in spite of what anyone else can say, my heart was never allowed to be darkened, so that it is open enough today to accept with open arms the blessings of my Lord Jesus Christ.

Make no mistake. My position was not arrived at without doubt. Consider Oliver Wendell Holmes: "To have doubted one's own first principles is the mark of a civilized man[34]."

> If I stand in Christ I stand in Truth.
> Understanding is the key to open another person's heart.
> To this end I tilt my head to dream
> So anyone can star in His name full steam.
> Understanding is real.
> It's a steal, it's so cheap. In fact, it's free, and full of grace
> Why wouldn't any be willing to see wisdom's face?
> Understanding is an act both of self-service and faith
> The courageous impulse demonstrates
> a higher source, a different source, than material.
> Seek to understand your neighbor—it's critical.
> Understanding draws a warm line.
> Warmth, in turn, draws kindness.
> Kindness draws agape.

What does it really mean to love God with all my heart, all my strength, all my mind and all my soul? How many Christians or any other belief system practice this every day? All day? I know I don't. We all fall short. But isn't it the reaching that matters? Isn't it not only the intention but also the process, the action, the creative twist? The creative twist in the sense that I have allowed my mind the flexibility to accept on faith alone some very old lines in a very old book? The printed word endures for a reason. To love God is a universal impulse. Many of our modern self-evident truths came, in fact, from the Bible.

Hence my native gratitude. Look back over my journey and see this has been a recurring theme. Without fully understanding why, and not needing an explanation, the fact is that my attitude of gratitude is deeply imbedded in the tracks of my mind and the core of my heart. For another example of embedded old writings, here's one from Cicero: "Gratitude is not only the greatest of virtues, but the parent of all virtues[35]."

Some truths are self-evident, say I, say you, and Jefferson. And, I'll wager that many will buy into this notion. Now, what better source of self-evident truths than the source of many of our self-evident truths, the Bible? In response I can sense the atheists, I can detect them rustling and quivering, but I do not hear them. My understanding of my own condition is that I can afford to ignore them and live in the light myself, even if they insist on embracing darkness.

Our technological advances have dazzled our senses to the point where we no longer see the simplicity of life. We are evolving into a new generation with uncertain futures. A good number of us slump our minds back, as if in a lazy boy, with a cold one, and a remote. But for anyone still thinking and aware, the possibility yet exists to elevate our lives, each of us, to a higher level of vibrations, from which compassion flows to understanding.

So let us invest in compassion. (This is actually where I think the atheists could seek to understand.) Compassion is living for one another. It flows from one's heart to another in agape. The heart is the key! It is openly loving one another in spirit; hurting inside for one another, through the heart.

Understanding led me to see more clearly the denials and obstacles put in front of me over the full span of my life in a different light, in which I could give myself to see my mother's pain. In understanding, with compassion, Ice began to melt before my eyes into my mother. Who was an excellent cook. And I still remember her fingers trembling on my shoulders that time at Nicky France's. Even my beautiful bodaciously intelligent estranged sister Lila also melted, or was rather transformed, from a scorpion to an eagle, through deeper understanding.

And MaryJane? She was the toughest to let go. Once an ally in a hurting past, now a saboteur in a joyful present, in understanding my reality as a child of God, I could no longer entertain her. Praise God, she is finally in my rear view mirror.

Understanding also led me to see import in these words of Aristotle's:

"Where your talents and the needs of the world cross lies your calling[36]."

My understanding of myself tells me for sure that I'm writing this book because I was born to do it. My grandmother told me so.

What needs does the world have today? What if not understanding between peoples? Consider people as all the same, regardless of language, location, rich or poor, all children of one loving God. If there must be different faiths on the planet let us at least all agree on this one item. What hurts you hurts me. What makes you happy is what makes me happy. Ultimately to understand this is to maintain peace.

> Understanding will lead me there.
> Understanding grows kindness like water grows grass.
> Understanding tells me to put it off for a time.
> Then Understanding comes to me, not me to it.
> Understanding tells me my secrets,
> And forces my hand to submit to higher knowledge.
> By way, of which, is kindness.

ON KINDNESS

When you breathe out truth, you inhale understanding. When you take in understanding you are warmed, and exhale kindness. Why? It is a natural response from a human person, that's why. When your heart is set on higher vibrations, low pulse but strong vibrations, any charitable act toward another will result in a kindness in return. Not as a quid-pro-quo but as a sharing, a loving, a natural mirroring.

With understanding that I as well as anyone may be misled, I still find this happy glow inside of me that is Christ. At twenty-two, long before I came to Christ, His example for exhibiting kindness to be my path was my choice, and consider not for one moment that my gratitude is lacking for the use of His example even while in darkness.

What is kindness? It is that ineffable quality of agape love, selfless giving of something good to another. Kindness is understanding, as it were, that somehow we are all one, and by doing good to another we are doing good to ourselves. But we cannot simply do good for ourselves without doing good to others, or the meat won't be good even for the dogs. Somehow selfless giving is married to self-interest. Bringing kindness to others brings peace back to us.

Kindness allows me even to forgive the mother of my children, as I understand she did the best she could in her own cage of fear. She was a good and nurturing mother of my children, just as I thought she would be. Kindness allows forgiveness to fall on her and her third husband, who after all was good to my kids. Kindness for myself allowed me to consider that just maybe my former pursuit of the doctorate was in a way an effort to gain my mother's approval, and when she checked out my plan went south behind me. But kindness to myself allows me to see, even as a joyful Christian, the chuckling Buddha sitting on my shoulder, gently laughing at the foolish human. Gently laughing, so much folly. As Eddie Edwards once said, "You can't take life too seriously since you'll never get out of it alive anyway." So I laugh a lot, often at myself, sometimes at most unlikely moments.

Kindness encompasses a wide spectrum of possibilities. But all are positive, as I accept kindness is a positive act. How can sworn enemies be offered kindness? What will they do with it? We must remain secure in agape love, never fear, kindness hold dear, as giving a light to the world.

"Better to light one candle than to curse the darkness[37]."

Kindness allows one to look at political opponents with compassion; at assaulters with the other cheek; without it one is lost to darkness. And there can be no greater, more hurtful darkness than not knowing kindness. Think of all the hurting people in your neighborhood. What would Jesus do for them? What will you do for the least of your people? What if we all actually felt as we are one in spirit? All of us on the planet? Brothers and sisters under the skin? All citizens of Earth. One kindness shown to any one of us helps every one of us. One hurt, all are hurt. It is just so critical for the real way the world works, that we all begin anew with a spirit of kindness for one another. It all starts in a heart that not only beats. The true heart not only beats.

Another word sometimes used for kindness is love.

"If I speak in the tongues of mortals and of angels, but do not have love, I am a noisy gong or a clanging cymbal. And if I have prophetic powers, and understand all mysteries and all knowledge, and if I have all faith, so as to remove mountains, but do not have love, I am nothing. If I give away all my possessions, and if I hand over my body so that I may boast, but do not have love, I gain nothing[38]." Then, some 1,600 years later, Francis Bacon:

> "There is in man's nature a secret inclination and motion towards love of others, which if it be not spent on some one or a few, does naturally spread itself towards many, and makes men become more humane and charitable[39]."

Light one candle for kindness today.

ON PEACE

Necessary to note is my own inner peace, in knowing the love of my God and knowing that my Lord and Savior Jesus Christ is in my corner. Whether through a form such as my Furnace Room Friend, in times of patience tried, or in a higher vibrating moment like an insight popping into a still-young head, the Assuror promised by Jesus was there, to my knowledge or not.

Non-Christians tell me they don't want to be part of any religion that says either you're in or you're going to hell. It's our way or the highway. But that's not the choice. The actual choice is to accept the truth as it has been written and diligently studied for 2,000 years, or not. It is not an unfeeling God that allows persons to go to hell; it's the person's own hubris and darkness of mind. What, in the end, would be lost if you accept Christ in your heart? You would live a God-loving, God-fearing life, righteous to all, and then, if the Word is true, you'd have eternal life. If it proves not to be true, and that's a risk I willingly take, given the stakes, then at least the righteous life was led. From this angle it does appear that the choice is rather starkly clear.

In the event that there will remain those for whom the Christian message for some (ungodly) reason is not received open–heartedly, we are left to the simple directions of my Lord: Love God with all your heart and soul and mind; and love your neighbor as yourself. My wish is not to judge any other; my wish, now that I have found the truth that set me free, is simply and as powerfully as possible glorify the Name of the Lord. If that in any way comes to pass through the dissemination of these pages, my peace will be even deeper, knowing that I fulfilled my grandmother's direction, and wrote a book about my Father. My heart is happy to have had a chance to introduce Eddie Edwards.

But just as my Dad was struck down by a weapon of war, today we have wars all around us. Here's an admission of my own personal chagrin, when considering this may be read outside the United States of America, and recognizing the utter irony of an American writing about peace while residing in the biggest war-mongering nation on planet Earth. America is always at war. Remember how absurd Ronald Reagan's invasion of Granada seemed? The unseen hand that guides the ship of American foreign policy, that once-festering tumor of which we were warned by President Eisenhower's farewell address, the military-industrial complex, now appears to have almost complete control. I say almost complete because for all the insane money they are making, and all the inside games they play, and all the success for evil they devise, theirs is temporal, while mine is permanent.

Do all you who watch America from abroad know the American people wish to be kind, but their government is sold off to a military-industrial complex whose only eventual demise must be the lifting of people's awareness past their plug in drug television sets? America, wake up!

Anyone remember the first images of the big blue marble in space? Did anyone besides me feel a certain ineffable hope for such a beautiful planet? Forgive me, gentle reader, as I am compelled by the thought of such magnificent beauty to say praise be to our Creator, God, Jehovah. How could anything else have created such wonders? The news, as it is called, chatters over rivalries and brutalities. America, wake up! But this reminds me that my Lord Jesus Christ told us there will be wars and rumors of wars to the end of days. I just wish my country didn't have to be so active in it. America, the land of progress, we've had a good run. Who knows how long this experiment can last? Wake up!

But peace in the world begins with peace in our hearts. Sometimes it just seems too ponderous a task to try to move justice or peace, but we can always attend to the peace within. Even when storms swirl outside our heads, bliss stands ready to offer an inside kiss.

What would each of us in our most lucid moments wish for our neighbors if not peace? Most of us, it would be hoped, have learned by now that to engender another's peace is to add to our own. To help another is to help yourself. We truly cannot hurt anyone without hurting all of us. Peace does not refer only to a lack of violence, or mere cessation of hostilities. True peace is more active, when the people involved share the higher notions of brotherhood and shared experience. Here we are astride this beautiful planet, spinning in space, at best we are temporary caretakers of this place. Isn't it time we all opened our minds just a little bit?

What possible partisan argument tops the need for peace? But peace implies justice, and sometimes justice must be won before peace arrives. Nevertheless, regarding simple personal inner peace, my experience is that it follows a feeling of kindness. Truth leads to Understanding leads to Kindness leads to Peace. This is what I wish for my gentle reader.

My journey has taken me around many corners, among many different people, cultures, languages, through many books, old and new, all the way to where I sit today, in the lap of Christ, wishing for all the world to see the light, and to live together on the Big Blue Marble in peace and harmony, as that is our collective destiny.

We live on a planet of wonder and delight, beauty, morning, night; stars above, mystic chords below, rain, sleet, sun, snow. Baby's smiles, hundreds of miles of flowers, intrinsic powers; colors, beasts, fruits and berries, fragrance carried on winds of grace, so much for which to be grateful in this wondrous place. No matter what may lie ahead, it does not move me to worry or doubt; our destiny is the Kingdom of Heaven, within and without. And to the types who jeer and shout, the end is near, or casting doubt, I say, as for me, I'm with the One who said

> "And this is the will of him who sent me, that I shall lose nothing of it all and raise it up on the last day[40]."

Thank you, Father God Jehovah
Thank you, Lord Jesus Christ.
Thank you, Furnace Room Friend
Thank you, Grandma.
And to every good soul which has touched mine,
From my not only beating heart to yours, Peace.

A BRIEF BIOGRAPHY OF LESTER RIVERS

Born and raised one-quarter mile from Lake Superior, on the east end of Duluth, Minnesota.

Worked as:

Golf Caddy, Snack Bar Operator, Railroad Switchman, Merchant Marine deckhand, Railroad Fireman, Merchant Marine Deckwatch, gravedigger, janitor, bank coin teller, bookstore cashier, cement laborer, pedicab driver, assistant manager of a McDonald's, city bus driver, college instructor, television news reporter, public information officer, political candidate, executive director of a non-profit special event, corporate sponsorship salesman for an NBA team, financial advisor, insurance agent.

Travels:

By 23, hitch-hiked in fourteen countries and forty states.

Now 18 countries, 46 states, New York City 42 times, Mexico 27 times, Europe three times, and Nome, Alaska twice.

ENDNOTES

1 Ralph Waldo Emerson, Essay on Self Reliance
2 Henry David Thoreau, Journal
3 The Sayings of Confucius, VII, 27
4 IBID, VIII, 2
5 Emerson, Essay on Self Reliance
6 The Golden Sayings of Epictetus, XXXI
7 IBID, XXXIII
8 The Dalai Llama, The Art of Happiness
9 Gary Zukav, Seat of the Soul
10 Dalai Llama, Compassion and the Individual
11 Abraham Lincoln, Second Inaugural Address
12 Friedrich Nietzsche, Beyond Good and Evil
13 George Ripley, Martineau's Rationale
14 Samuel Taylor Coleridge, Famous Quotes
15 Isaiah 53: 3
16 Acts 10: 39-41
17 Ripley, Jesus Christ, Yesterday, Today and Forever
18 G. K. Chesterton, What's wrong with the world, 1910
19 IBID, ILN, 1-3-31
20 IBID, LIN, 9-30-33
21 Emerson, The Over Soul
22 Albert Einstein, Famous Quotes
23 U.S. Declaration of Independence
24 Proverbs 20-22
25 Proverbs 1:7

26 Sir Francis Bacon, Essay on Atheism
27 Chesterton, What's wrong with the World. 1910
28 IBID., The Speaker, 12/15/1900
29 IBID., What's wrong with the world, 1910
30 The Sayings of Confucius, The Wisdom of Confucius
31 Lao Tzu, Tao Te Ching
32 Chesterton, Where all roads lead, 1932
33 Thomas Aquinas, Summa Theologica
34 Oliver Wendell Holmes, Jr., Ideals and Doubts, 1915
35 Cicero, Pro Plancio, 54 B.C.
36 Aristotle, Nicomachean Ethics
37 Chinese Proverb
38 1 Corinthians 13: 1-3
39 Sir Francis Bacon, Essay, Of Love, 1625
40 John 6: 39